ARCHIE COMIC PUBLICATION

THE ADVENTURES OF

Little Archie

DEDICATED TO THE MEMORY OF
PRESIDENT AND CO-PUBLISHER
RICHARD H. GOLDWATER
1936-2007

CHAIRMAN AND CO-PUBLISHER
MICHAEL I. SILBERKLEIT

VP/ EDITOR-IN-CHIEF
VICTOR GORELICK

VP/DIRECTOR OF CIRCULATION
FRED MAUSSER

MANAGING EDITOR
MIKE PELLERITO

COMPILATION EDITOR
PAUL CASTIGLIA

ART DIRECTOR
JOE PEP

COVER ART
BOB BOLLING
BOB SMITH

COVER COLORIST
ROSARIO "TITO" PEÑA

PRODUCTION
STEPHEN OSWALD
CARLOS ANTUNES
JOE MORCIGLIO

The Stories, Characters and Incidents in this
publication are entirely fictional.
This publication contains material that was
originally created in a less racially and socially
sensitive time in our society and reflects
attitudes that may be interpreted as offensive
today. The stories are reprinted here without
alteration for historical reference.

The Adventures of Little Archie
Volume 2, 2008. Printed in Canada.
Published by Archie Comic Publications,
Inc., 325 Fayette Avenue, Mamaroneck,
New York 10543-2318. Archie characters
created by John L. Goldwater; the
likenesses of the Archie characters were
created by Bob Montana. The individual
characters' names and likenesses are the
exclusive trademarks of Archie Comic Publications, Inc.

ISBN-13: 978-1-879794-28-3
ISBN-10: 1-879794-28-4

www.archiecomics.com

TABLE OF CONTENTS

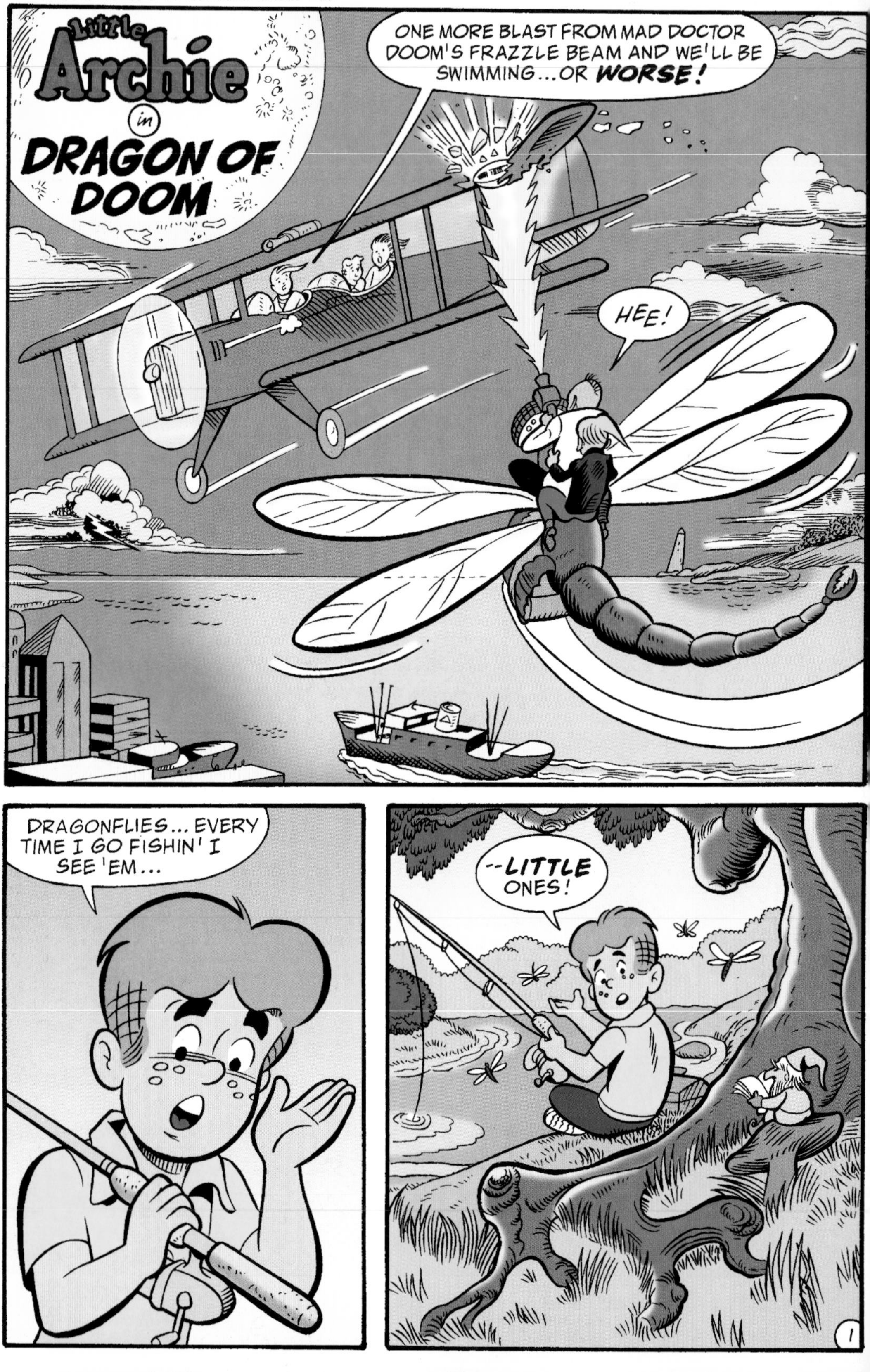
Little Archie
in
DRAGON OF DOOM
ONE MORE BLAST FROM MAD DOCTOR DOOM'S FRAZZLE BEAM AND WE'LL BE SWIMMING...OR WORSE!
HEE!
DRAGONFLIES... EVERY TIME I GO FISHIN' I SEE 'EM...
--LITTLE ONES!
1

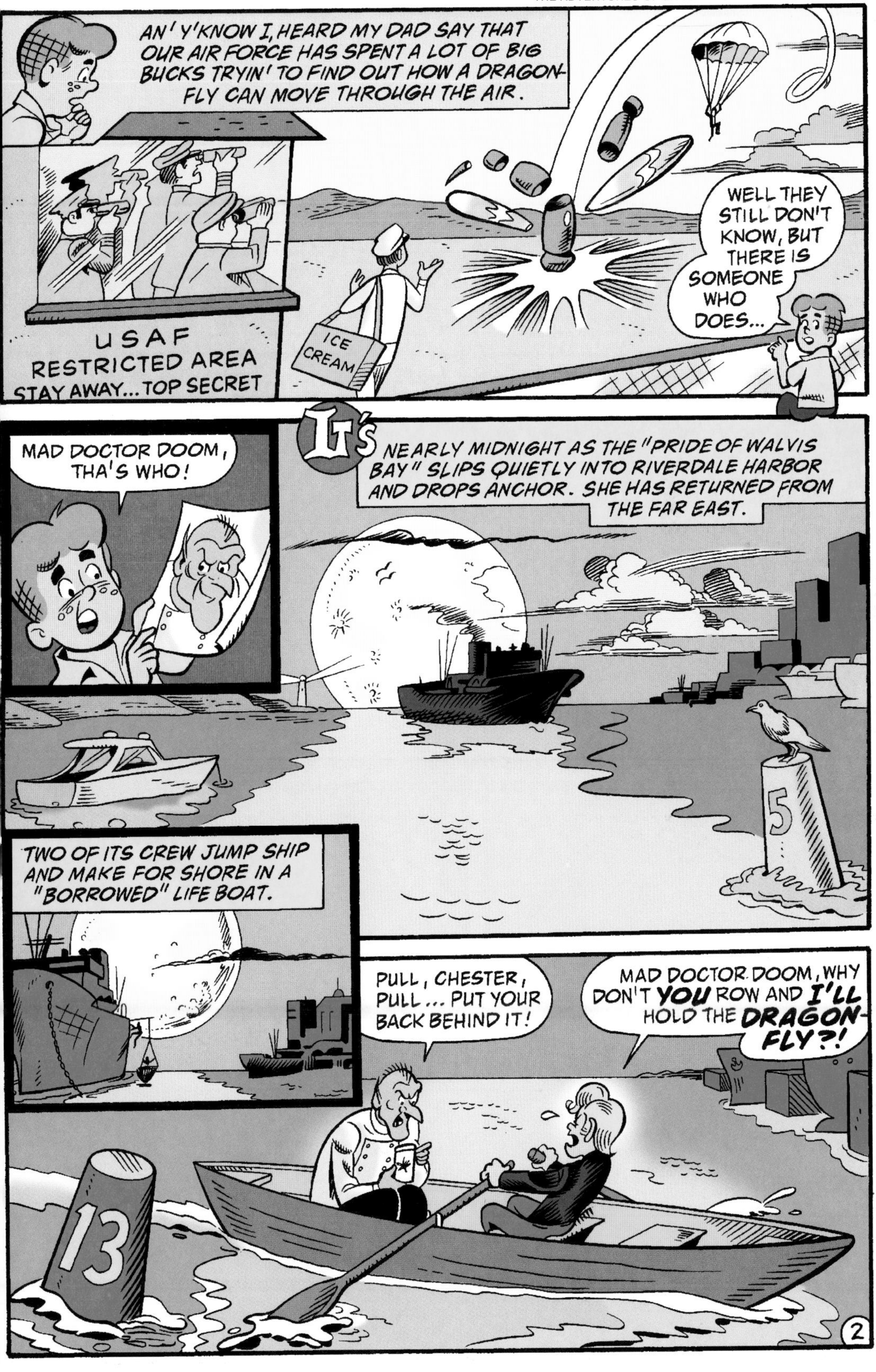
AN' Y'KNOW I, HEARD MY DAD SAY THAT OUR AIR FORCE HAS SPENT A LOT OF BIG BUCKS TRYIN' TO FIND OUT HOW A DRAGON-FLY CAN MOVE THROUGH THE AIR.
USAF RESTRICTED AREA STAY AWAY... TOP SECRET
ICE CREAM
WELL THEY STILL DON'T KNOW, BUT THERE IS SOMEONE WHO DOES...
MAD DOCTOR DOOM, THA'S WHO!
IT'S NEARLY MIDNIGHT AS THE "PRIDE OF WALVIS BAY" SLIPS QUIETLY INTO RIVERDALE HARBOR AND DROPS ANCHOR. SHE HAS RETURNED FROM THE FAR EAST.
5
TWO OF ITS CREW JUMP SHIP AND MAKE FOR SHORE IN A "BORROWED" LIFE BOAT.
PULL, CHESTER, PULL... PUT YOUR BACK BEHIND IT!
MAD DOCTOR DOOM, WHY DON'T YOU ROW AND I'LL HOLD THE DRAGON-FLY?!
13
2

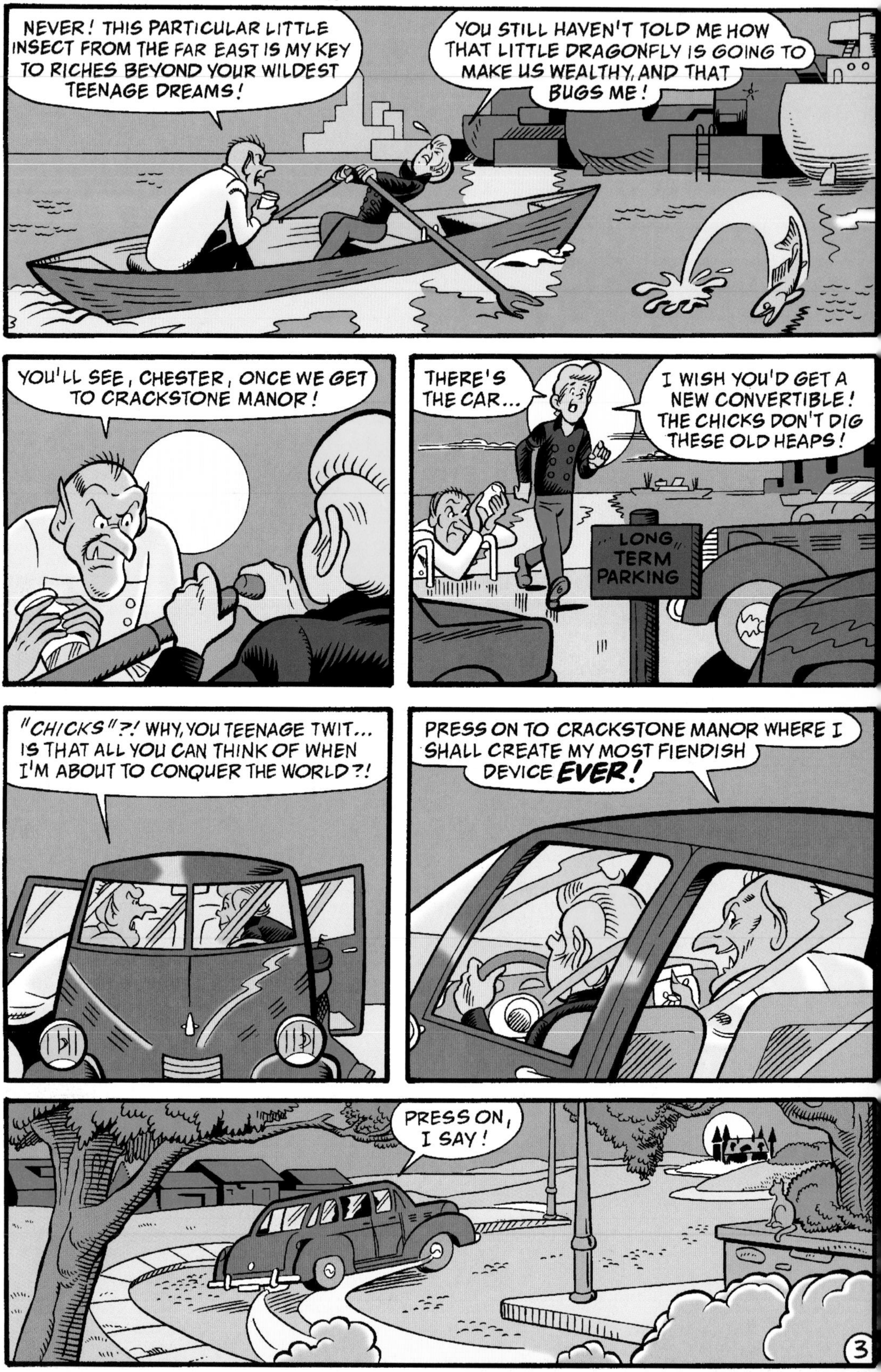
NEVER! THIS PARTICULAR LITTLE INSECT FROM THE FAR EAST IS MY KEY TO RICHES BEYOND YOUR WILDEST TEENAGE DREAMS!
YOU STILL HAVEN'T TOLD ME HOW THAT LITTLE DRAGONFLY IS GOING TO MAKE US WEALTHY, AND THAT BUGS ME!
YOU'LL SEE, CHESTER, ONCE WE GET TO CRACKSTONE MANOR!
THERE'S THE CAR...
I WISH YOU'D GET A NEW CONVERTIBLE! THE CHICKS DON'T DIG THESE OLD HEAPS!
LONG TERM PARKING
"CHICKS"?! WHY, YOU TEENAGE TWIT... IS THAT ALL YOU CAN THINK OF WHEN I'M ABOUT TO CONQUER THE WORLD?!
PRESS ON TO CRACKSTONE MANOR WHERE I SHALL CREATE MY MOST FIENDISH DEVICE EVER!
PRESS ON, I SAY!
3

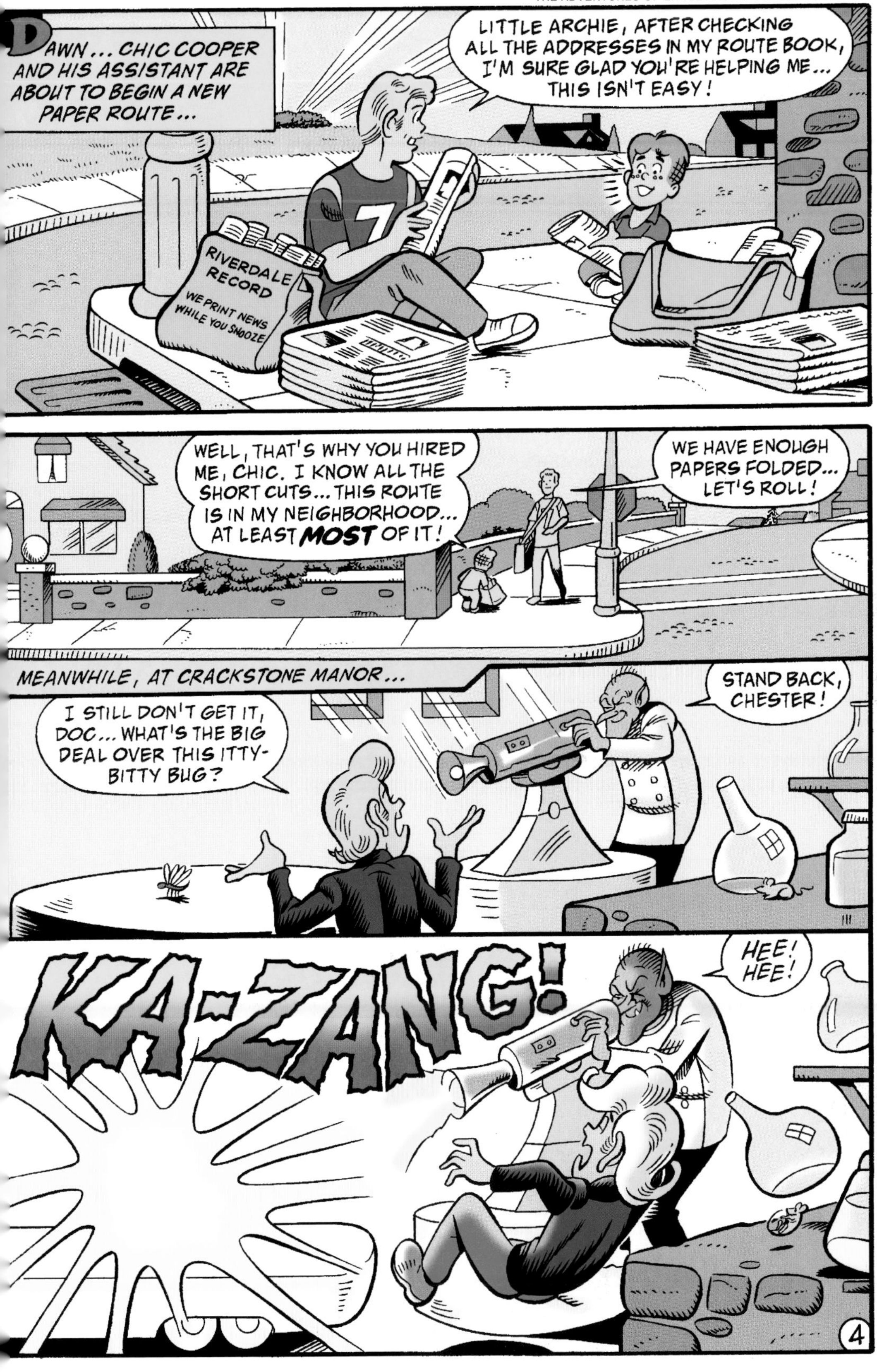
DAWN... CHIC COOPER AND HIS ASSISTANT ARE ABOUT TO BEGIN A NEW PAPER ROUTE...
LITTLE ARCHIE, AFTER CHECKING ALL THE ADDRESSES IN MY ROUTE BOOK, I'M SURE GLAD YOU'RE HELPING ME... THIS ISN'T EASY!
RIVERDALE RECORD
WE PRINT NEWS WHILE YOU SNOOZE
WELL, THAT'S WHY YOU HIRED ME, CHIC. I KNOW ALL THE SHORT CUTS... THIS ROUTE IS IN MY NEIGHBORHOOD... AT LEAST MOST OF IT!
WE HAVE ENOUGH PAPERS FOLDED... LET'S ROLL!
MEANWHILE, AT CRACKSTONE MANOR...
I STILL DON'T GET IT, DOC... WHAT'S THE BIG DEAL OVER THIS ITTY-BITTY BUG?
STAND BACK, CHESTER!
KA-ZANG!
HEE! HEE!
4

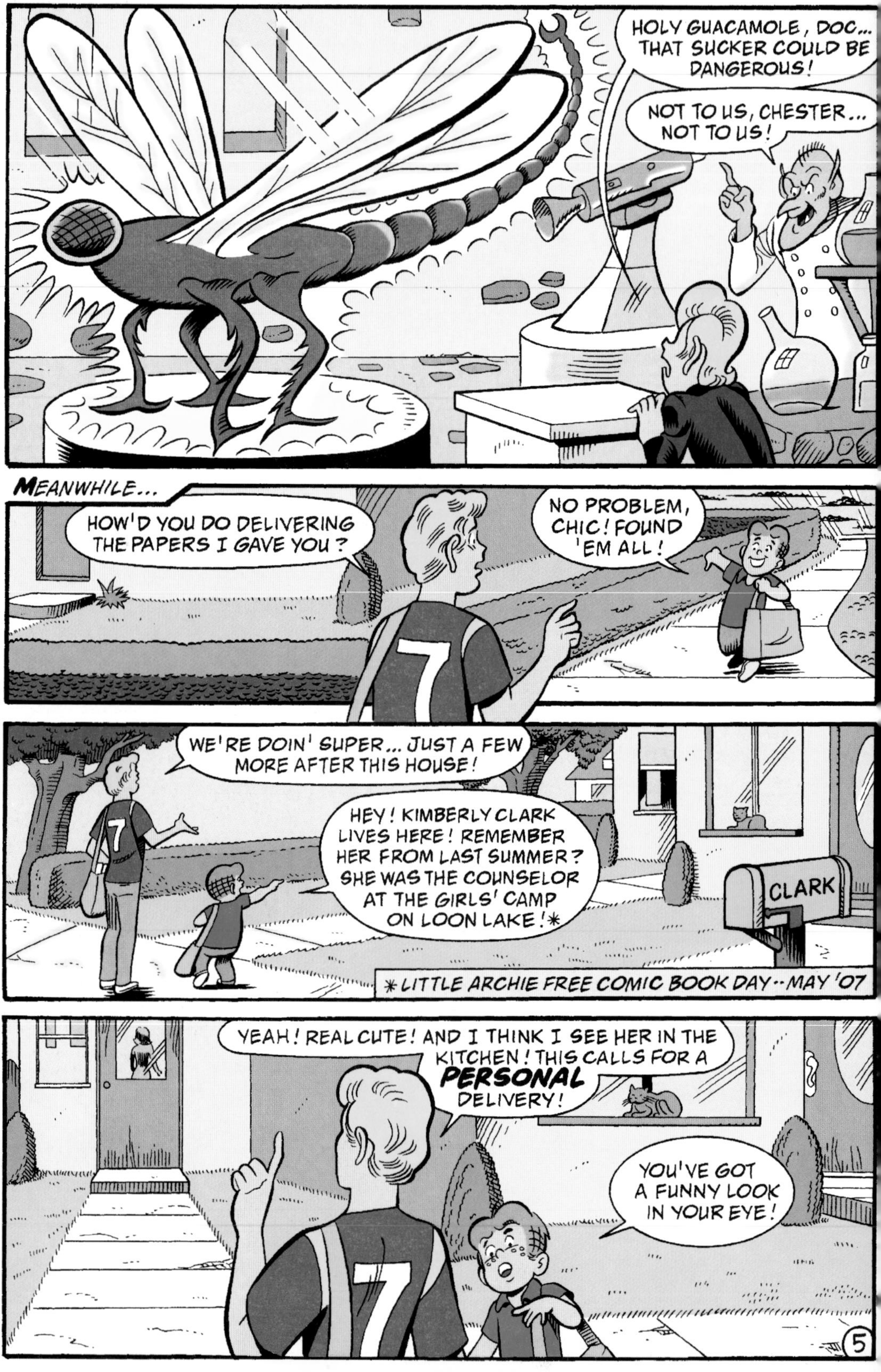
HOLY GUACAMOLE, DOC... THAT SUCKER COULD BE DANGEROUS!
NOT TO US, CHESTER... NOT TO US!
MEANWHILE...
HOW'D YOU DO DELIVERING THE PAPERS I GAVE YOU?
NO PROBLEM, CHIC! FOUND 'EM ALL!
WE'RE DOIN' SUPER... JUST A FEW MORE AFTER THIS HOUSE!
HEY! KIMBERLY CLARK LIVES HERE! REMEMBER HER FROM LAST SUMMER? SHE WAS THE COUNSELOR AT THE GIRLS' CAMP ON LOON LAKE!*
CLARK
*LITTLE ARCHIE FREE COMIC BOOK DAY--MAY '07
YEAH! REAL CUTE! AND I THINK I SEE HER IN THE KITCHEN! THIS CALLS FOR A PERSONAL DELIVERY!
YOU'VE GOT A FUNNY LOOK IN YOUR EYE!
5

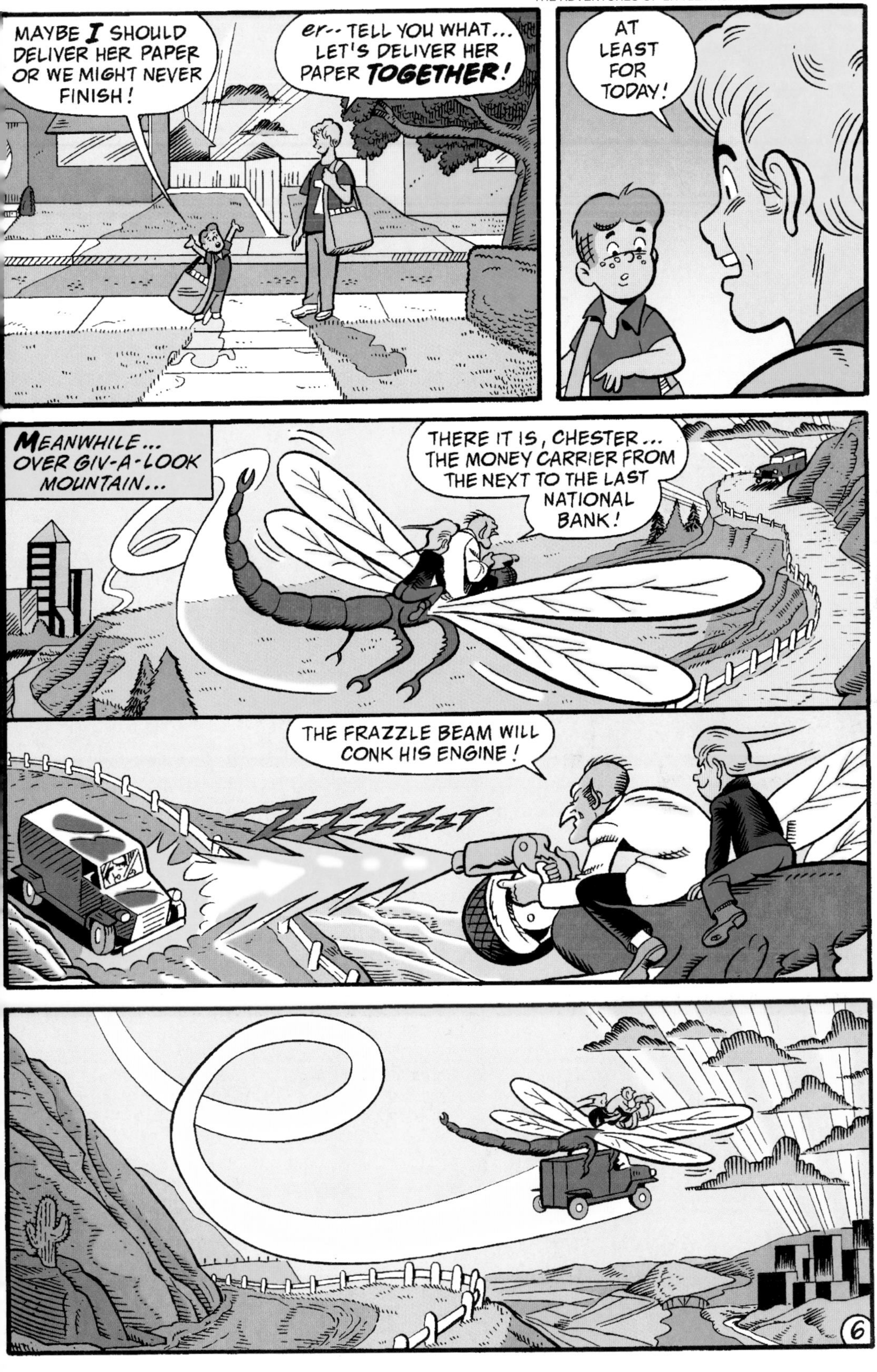
MAYBE I SHOULD DELIVER HER PAPER OR WE MIGHT NEVER FINISH!
er-- TELL YOU WHAT... LET'S DELIVER HER PAPER TOGETHER!
AT LEAST FOR TODAY!
MEANWHILE... OVER GIV-A-LOOK MOUNTAIN...
THERE IT IS, CHESTER... THE MONEY CARRIER FROM THE NEXT TO THE LAST NATIONAL BANK!
THE FRAZZLE BEAM WILL CONK HIS ENGINE!
ZZZZZZT
6

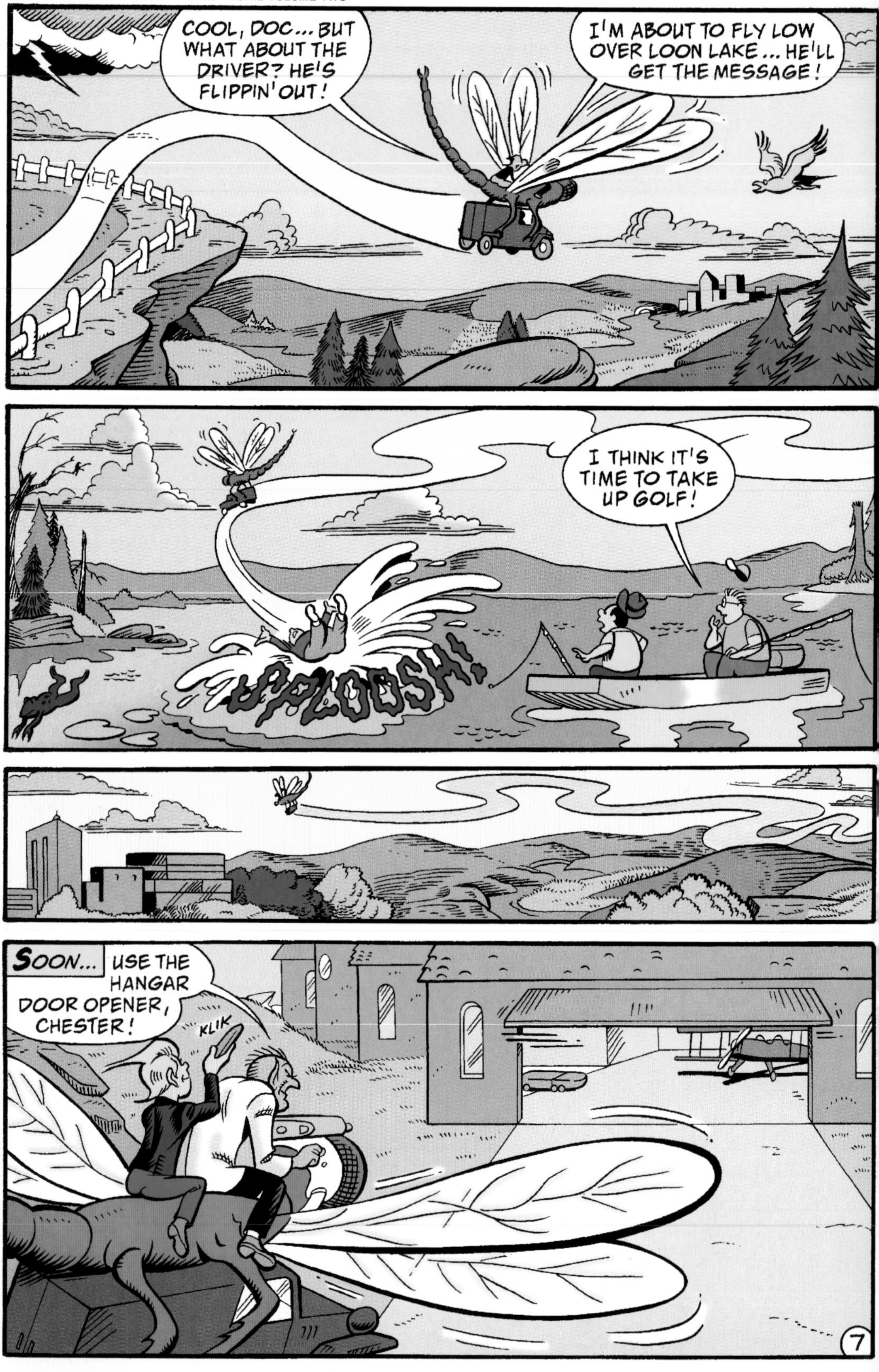
COOL, DOC... BUT WHAT ABOUT THE DRIVER? HE'S FLIPPIN' OUT!
I'M ABOUT TO FLY LOW OVER LOON LAKE... HE'LL GET THE MESSAGE!
I THINK IT'S TIME TO TAKE UP GOLF!
SPLOOSH!
SOON...
USE THE HANGAR DOOR OPENER, CHESTER!
KLIK
7

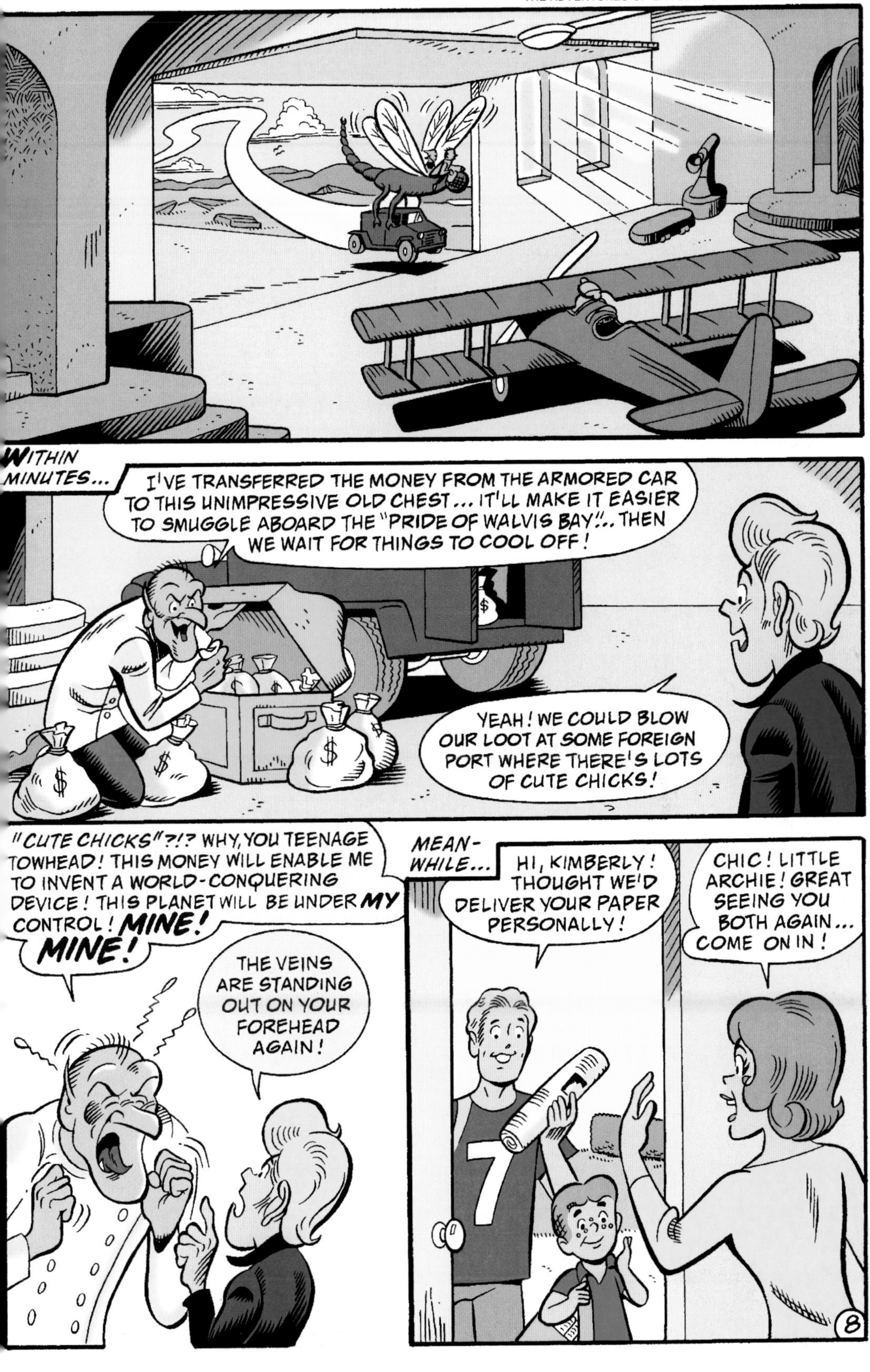
WITHIN MINUTES...
I'VE TRANSFERRED THE MONEY FROM THE ARMORED CAR TO THIS UNIMPRESSIVE OLD CHEST... IT'LL MAKE IT EASIER TO SMUGGLE ABOARD THE "PRIDE OF WALVIS BAY"... THEN WE WAIT FOR THINGS TO COOL OFF!
YEAH! WE COULD BLOW OUR LOOT AT SOME FOREIGN PORT WHERE THERE'S LOTS OF CUTE CHICKS!
"CUTE CHICKS"?!? WHY, YOU TEENAGE TOWHEAD! THIS MONEY WILL ENABLE ME TO INVENT A WORLD-CONQUERING DEVICE! THIS PLANET WILL BE UNDER MY CONTROL! MINE! MINE!
THE VEINS ARE STANDING OUT ON YOUR FOREHEAD AGAIN!
MEAN-WHILE...
HI, KIMBERLY! THOUGHT WE'D DELIVER YOUR PAPER PERSONALLY!
CHIC! LITTLE ARCHIE! GREAT SEEING YOU BOTH AGAIN... COME ON IN!
8

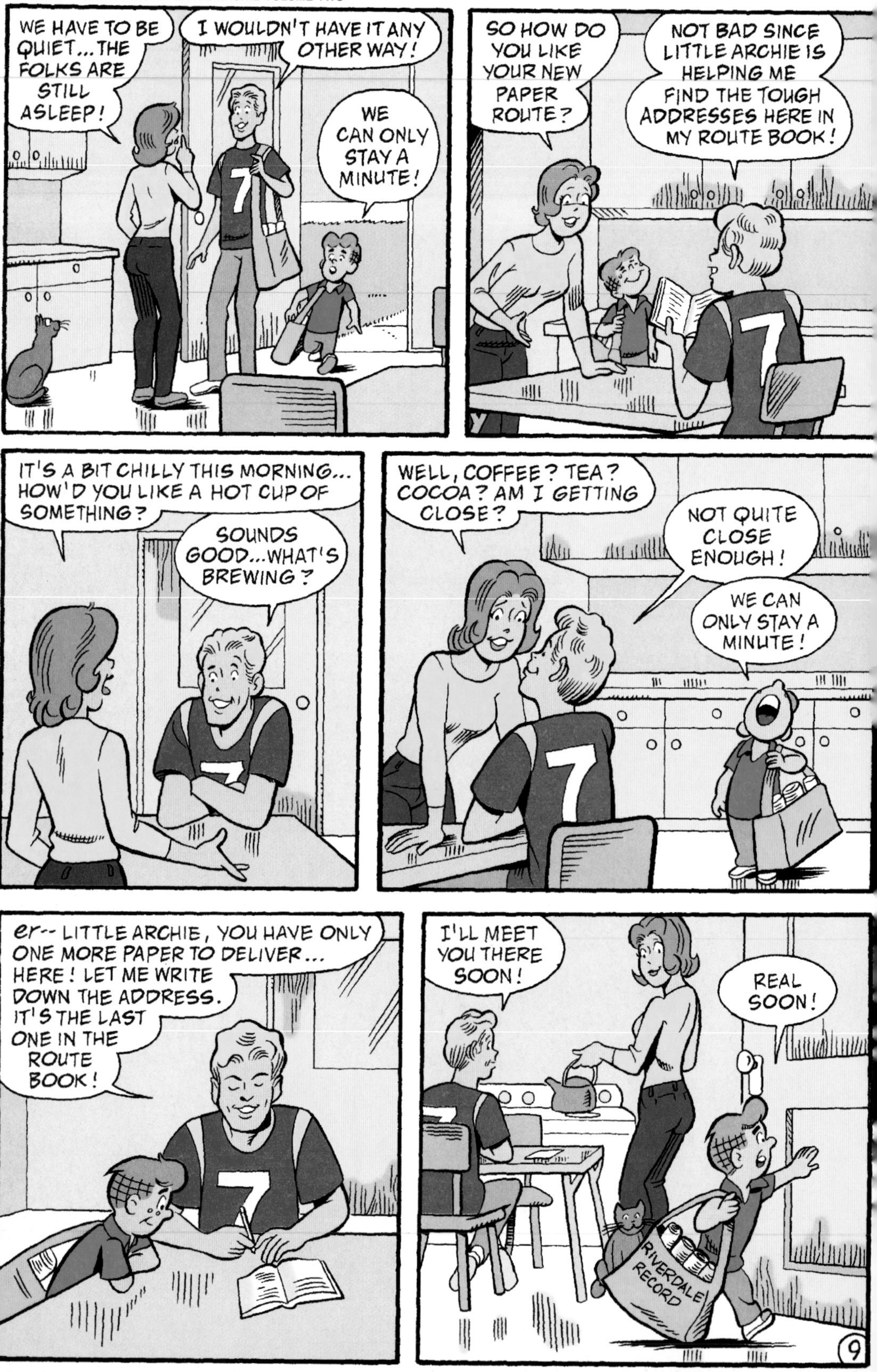
WE HAVE TO BE QUIET... THE FOLKS ARE STILL ASLEEP!
I WOULDN'T HAVE IT ANY OTHER WAY!
WE CAN ONLY STAY A MINUTE!
SO HOW DO YOU LIKE YOUR NEW PAPER ROUTE?
NOT BAD SINCE LITTLE ARCHIE IS HELPING ME FIND THE TOUGH ADDRESSES HERE IN MY ROUTE BOOK!
IT'S A BIT CHILLY THIS MORNING... HOW'D YOU LIKE A HOT CUP OF SOMETHING?
SOUNDS GOOD... WHAT'S BREWING?
WELL, COFFEE? TEA? COCOA? AM I GETTING CLOSE?
NOT QUITE CLOSE ENOUGH!
WE CAN ONLY STAY A MINUTE!
er-- LITTLE ARCHIE, YOU HAVE ONLY ONE MORE PAPER TO DELIVER... HERE! LET ME WRITE DOWN THE ADDRESS. IT'S THE LAST ONE IN THE ROUTE BOOK!
I'LL MEET YOU THERE SOON!
REAL SOON!
RIVERDALE RECORD
9

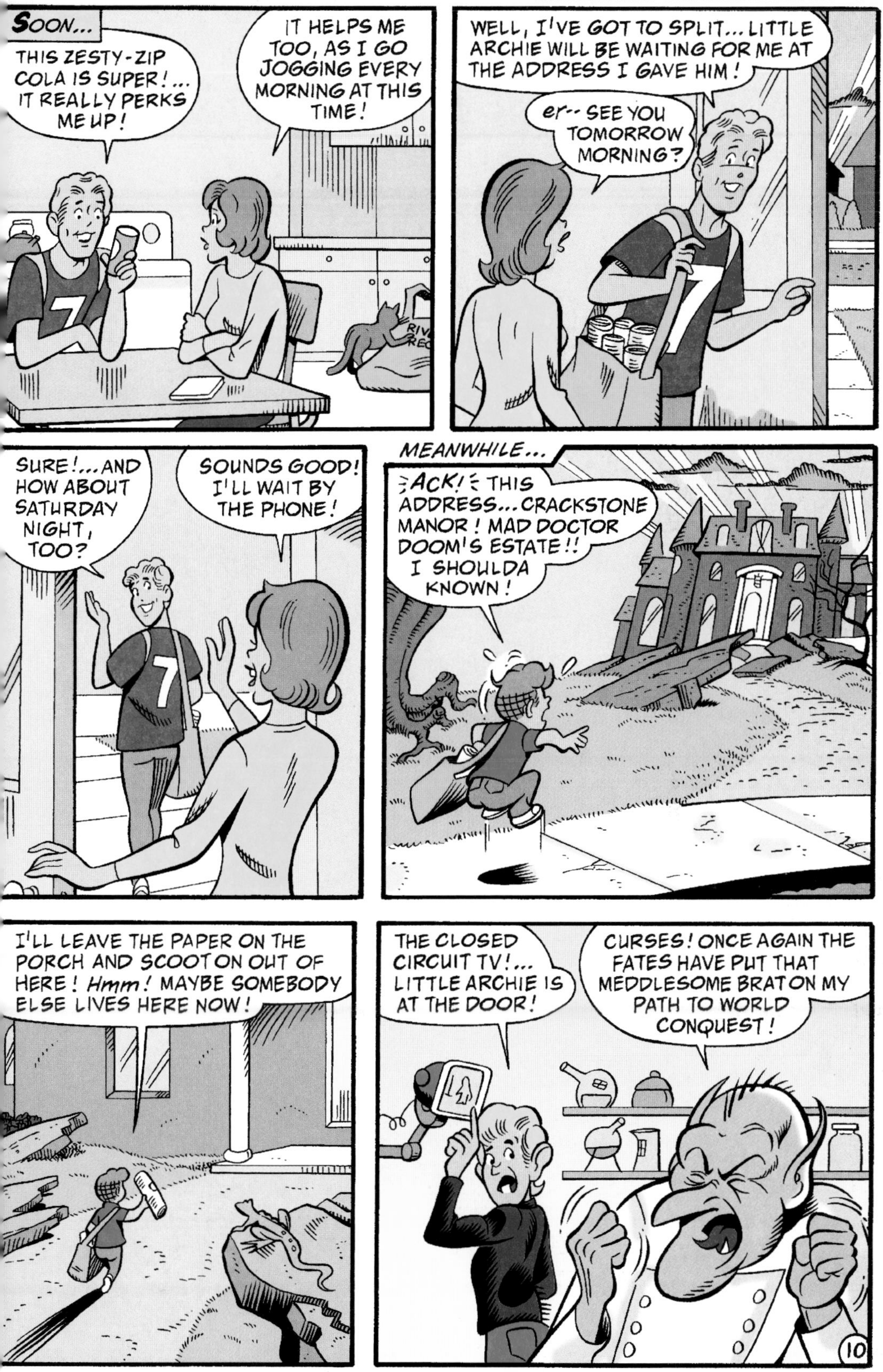
SOON...
THIS ZESTY-ZIP COLA IS SUPER!... IT REALLY PERKS ME UP!
IT HELPS ME TOO, AS I GO JOGGING EVERY MORNING AT THIS TIME!
WELL, I'VE GOT TO SPLIT... LITTLE ARCHIE WILL BE WAITING FOR ME AT THE ADDRESS I GAVE HIM!
er-- SEE YOU TOMORROW MORNING?
SURE!... AND HOW ABOUT SATURDAY NIGHT, TOO?
SOUNDS GOOD! I'LL WAIT BY THE PHONE!
MEANWHILE...
ACK! THIS ADDRESS... CRACKSTONE MANOR! MAD DOCTOR DOOM'S ESTATE!! I SHOULDA KNOWN!
I'LL LEAVE THE PAPER ON THE PORCH AND SCOOT ON OUT OF HERE! Hmm! MAYBE SOMEBODY ELSE LIVES HERE NOW!
THE CLOSED CIRCUIT TV!... LITTLE ARCHIE IS AT THE DOOR!
CURSES! ONCE AGAIN THE FATES HAVE PUT THAT MEDDLESOME BRAT ON MY PATH TO WORLD CONQUEST!
10

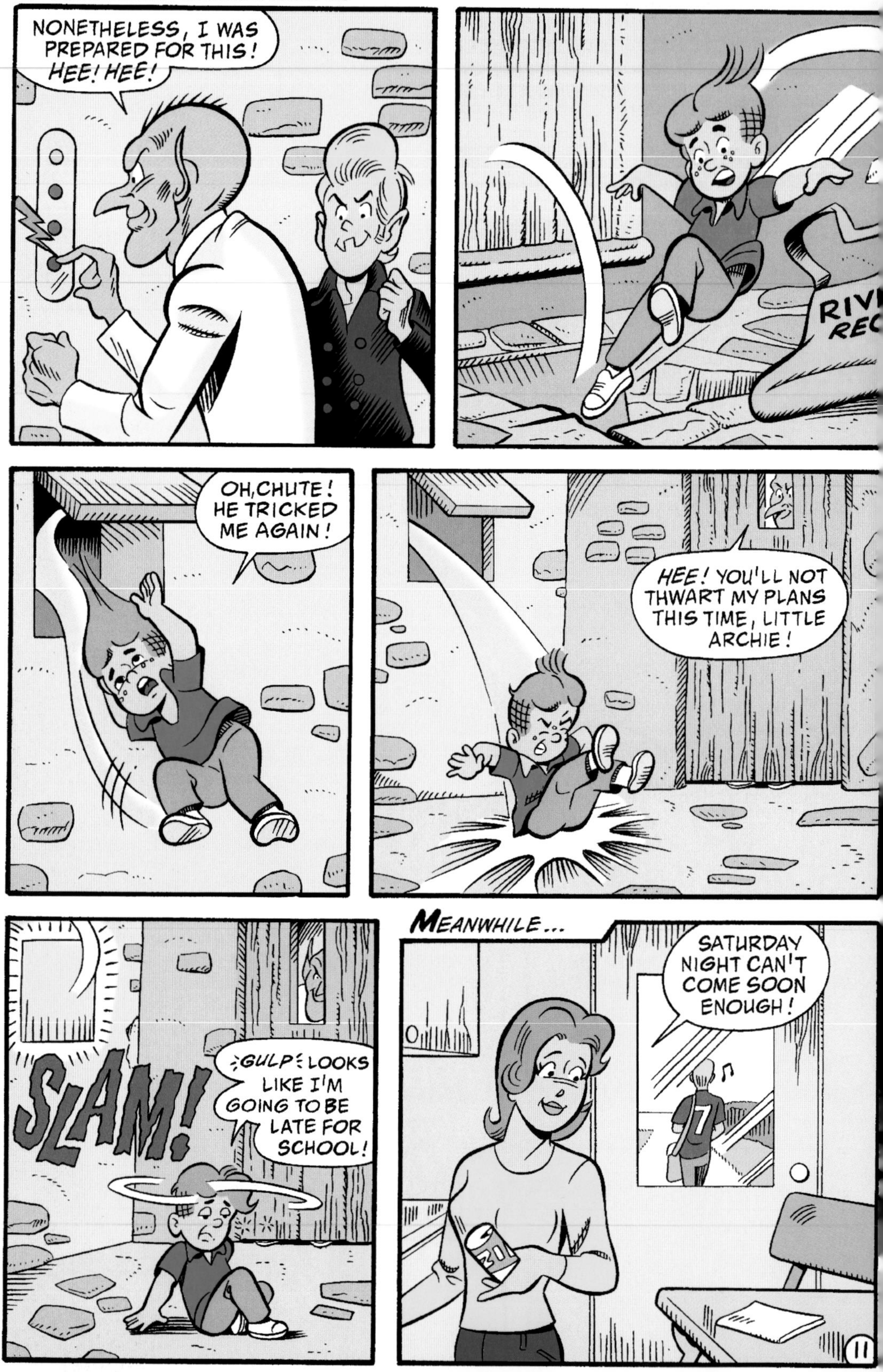
NONETHELESS, I WAS PREPARED FOR THIS! HEE! HEE!
RIV
REC
OH, CHUTE! HE TRICKED ME AGAIN!
HEE! YOU'LL NOT THWART MY PLANS THIS TIME, LITTLE ARCHIE!
SLAM!
:GULP: LOOKS LIKE I'M GOING TO BE LATE FOR SCHOOL!
MEANWHILE...
SATURDAY NIGHT CAN'T COME SOON ENOUGH!
7
11

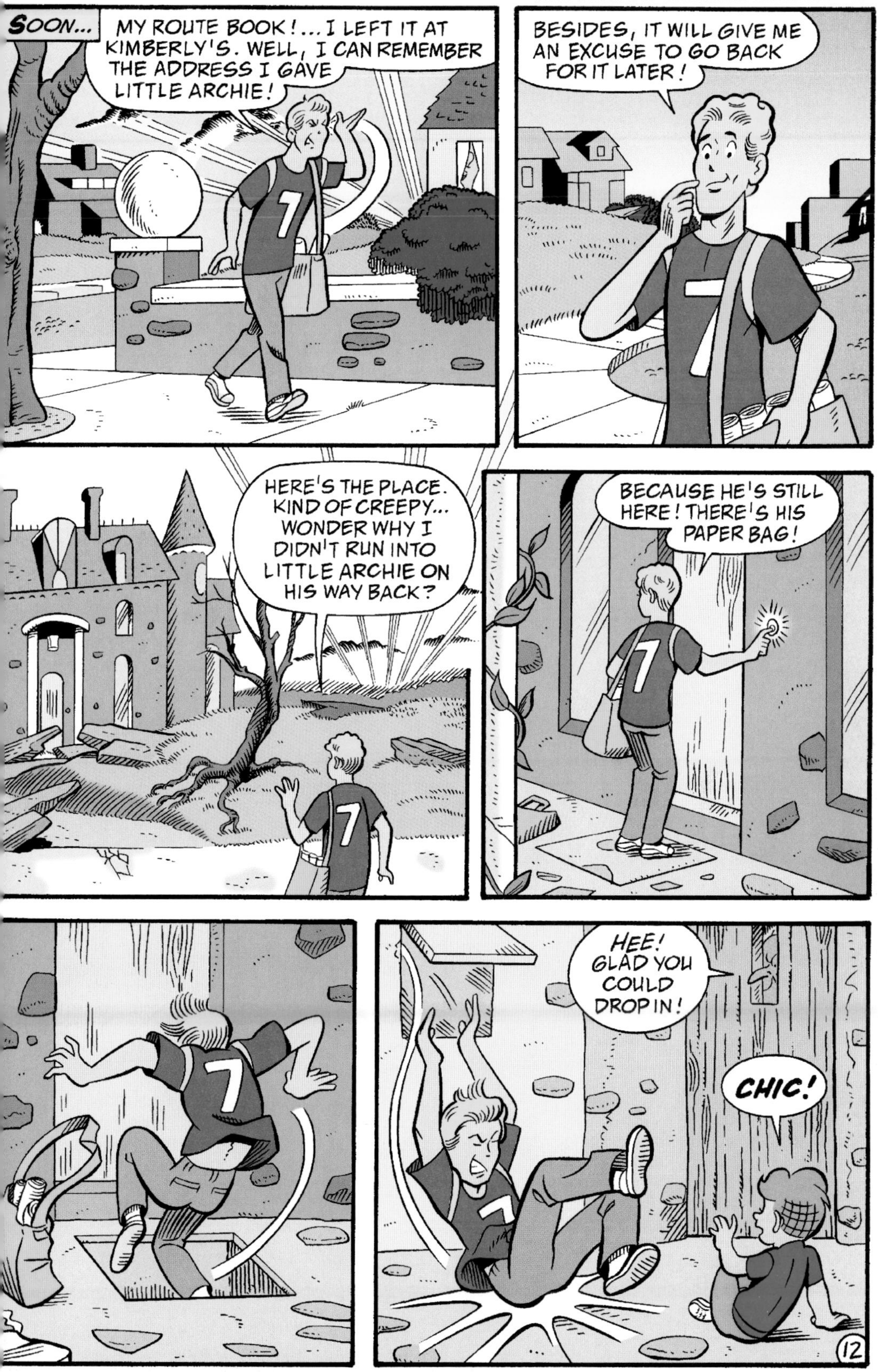
SOON...
MY ROUTE BOOK! ... I LEFT IT AT KIMBERLY'S. WELL, I CAN REMEMBER THE ADDRESS I GAVE LITTLE ARCHIE!
BESIDES, IT WILL GIVE ME AN EXCUSE TO GO BACK FOR IT LATER!
HERE'S THE PLACE. KIND OF CREEPY... WONDER WHY I DIDN'T RUN INTO LITTLE ARCHIE ON HIS WAY BACK?
BECAUSE HE'S STILL HERE! THERE'S HIS PAPER BAG!
HEE! GLAD YOU COULD DROP IN!
CHIC!
12

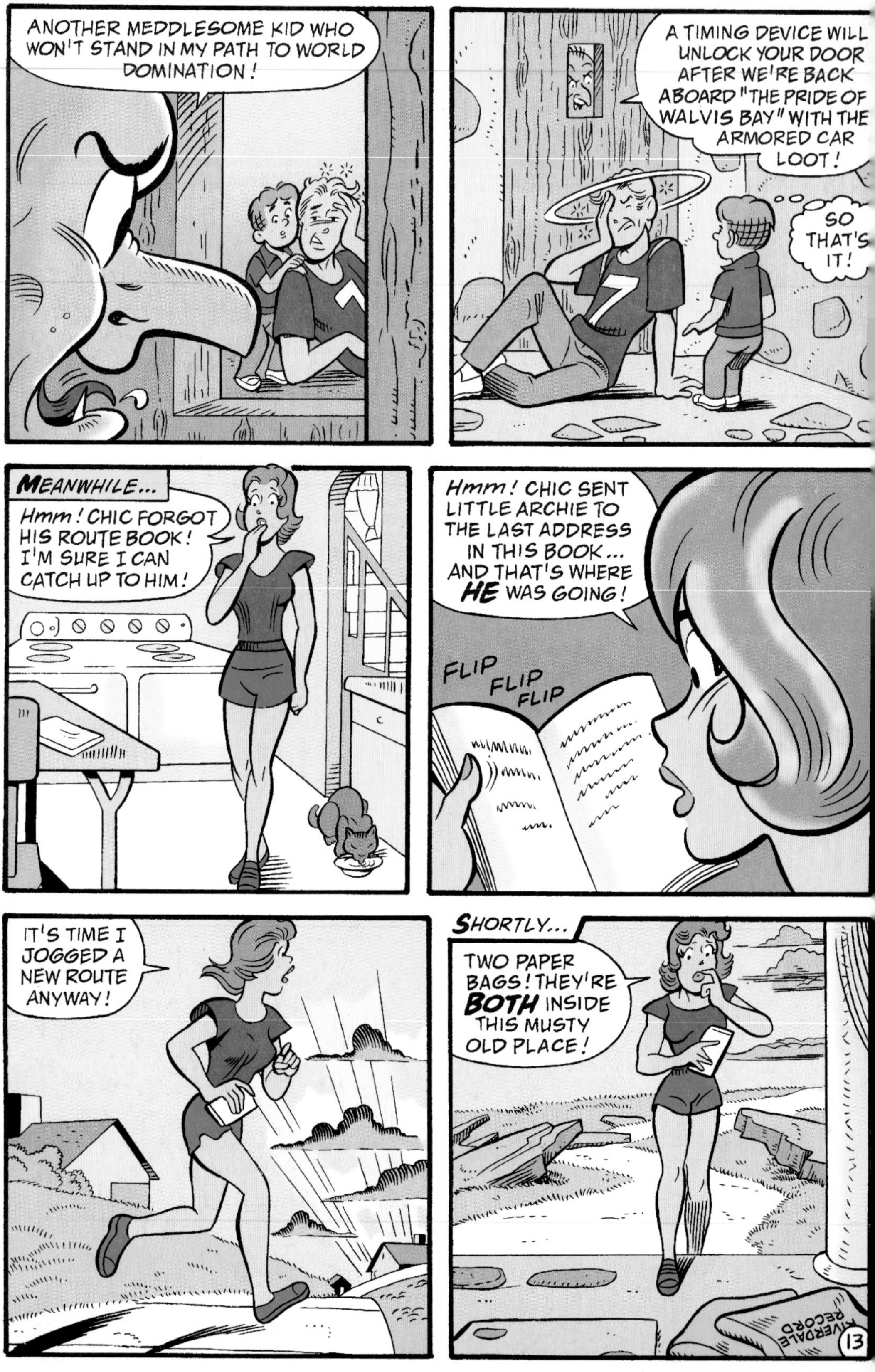

ANOTHER MEDDLESOME KID WHO WON'T STAND IN MY PATH TO WORLD DOMINATION!
A TIMING DEVICE WILL UNLOCK YOUR DOOR AFTER WE'RE BACK ABOARD "THE PRIDE OF WALVIS BAY" WITH THE ARMORED CAR LOOT!
SO THAT'S IT!
MEANWHILE...
Hmm! CHIC FORGOT HIS ROUTE BOOK! I'M SURE I CAN CATCH UP TO HIM!
Hmm! CHIC SENT LITTLE ARCHIE TO THE LAST ADDRESS IN THIS BOOK... AND THAT'S WHERE HE WAS GOING!
FLIP FLIP FLIP
IT'S TIME I JOGGED A NEW ROUTE ANYWAY!
SHORTLY...
TWO PAPER BAGS! THEY'RE BOTH INSIDE THIS MUSTY OLD PLACE!
RIVERDALE RECORD
13

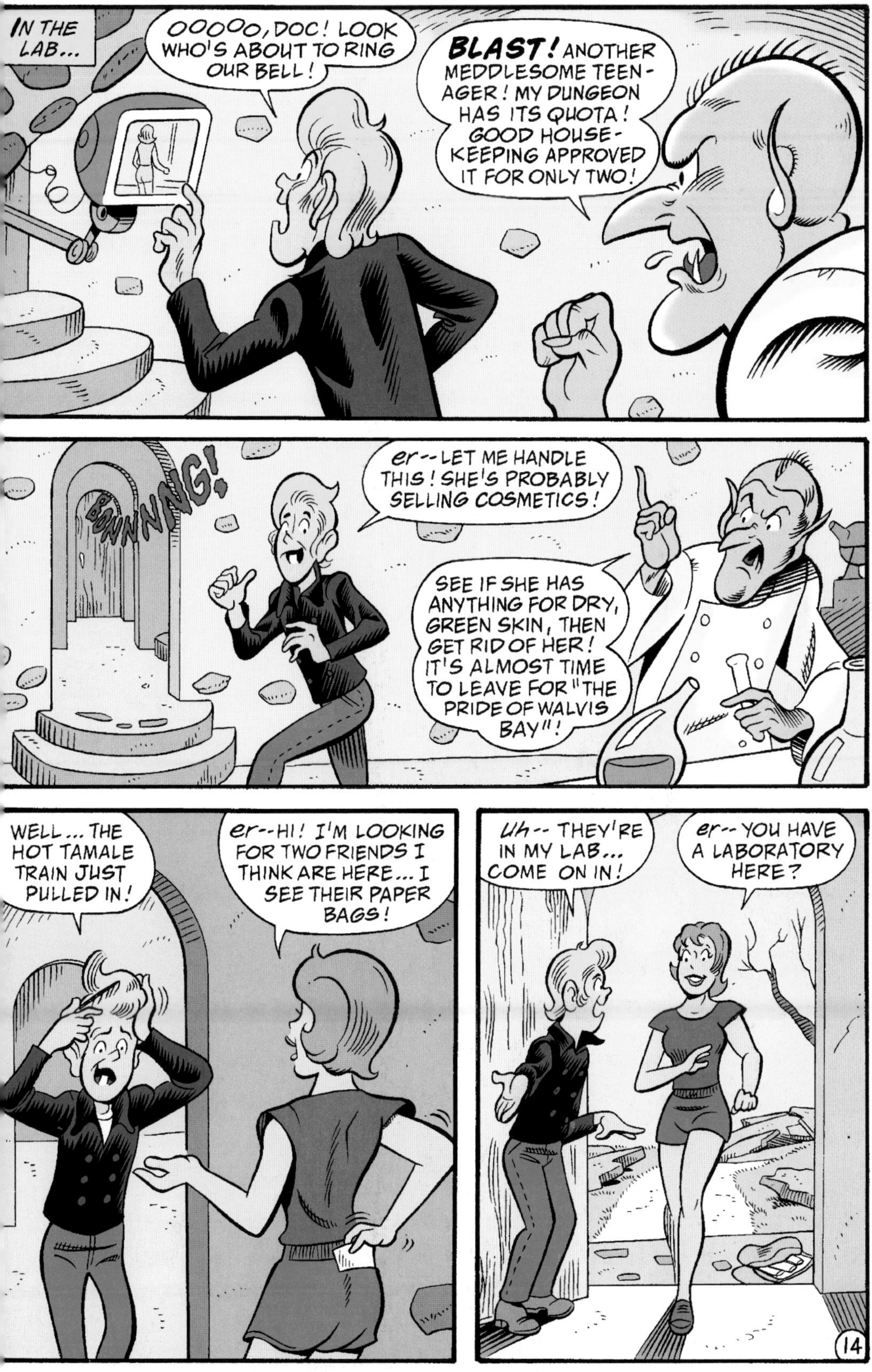
IN THE LAB...
OOOOO, DOC! LOOK WHO'S ABOUT TO RING OUR BELL!
BLAST! ANOTHER MEDDLESOME TEEN-AGER! MY DUNGEON HAS ITS QUOTA! GOOD HOUSE-KEEPING APPROVED IT FOR ONLY TWO!
BONNNNG!
er-- LET ME HANDLE THIS! SHE'S PROBABLY SELLING COSMETICS!
SEE IF SHE HAS ANYTHING FOR DRY, GREEN SKIN, THEN GET RID OF HER! IT'S ALMOST TIME TO LEAVE FOR "THE PRIDE OF WALVIS BAY"!
WELL ... THE HOT TAMALE TRAIN JUST PULLED IN!
er--HI! I'M LOOKING FOR TWO FRIENDS I THINK ARE HERE... I SEE THEIR PAPER BAGS!
uh-- THEY'RE IN MY LAB... COME ON IN!
er-- YOU HAVE A LABORATORY HERE?
14

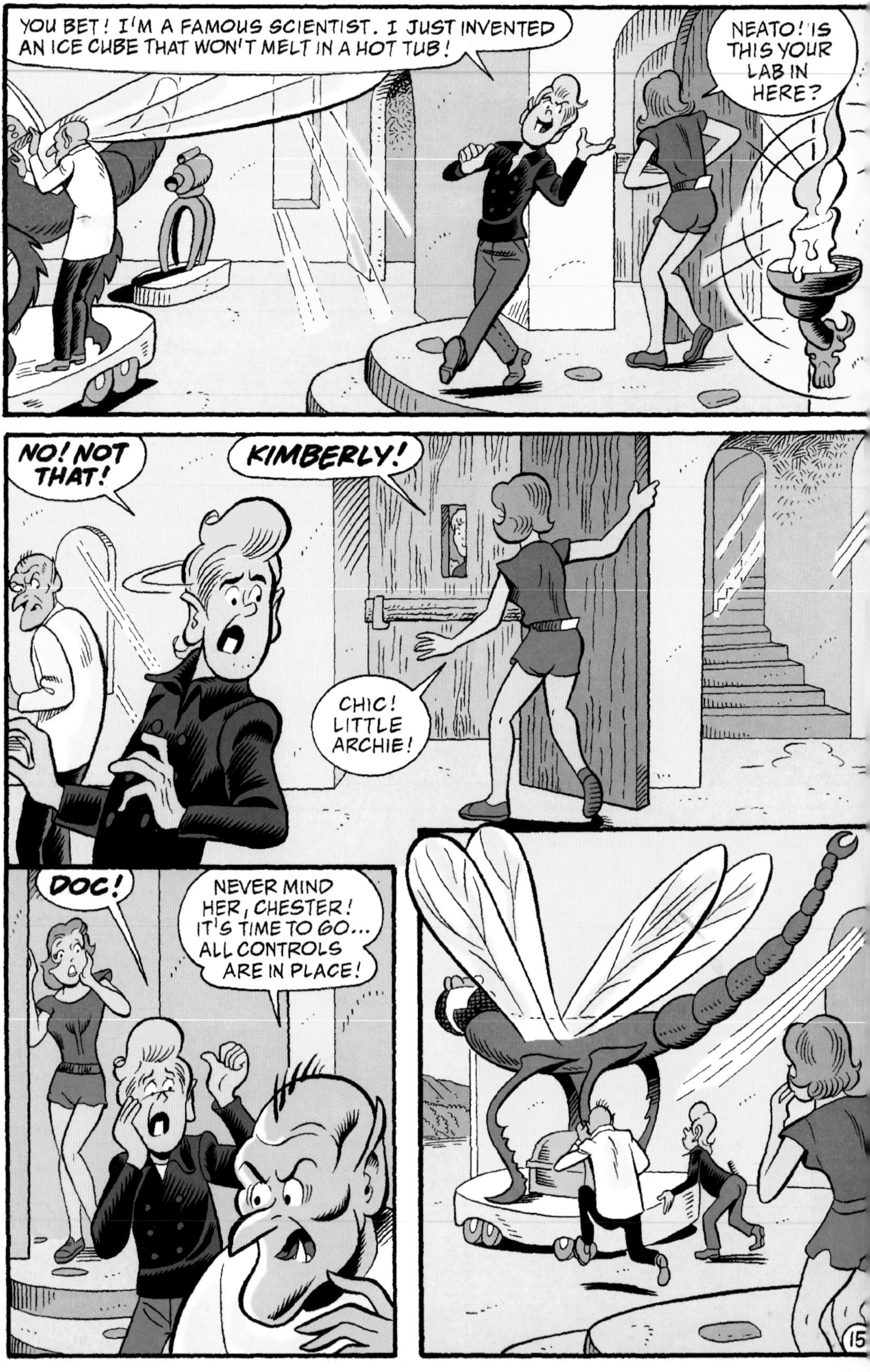
YOU BET! I'M A FAMOUS SCIENTIST. I JUST INVENTED AN ICE CUBE THAT WON'T MELT IN A HOT TUB!
NEATO! IS THIS YOUR LAB IN HERE?
NO! NOT THAT!
KIMBERLY!
CHIC! LITTLE ARCHIE!
DOC!
NEVER MIND HER, CHESTER! IT'S TIME TO GO... ALL CONTROLS ARE IN PLACE!
15

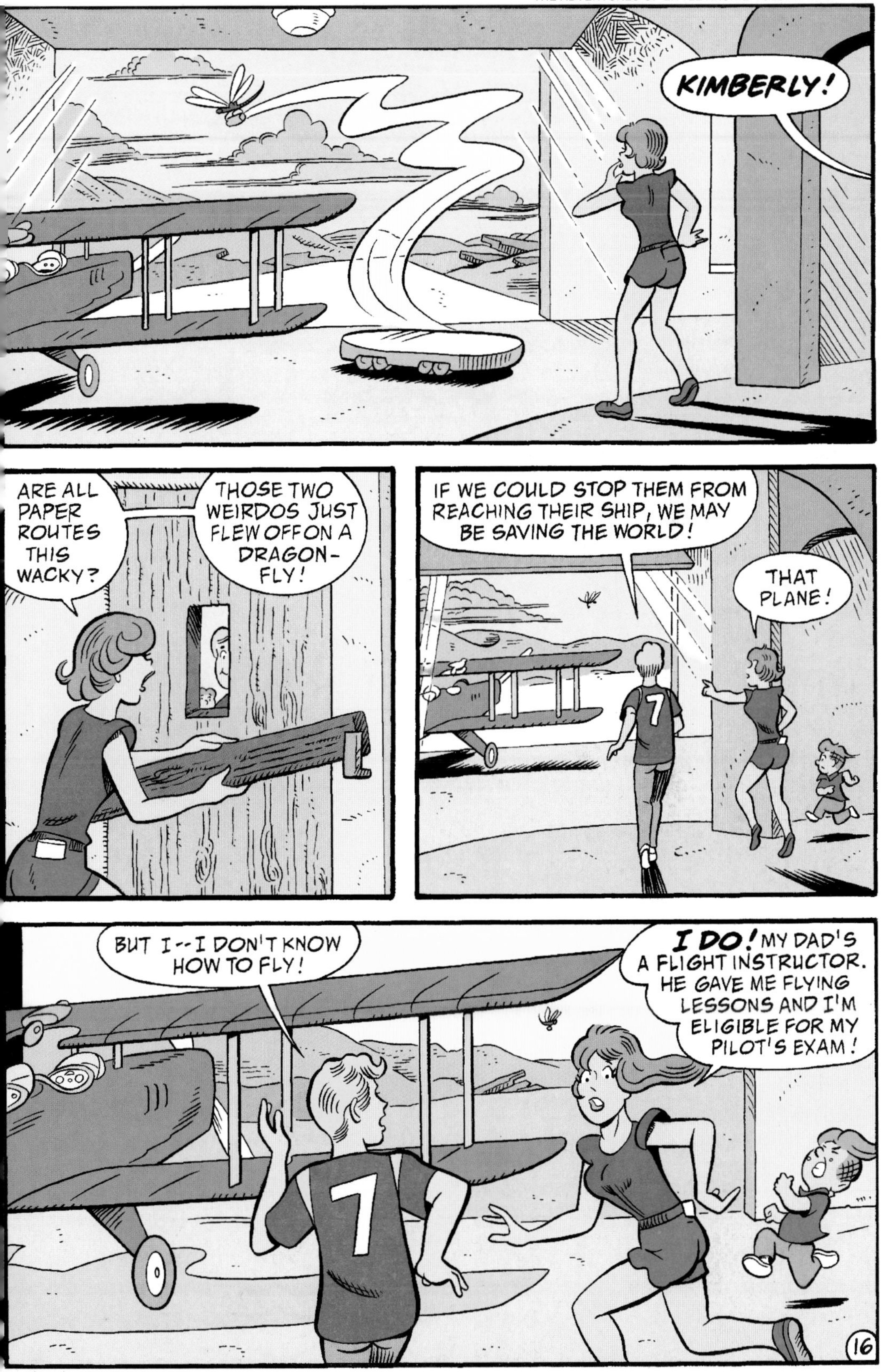
KIMBERLY!
ARE ALL PAPER ROUTES THIS WACKY?
THOSE TWO WEIRDOS JUST FLEW OFF ON A DRAGON-FLY!
IF WE COULD STOP THEM FROM REACHING THEIR SHIP, WE MAY BE SAVING THE WORLD!
THAT PLANE!
BUT I--I DON'T KNOW HOW TO FLY!
I DO! MY DAD'S A FLIGHT INSTRUCTOR. HE GAVE ME FLYING LESSONS AND I'M ELIGIBLE FOR MY PILOT'S EXAM!
16

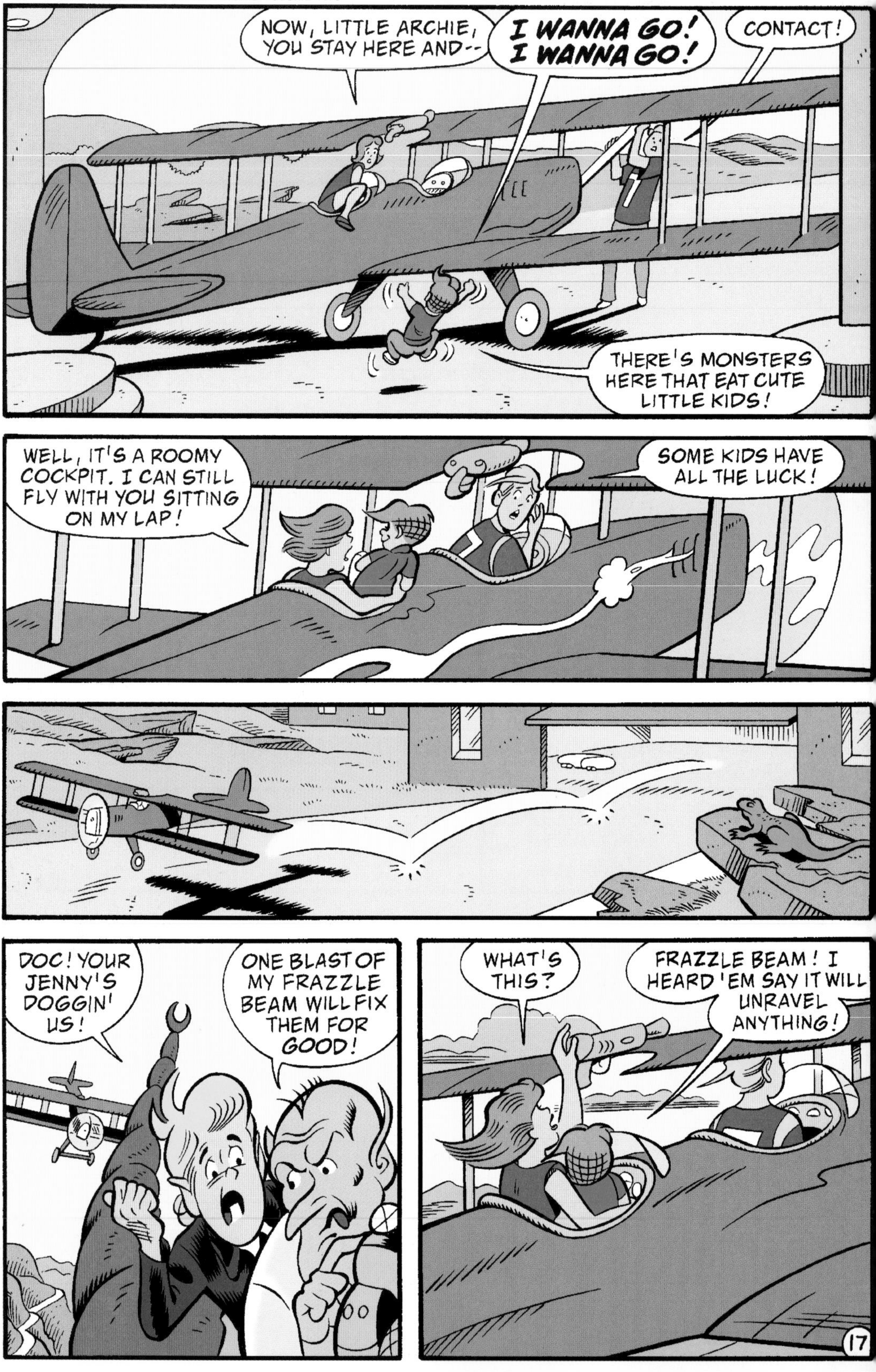
NOW, LITTLE ARCHIE, YOU STAY HERE AND--
I WANNA GO! I WANNA GO!
CONTACT!
THERE'S MONSTERS HERE THAT EAT CUTE LITTLE KIDS!
WELL, IT'S A ROOMY COCKPIT. I CAN STILL FLY WITH YOU SITTING ON MY LAP!
SOME KIDS HAVE ALL THE LUCK!
DOC! YOUR JENNY'S DOGGIN' US!
ONE BLAST OF MY FRAZZLE BEAM WILL FIX THEM FOR GOOD!
WHAT'S THIS?
FRAZZLE BEAM! I HEARD 'EM SAY IT WILL UNRAVEL ANYTHING!
17

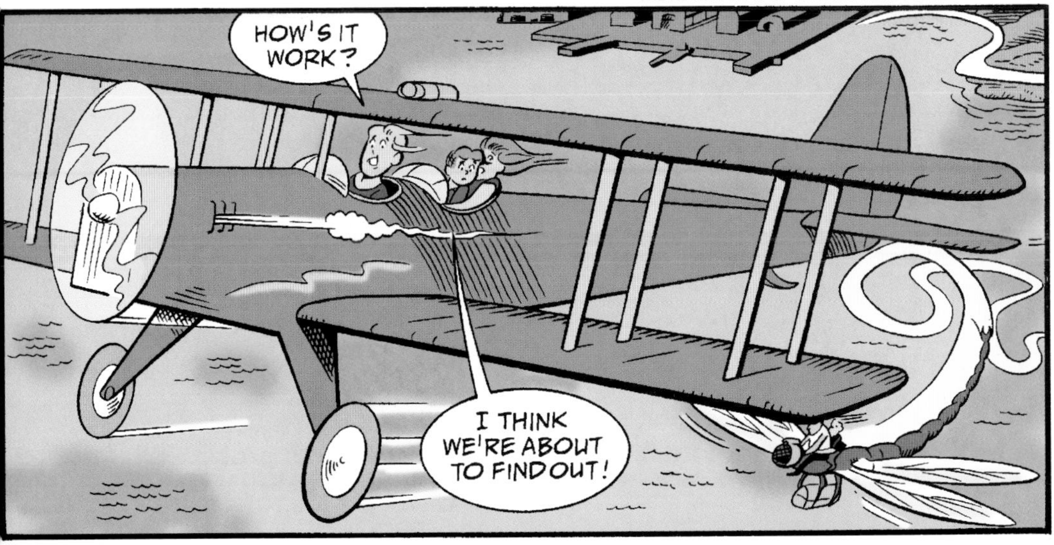
HOW'S IT WORK?
I THINK WE'RE ABOUT TO FIND OUT!

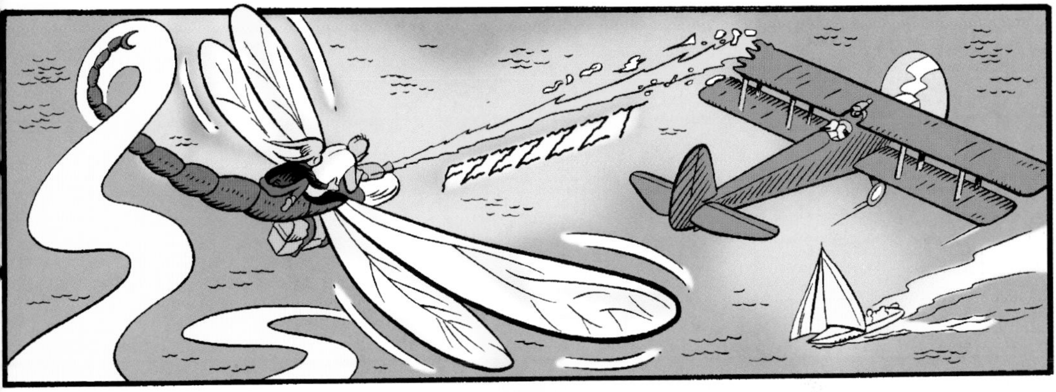
FZZZZZZT

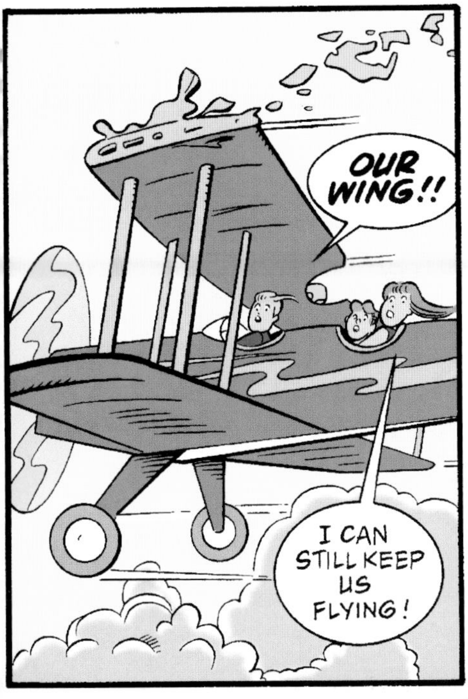
OUR WING!!
I CAN STILL KEEP US FLYING!

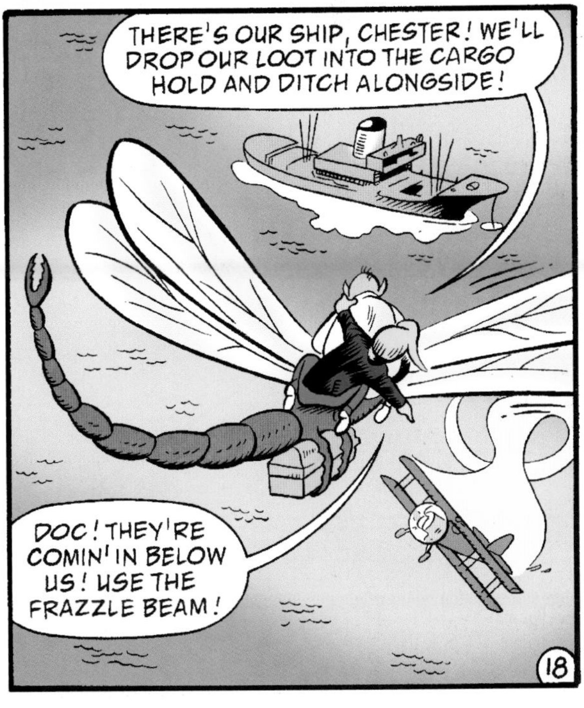
THERE'S OUR SHIP, CHESTER! WE'LL DROP OUR LOOT INTO THE CARGO HOLD AND DITCH ALONGSIDE!
DOC! THEY'RE COMIN' IN BELOW US! USE THE FRAZZLE BEAM!
18

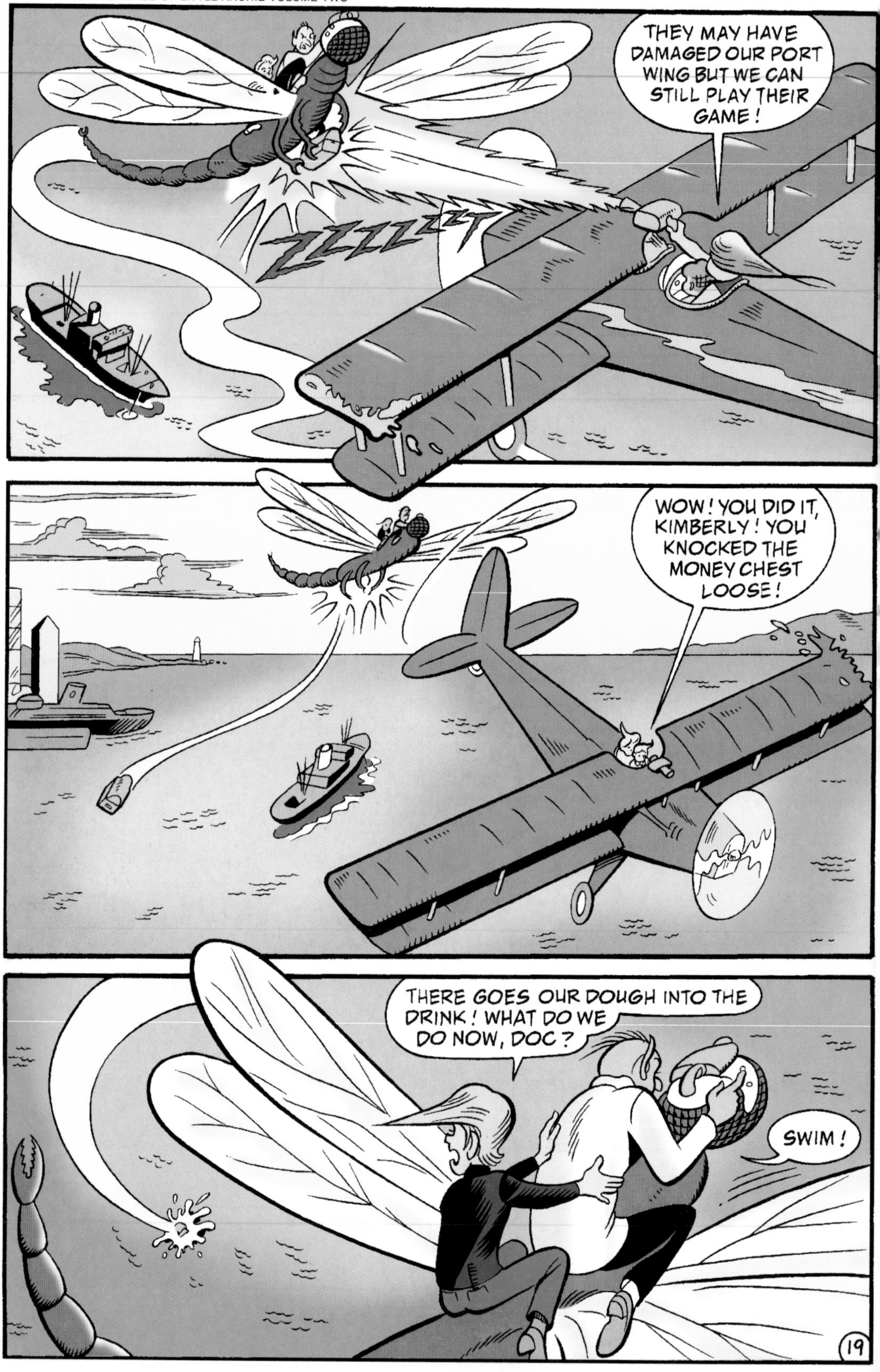
THEY MAY HAVE DAMAGED OUR PORT WING BUT WE CAN STILL PLAY THEIR GAME!
ZZZZZZZT
WOW! YOU DID IT, KIMBERLY! YOU KNOCKED THE MONEY CHEST LOOSE!
THERE GOES OUR DOUGH INTO THE DRINK! WHAT DO WE DO NOW, DOC?
SWIM!
19

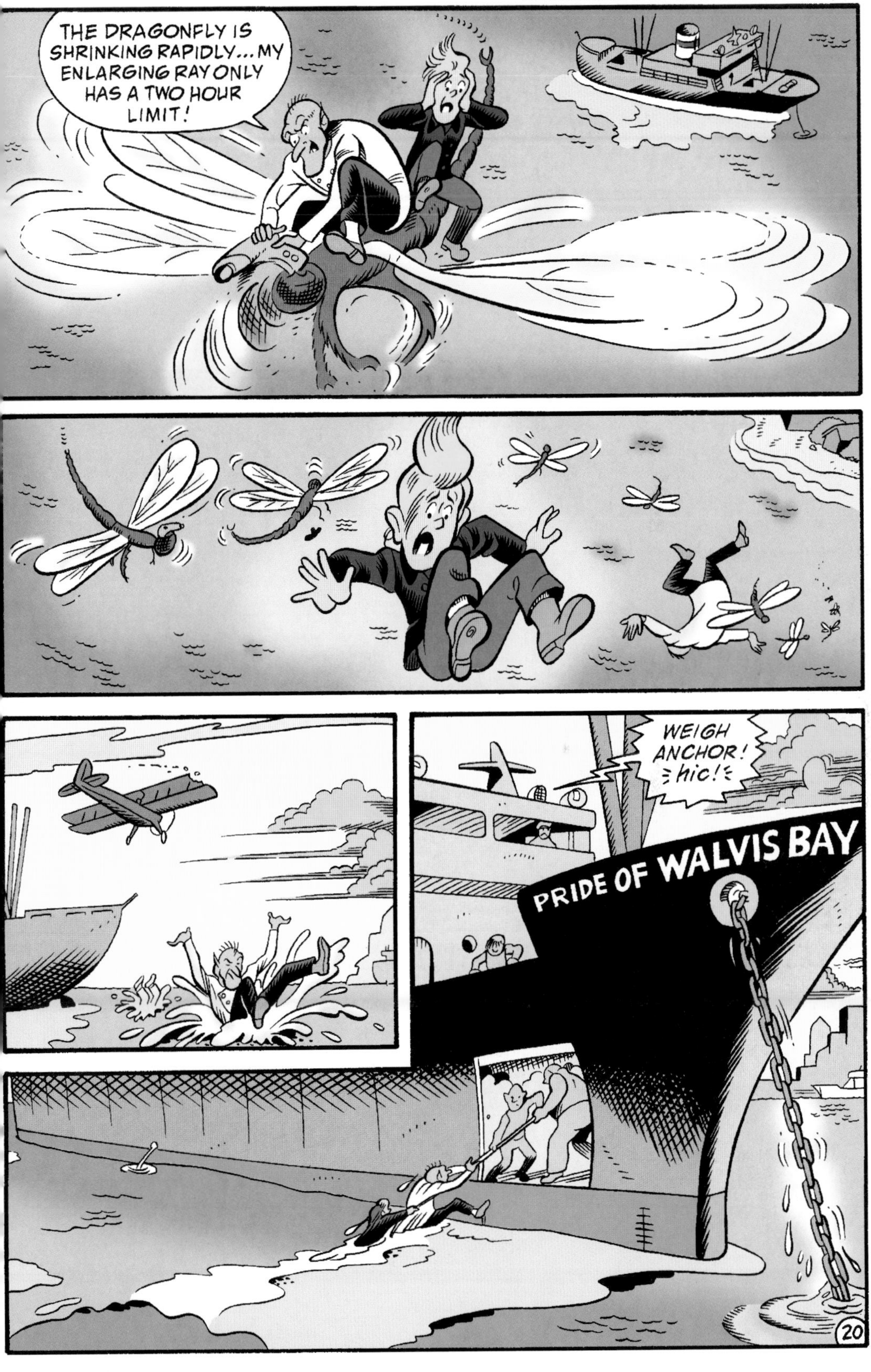
THE DRAGONFLY IS SHRINKING RAPIDLY... MY ENLARGING RAY ONLY HAS A TWO HOUR LIMIT!
WEIGH ANCHOR! hic!
PRIDE OF WALVIS BAY
20

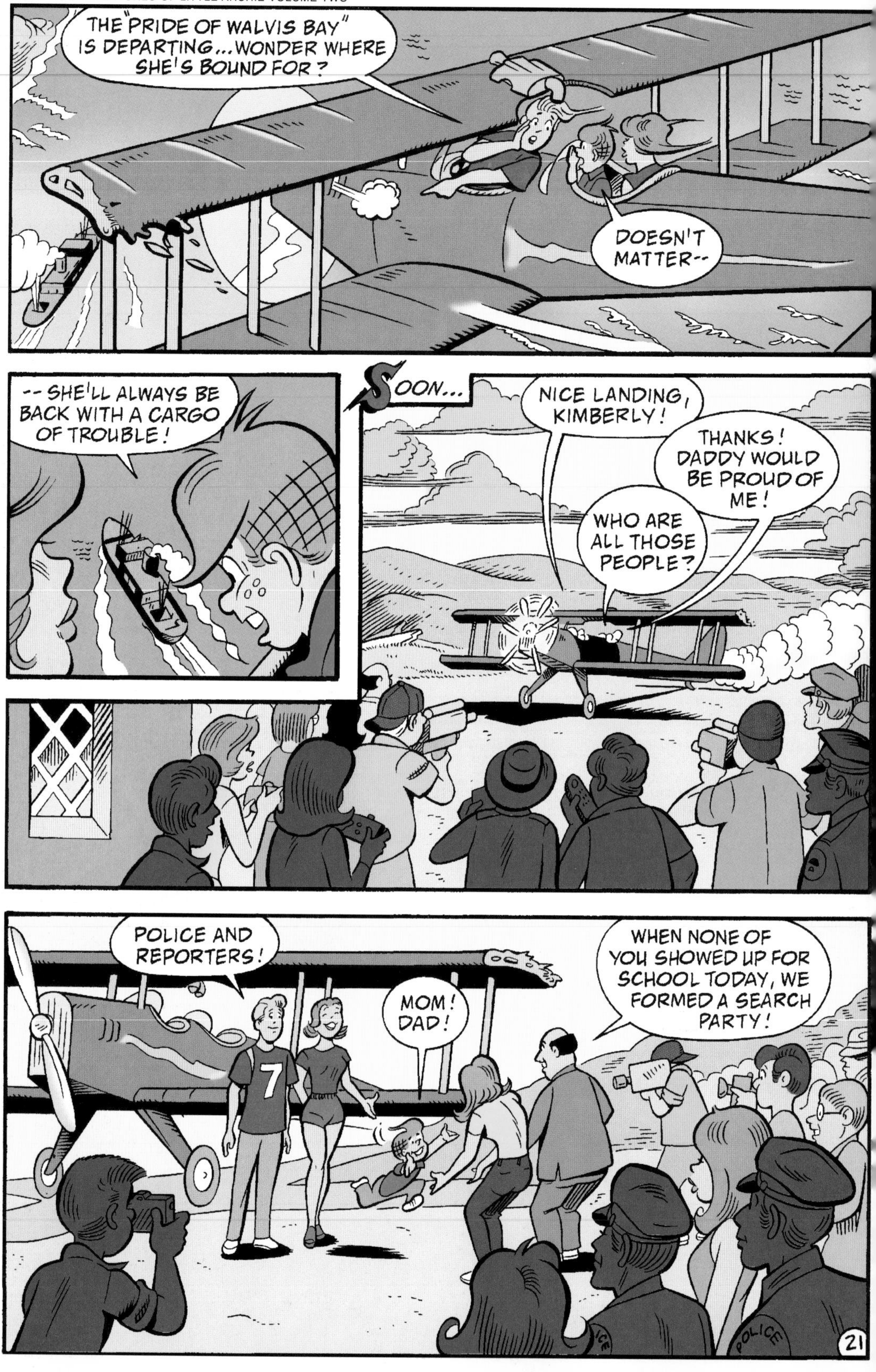
THE "PRIDE OF WALVIS BAY" IS DEPARTING...WONDER WHERE SHE'S BOUND FOR?
DOESN'T MATTER--
-- SHE'LL ALWAYS BE BACK WITH A CARGO OF TROUBLE!
SOON...
NICE LANDING, KIMBERLY!
THANKS! DADDY WOULD BE PROUD OF ME!
WHO ARE ALL THOSE PEOPLE?
POLICE AND REPORTERS!
MOM! DAD!
WHEN NONE OF YOU SHOWED UP FOR SCHOOL TODAY, WE FORMED A SEARCH PARTY!
POLICE
21

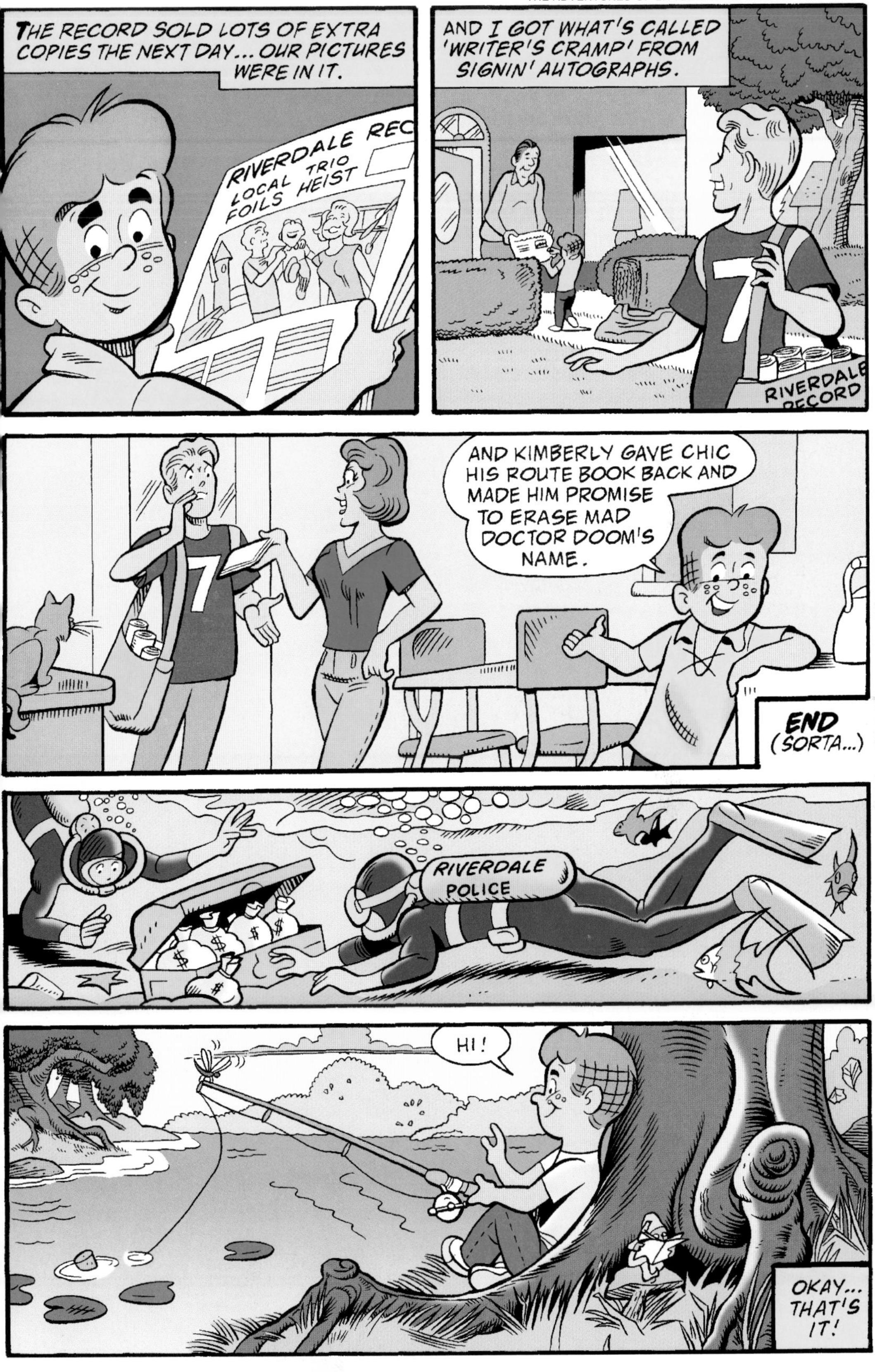
THE RECORD SOLD LOTS OF EXTRA COPIES THE NEXT DAY... OUR PICTURES WERE IN IT.
RIVERDALE REC
LOCAL TRIO FOILS HEIST
AND I GOT WHAT'S CALLED 'WRITER'S CRAMP' FROM SIGNIN' AUTOGRAPHS.
7
RIVERDALE RECORD
AND KIMBERLY GAVE CHIC HIS ROUTE BOOK BACK AND MADE HIM PROMISE TO ERASE MAD DOCTOR DOOM'S NAME.
END (SORTA...)
RIVERDALE POLICE
HI!
OKAY... THAT'S IT!

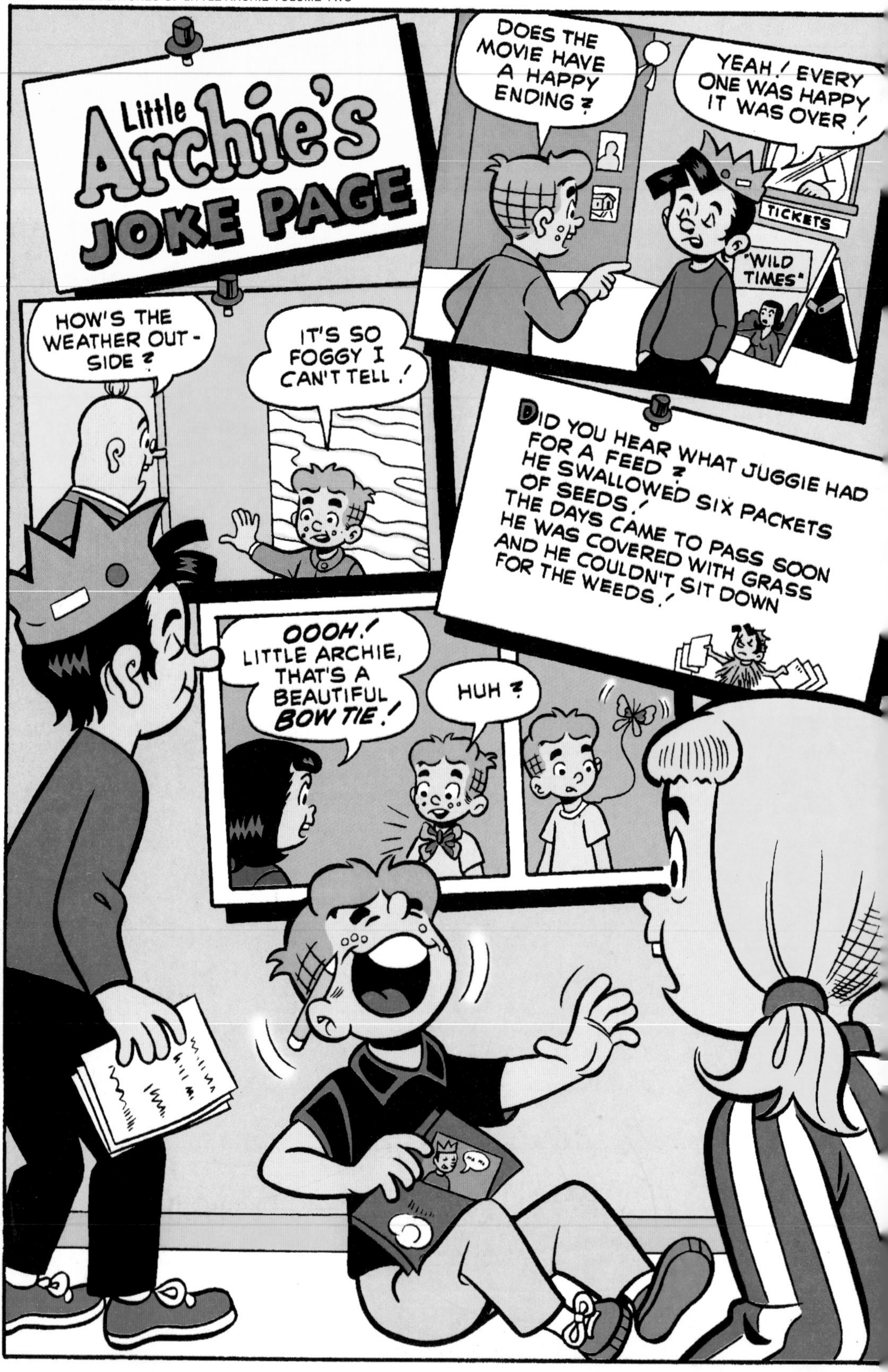
Little Archie's
JOKE PAGE
DOES THE MOVIE HAVE A HAPPY ENDING ?
YEAH ! EVERY ONE WAS HAPPY IT WAS OVER !
TICKETS
"WILD TIMES"
HOW'S THE WEATHER OUT-SIDE ?
IT'S SO FOGGY I CAN'T TELL !
DID YOU HEAR WHAT JUGGIE HAD FOR A FEED ? HE SWALLOWED SIX PACKETS OF SEEDS ! THE DAYS CAME TO PASS SOON HE WAS COVERED WITH GRASS AND HE COULDN'T SIT DOWN FOR THE WEEDS !
OOOH ! LITTLE ARCHIE, THAT'S A BEAUTIFUL BOW TIE !
HUH ?

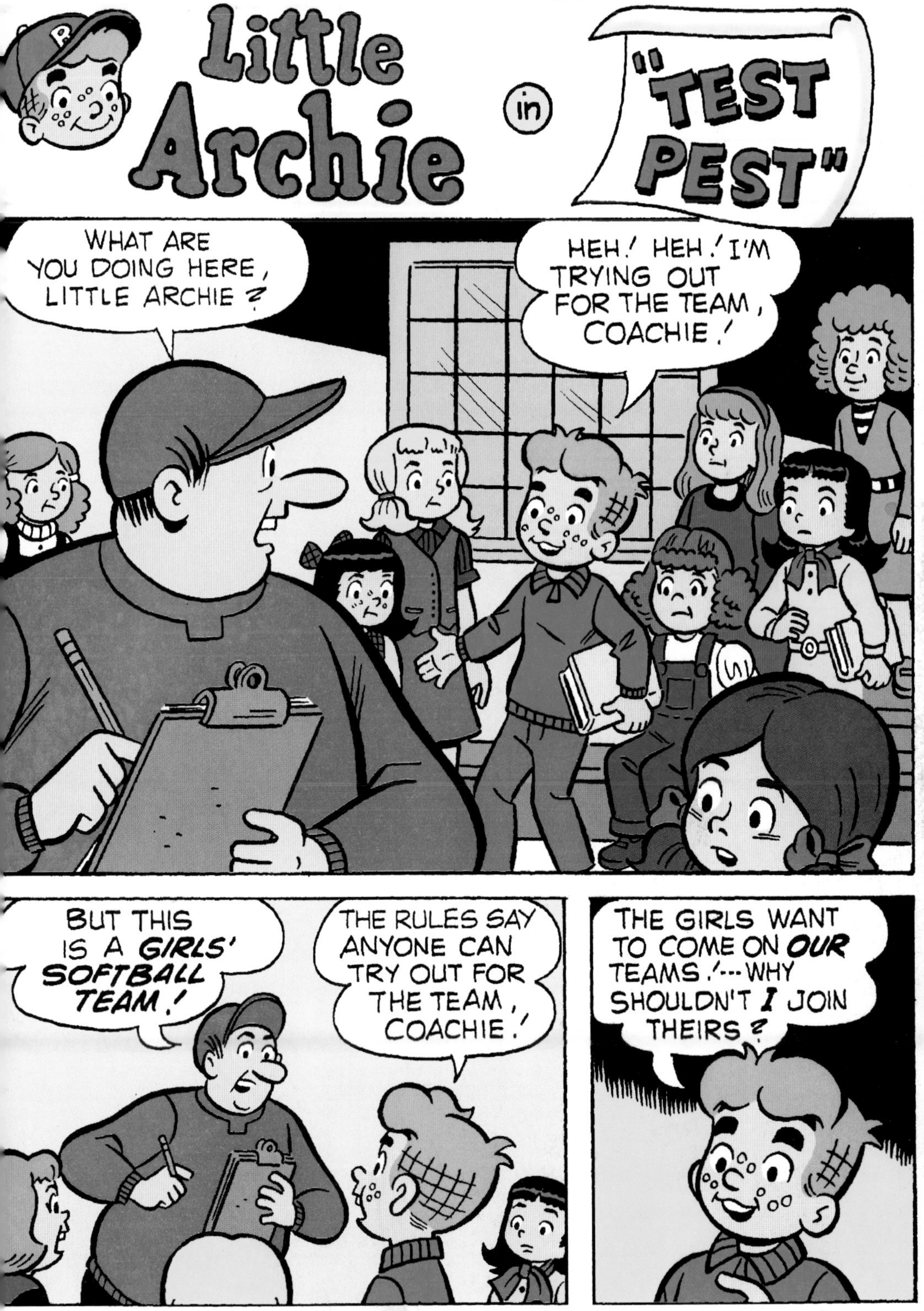
Little Archie in "TEST PEST"
WHAT ARE YOU DOING HERE, LITTLE ARCHIE?
HEH! HEH! I'M TRYING OUT FOR THE TEAM, COACHIE!
BUT THIS IS A GIRLS' SOFTBALL TEAM!
THE RULES SAY ANYONE CAN TRY OUT FOR THE TEAM, COACHIE!
THE GIRLS WANT TO COME ON OUR TEAMS!--- WHY SHOULDN'T I JOIN THEIRS?

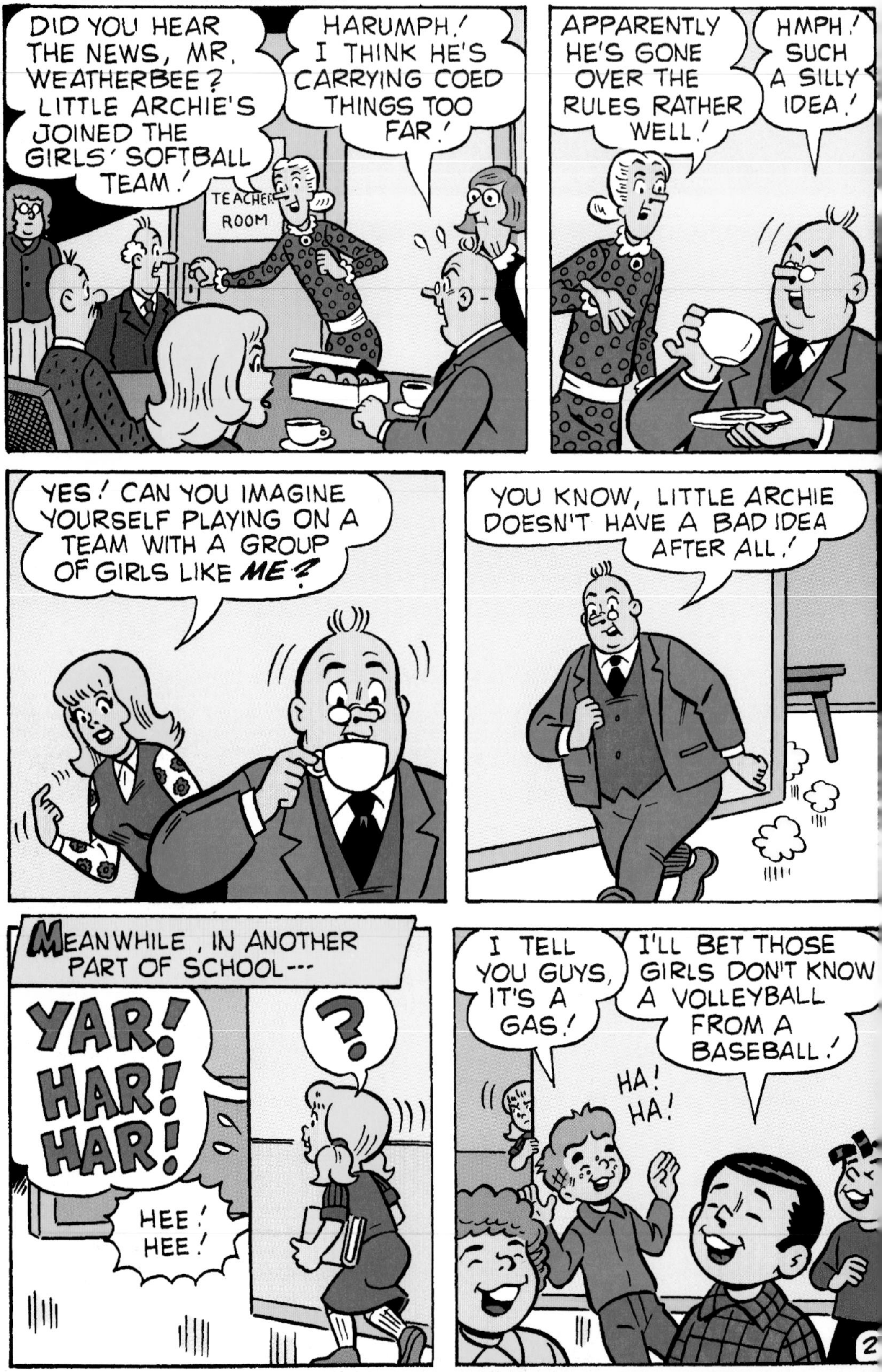
DID YOU HEAR THE NEWS, MR. WEATHERBEE? LITTLE ARCHIE'S JOINED THE GIRLS' SOFTBALL TEAM!
HARUMPH! I THINK HE'S CARRYING COED THINGS TOO FAR!
TEACHERS ROOM
APPARENTLY HE'S GONE OVER THE RULES RATHER WELL!
HMPH! SUCH A SILLY IDEA!
YES! CAN YOU IMAGINE YOURSELF PLAYING ON A TEAM WITH A GROUP OF GIRLS LIKE *ME*?
YOU KNOW, LITTLE ARCHIE DOESN'T HAVE A BAD IDEA AFTER ALL!
MEANWHILE, IN ANOTHER PART OF SCHOOL---
YAR! HAR! HAR!
HEE! HEE!
?
I TELL YOU GUYS, IT'S A GAS!
I'LL BET THOSE GIRLS DON'T KNOW A VOLLEYBALL FROM A BASEBALL!
HA! HA!
2

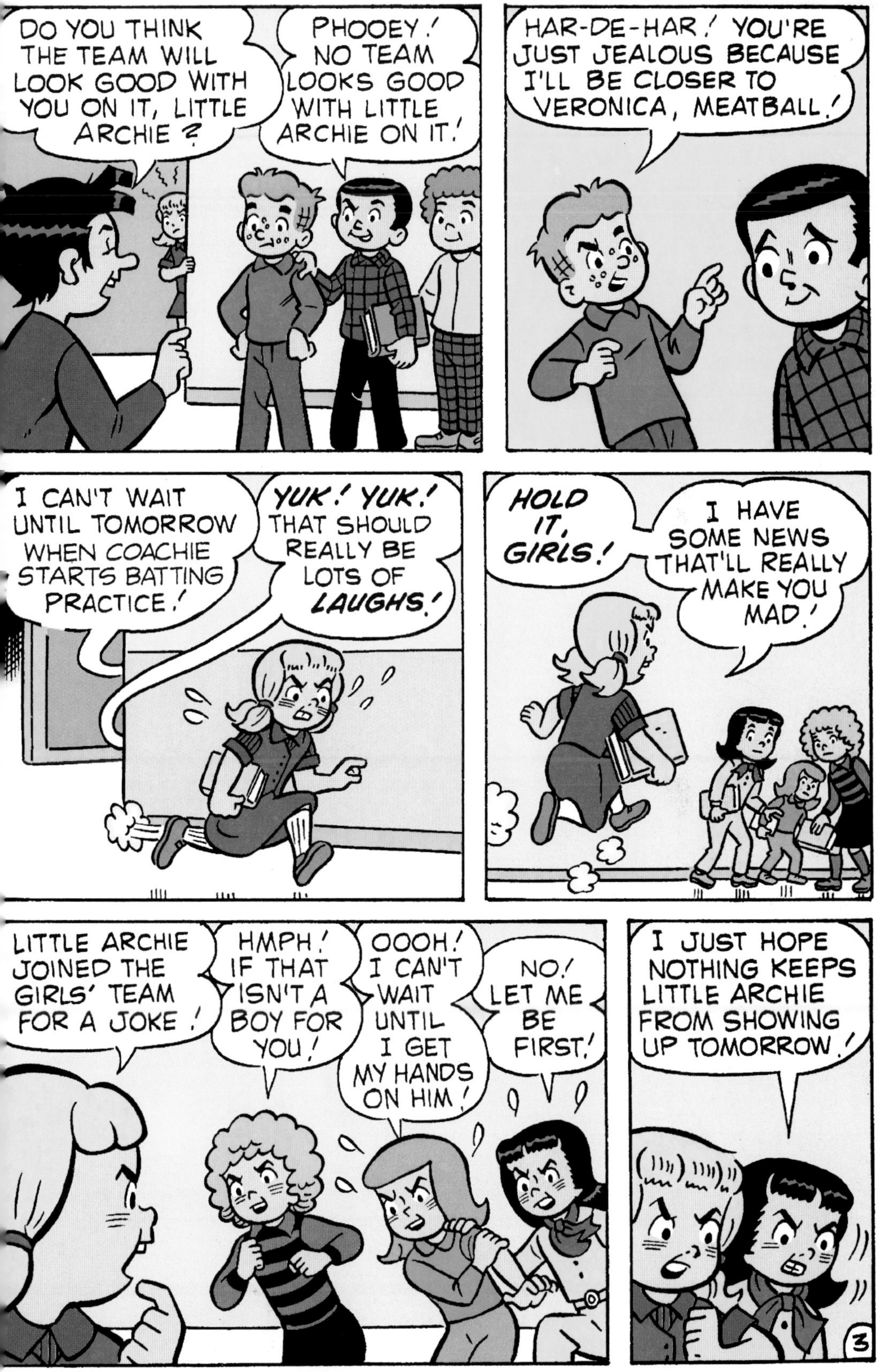
DO YOU THINK THE TEAM WILL LOOK GOOD WITH YOU ON IT, LITTLE ARCHIE?
PHOOEY! NO TEAM LOOKS GOOD WITH LITTLE ARCHIE ON IT!
HAR-DE-HAR! YOU'RE JUST JEALOUS BECAUSE I'LL BE CLOSER TO VERONICA, MEATBALL!
I CAN'T WAIT UNTIL TOMORROW WHEN COACHIE STARTS BATTING PRACTICE!
YUK! YUK! THAT SHOULD REALLY BE LOTS OF LAUGHS!
HOLD IT, GIRLS!
I HAVE SOME NEWS THAT'LL REALLY MAKE YOU MAD!
LITTLE ARCHIE JOINED THE GIRLS' TEAM FOR A JOKE!
HMPH! IF THAT ISN'T A BOY FOR YOU!
OOOH! I CAN'T WAIT UNTIL I GET MY HANDS ON HIM!
NO! LET ME BE FIRST!
I JUST HOPE NOTHING KEEPS LITTLE ARCHIE FROM SHOWING UP TOMORROW!
3

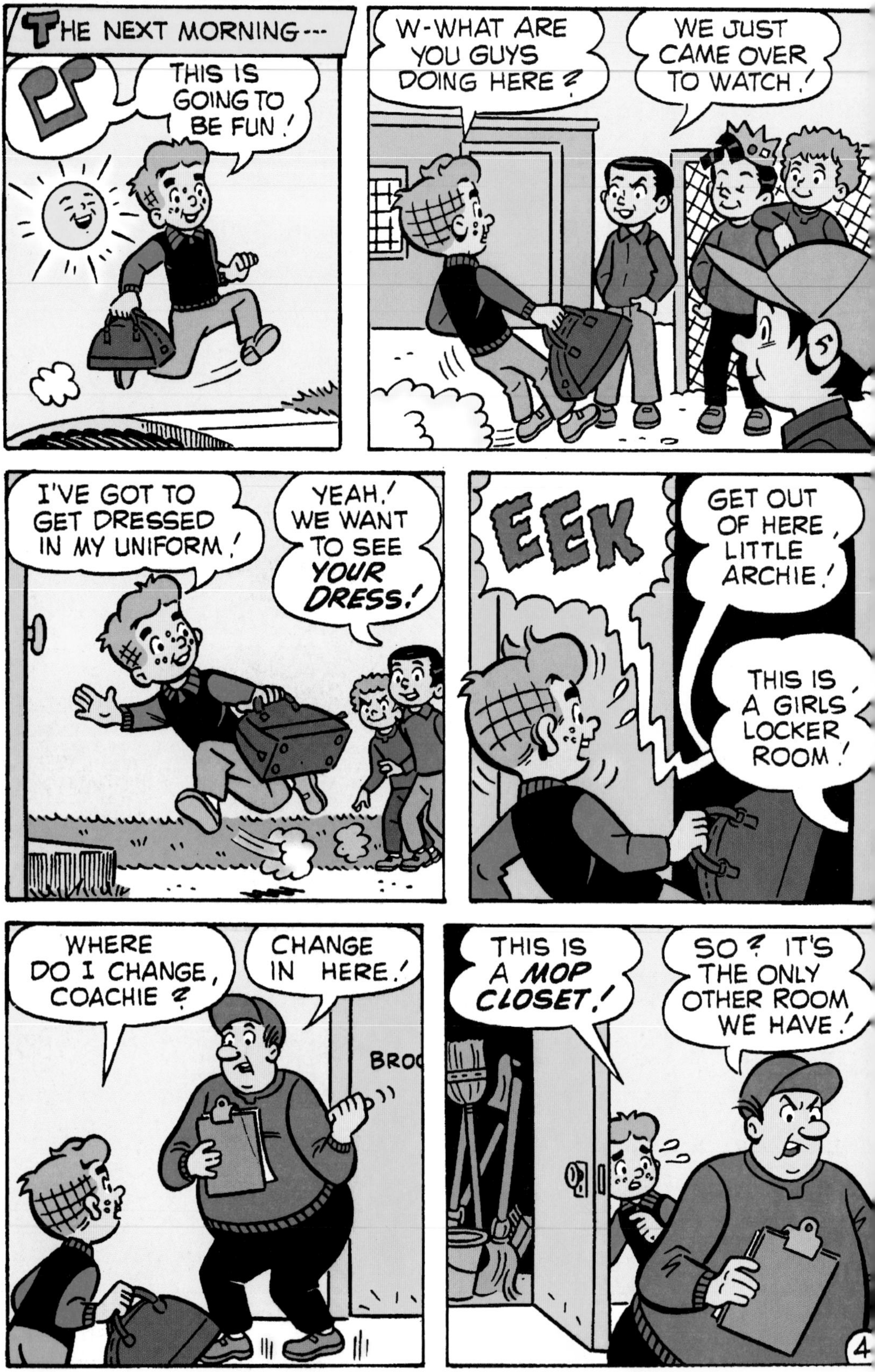
THE NEXT MORNING---
THIS IS GOING TO BE FUN!
W-WHAT ARE YOU GUYS DOING HERE?
WE JUST CAME OVER TO WATCH!
I'VE GOT TO GET DRESSED IN MY UNIFORM!
YEAH! WE WANT TO SEE YOUR DRESS!
EEK
GET OUT OF HERE, LITTLE ARCHIE!
THIS IS A GIRLS LOCKER ROOM!
WHERE DO I CHANGE, COACHIE?
CHANGE IN HERE!
BRO
THIS IS A MOP CLOSET!
SO? IT'S THE ONLY OTHER ROOM WE HAVE!
4

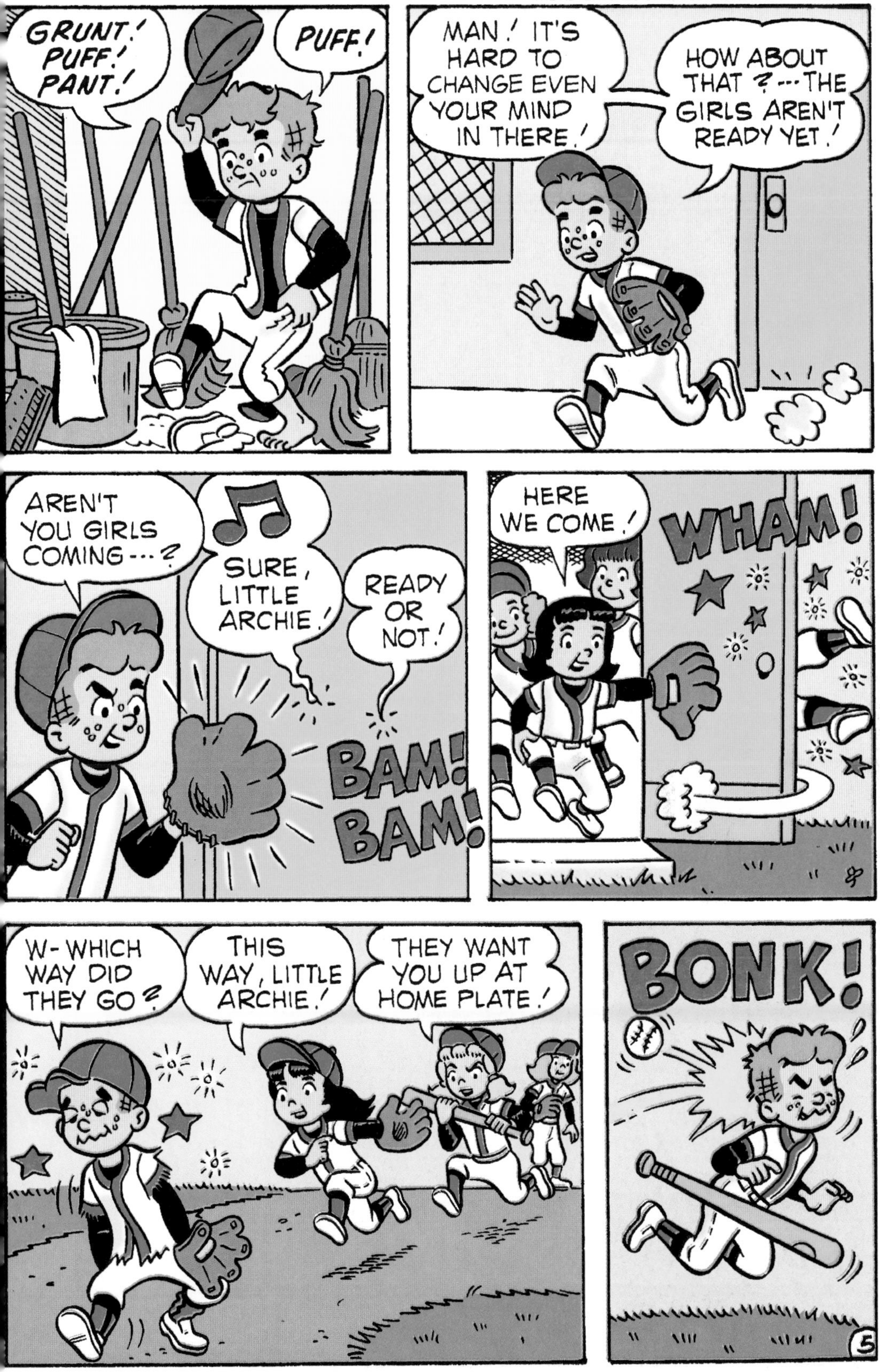
GRUNT! PUFF! PANT!
PUFF!
MAN! IT'S HARD TO CHANGE EVEN YOUR MIND IN THERE!
HOW ABOUT THAT? --- THE GIRLS AREN'T READY YET!
AREN'T YOU GIRLS COMING---?
SURE, LITTLE ARCHIE!
READY OR NOT!
BAM! BAM!
HERE WE COME!
WHAM!
W-WHICH WAY DID THEY GO?
THIS WAY, LITTLE ARCHIE!
THEY WANT YOU UP AT HOME PLATE!
BONK!
5

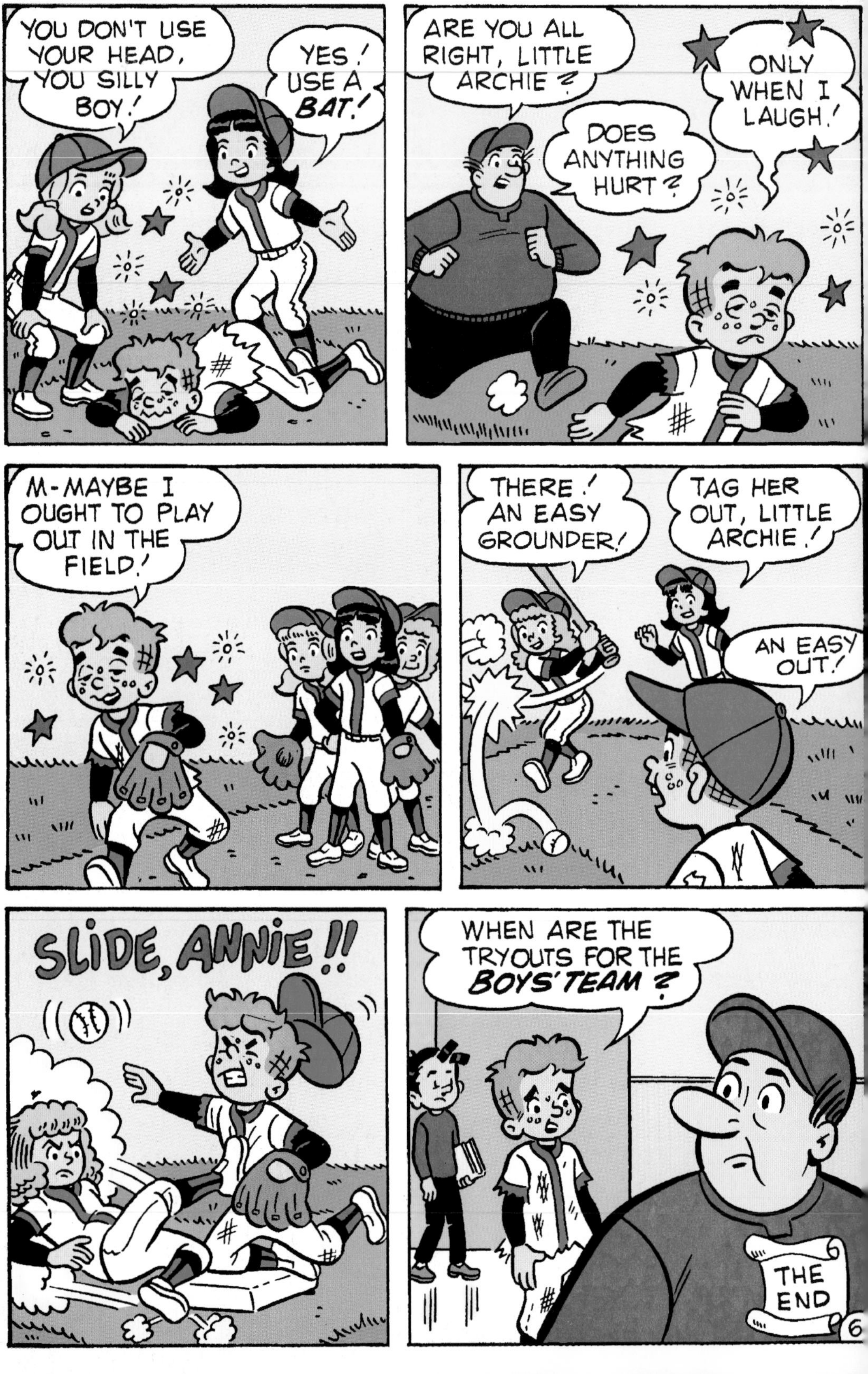
YOU DON'T USE YOUR HEAD, YOU SILLY BOY!
YES! USE A BAT!
ARE YOU ALL RIGHT, LITTLE ARCHIE?
DOES ANYTHING HURT?
ONLY WHEN I LAUGH!
M-MAYBE I OUGHT TO PLAY OUT IN THE FIELD!
THERE! AN EASY GROUNDER!
TAG HER OUT, LITTLE ARCHIE!
AN EASY OUT!
SLIDE, ANNIE!!
WHEN ARE THE TRYOUTS FOR THE BOYS' TEAM?
THE END
6

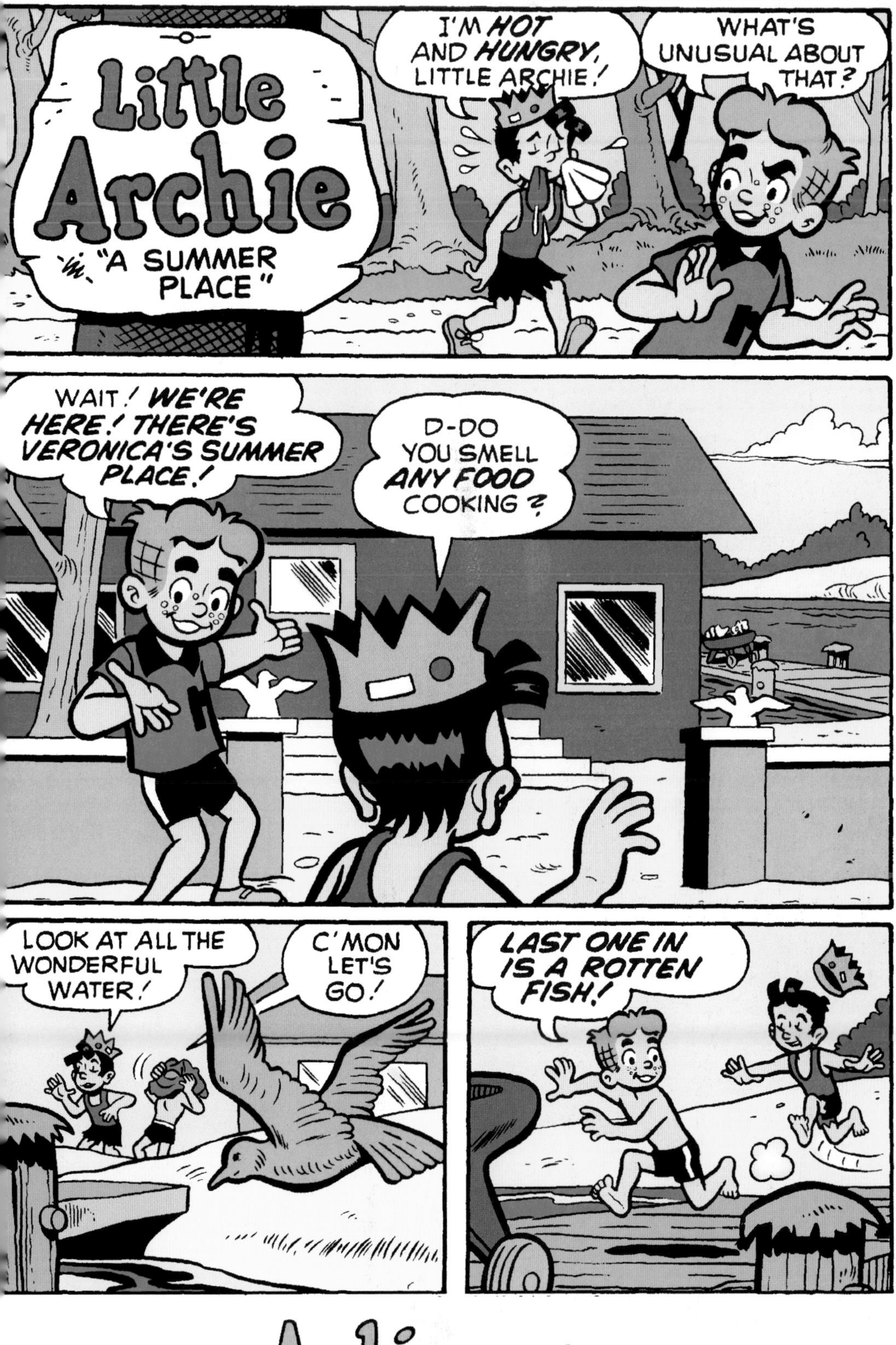
Little Archie
"A SUMMER PLACE"
I'M HOT AND HUNGRY, LITTLE ARCHIE!
WHAT'S UNUSUAL ABOUT THAT?
WAIT! WE'RE HERE! THERE'S VERONICA'S SUMMER PLACE!
D-DO YOU SMELL ANY FOOD COOKING?
LOOK AT ALL THE WONDERFUL WATER!
C'MON LET'S GO!
LAST ONE IN IS A ROTTEN FISH!

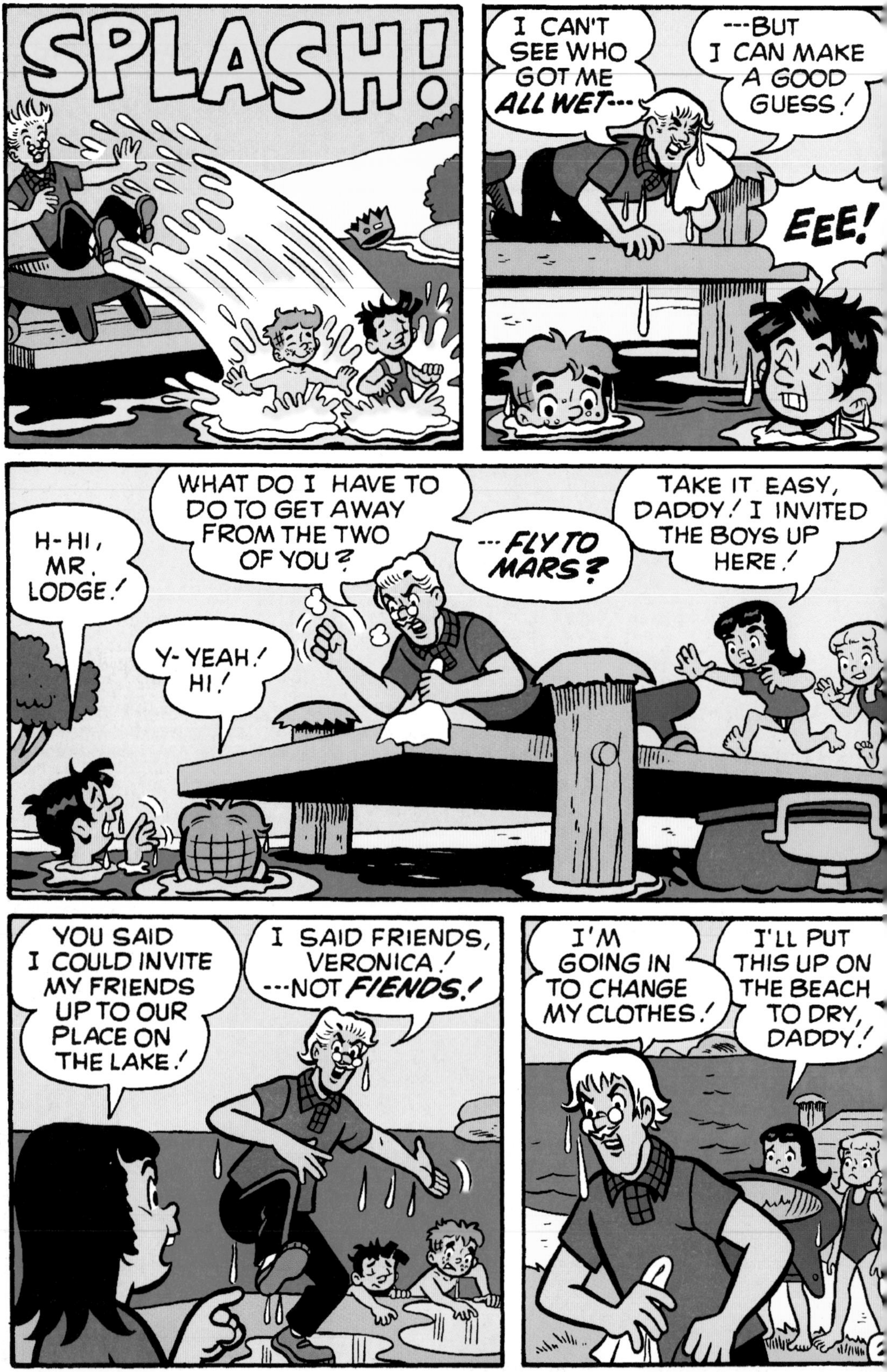
SPLASH!
I CAN'T SEE WHO GOT ME ALL WET---
---BUT I CAN MAKE A GOOD GUESS!
EEE!
H-HI, MR. LODGE!
Y-YEAH! HI!
WHAT DO I HAVE TO DO TO GET AWAY FROM THE TWO OF YOU?
---FLY TO MARS?
TAKE IT EASY, DADDY! I INVITED THE BOYS UP HERE!
YOU SAID I COULD INVITE MY FRIENDS UP TO OUR PLACE ON THE LAKE!
I SAID FRIENDS, VERONICA! ---NOT FIENDS!
I'M GOING IN TO CHANGE MY CLOTHES!
I'LL PUT THIS UP ON THE BEACH TO DRY, DADDY!

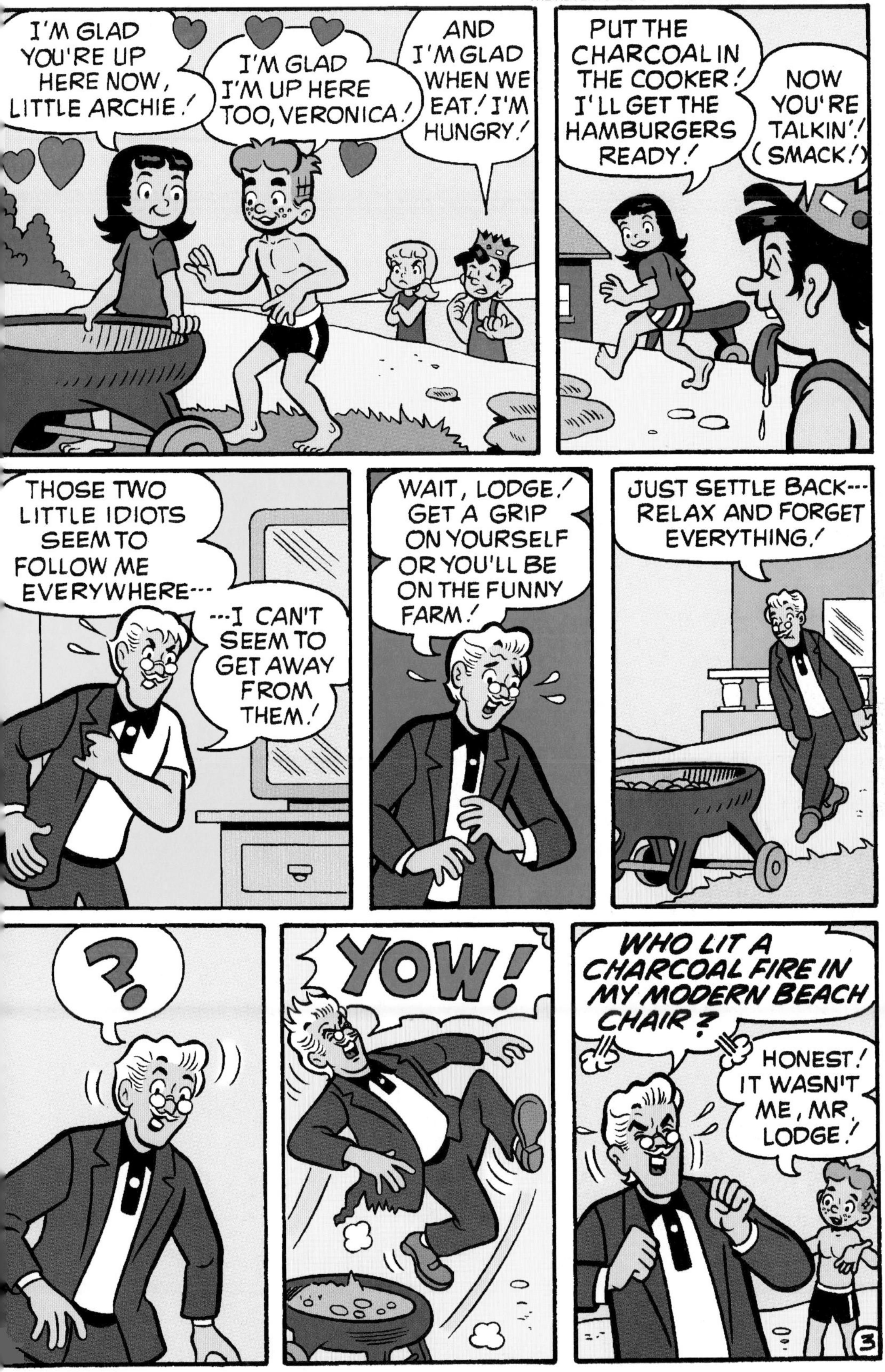
I'M GLAD YOU'RE UP HERE NOW, LITTLE ARCHIE!
I'M GLAD I'M UP HERE TOO, VERONICA!
AND I'M GLAD WHEN WE EAT! I'M HUNGRY!
PUT THE CHARCOAL IN THE COOKER! I'LL GET THE HAMBURGERS READY!
NOW YOU'RE TALKIN'! (SMACK!)
THOSE TWO LITTLE IDIOTS SEEM TO FOLLOW ME EVERYWHERE---
---I CAN'T SEEM TO GET AWAY FROM THEM!
WAIT, LODGE! GET A GRIP ON YOURSELF OR YOU'LL BE ON THE FUNNY FARM!
JUST SETTLE BACK--- RELAX AND FORGET EVERYTHING!
?
YOW!
WHO LIT A CHARCOAL FIRE IN MY MODERN BEACH CHAIR?
HONEST! IT WASN'T ME, MR. LODGE!
3

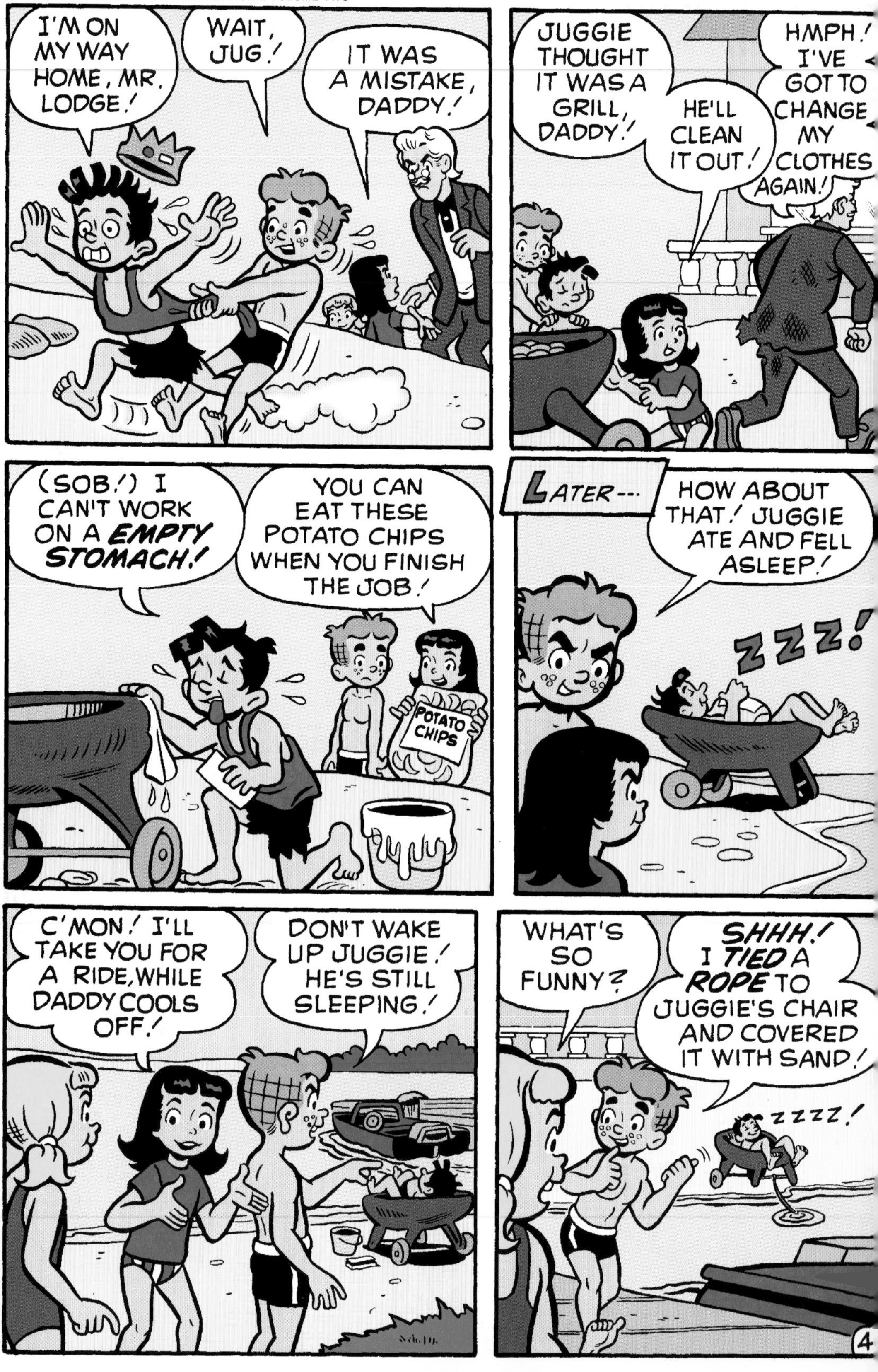
I'M ON MY WAY HOME, MR. LODGE!
WAIT, JUG!
IT WAS A MISTAKE, DADDY!
JUGGIE THOUGHT IT WAS A GRILL, DADDY!
HE'LL CLEAN IT OUT!
HMPH! I'VE GOT TO CHANGE MY CLOTHES AGAIN!
(SOB!) I CAN'T WORK ON A EMPTY STOMACH!
YOU CAN EAT THESE POTATO CHIPS WHEN YOU FINISH THE JOB!
POTATO CHIPS
LATER---
HOW ABOUT THAT! JUGGIE ATE AND FELL ASLEEP!
Z Z Z!
C'MON! I'LL TAKE YOU FOR A RIDE, WHILE DADDY COOLS OFF!
DON'T WAKE UP JUGGIE! HE'S STILL SLEEPING!
WHAT'S SO FUNNY?
SHHH! I TIED A ROPE TO JUGGIE'S CHAIR AND COVERED IT WITH SAND!
Z Z Z Z!
4

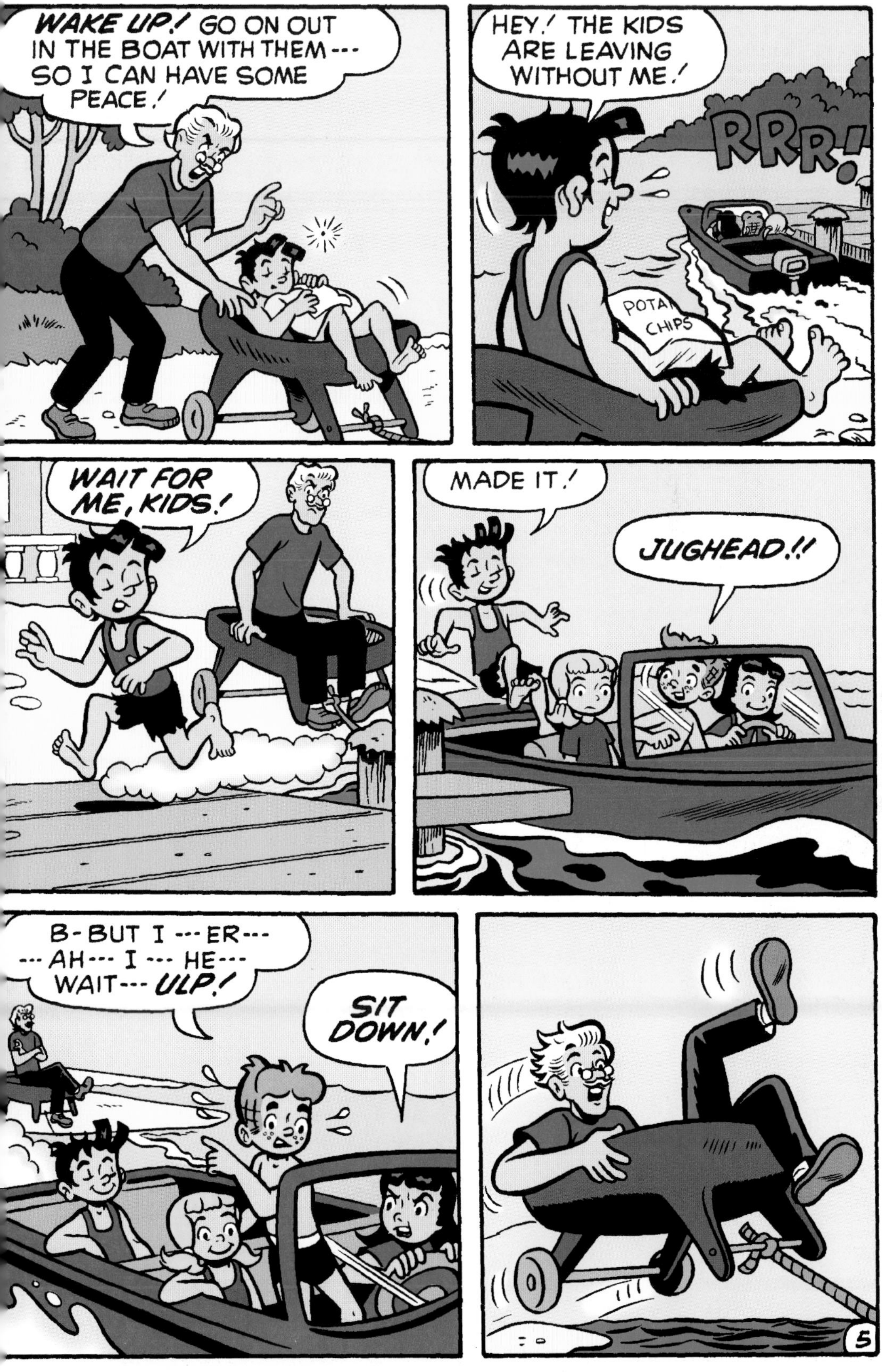
WAKE UP! GO ON OUT IN THE BOAT WITH THEM--- SO I CAN HAVE SOME PEACE!
HEY! THE KIDS ARE LEAVING WITHOUT ME!
RRR!
POTA CHIPS
WAIT FOR ME, KIDS!
MADE IT!
JUGHEAD!!
B-BUT I --- ER--- --- AH--- I --- HE--- WAIT--- ULP!
SIT DOWN!
5

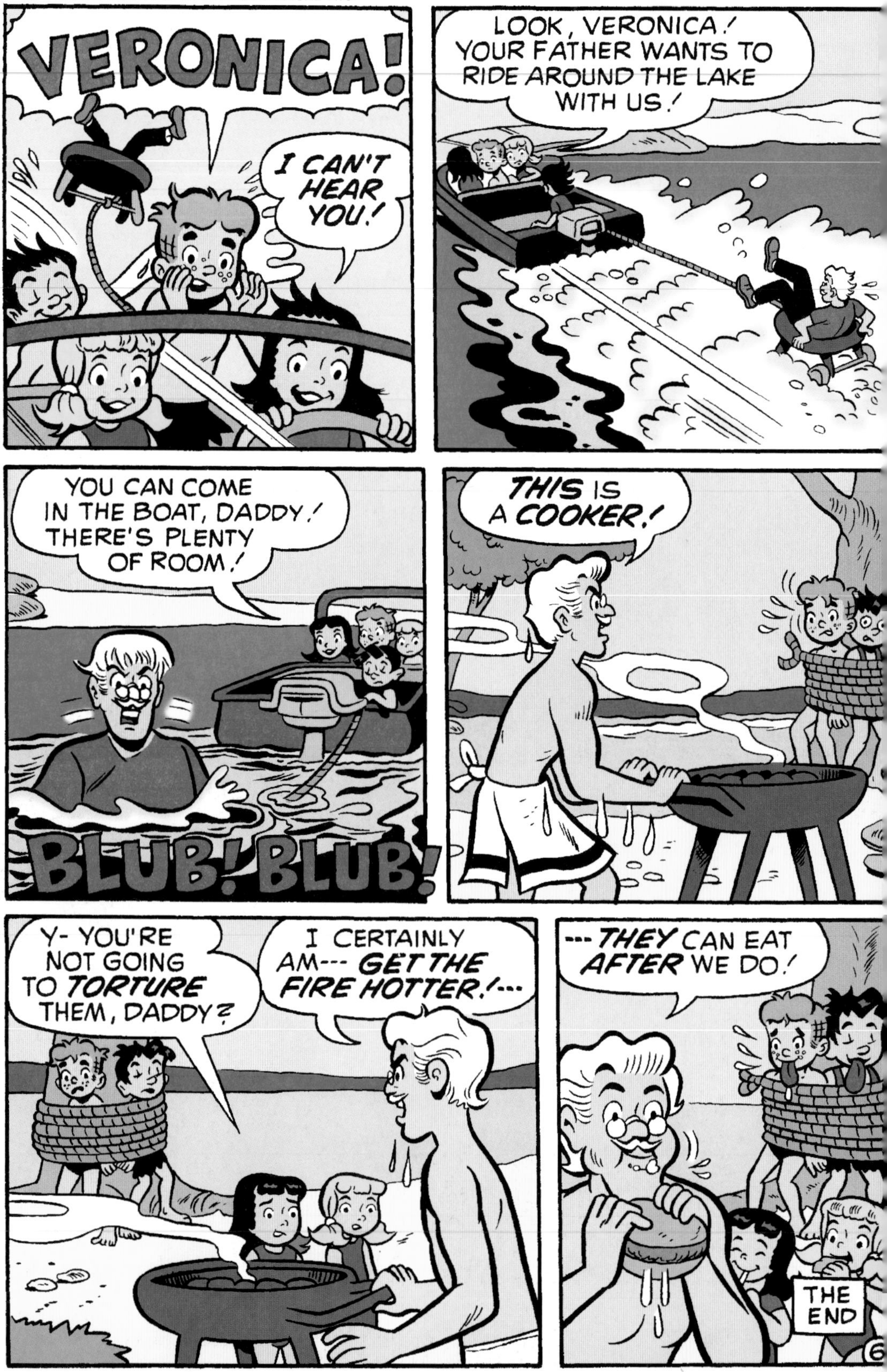
VERONICA!
I CAN'T HEAR YOU!
LOOK, VERONICA! YOUR FATHER WANTS TO RIDE AROUND THE LAKE WITH US!
YOU CAN COME IN THE BOAT, DADDY! THERE'S PLENTY OF ROOM!
BLUB! BLUB!
THIS IS A COOKER!
Y- YOU'RE NOT GOING TO TORTURE THEM, DADDY?
I CERTAINLY AM--- GET THE FIRE HOTTER!---
---THEY CAN EAT AFTER WE DO!
THE END
6

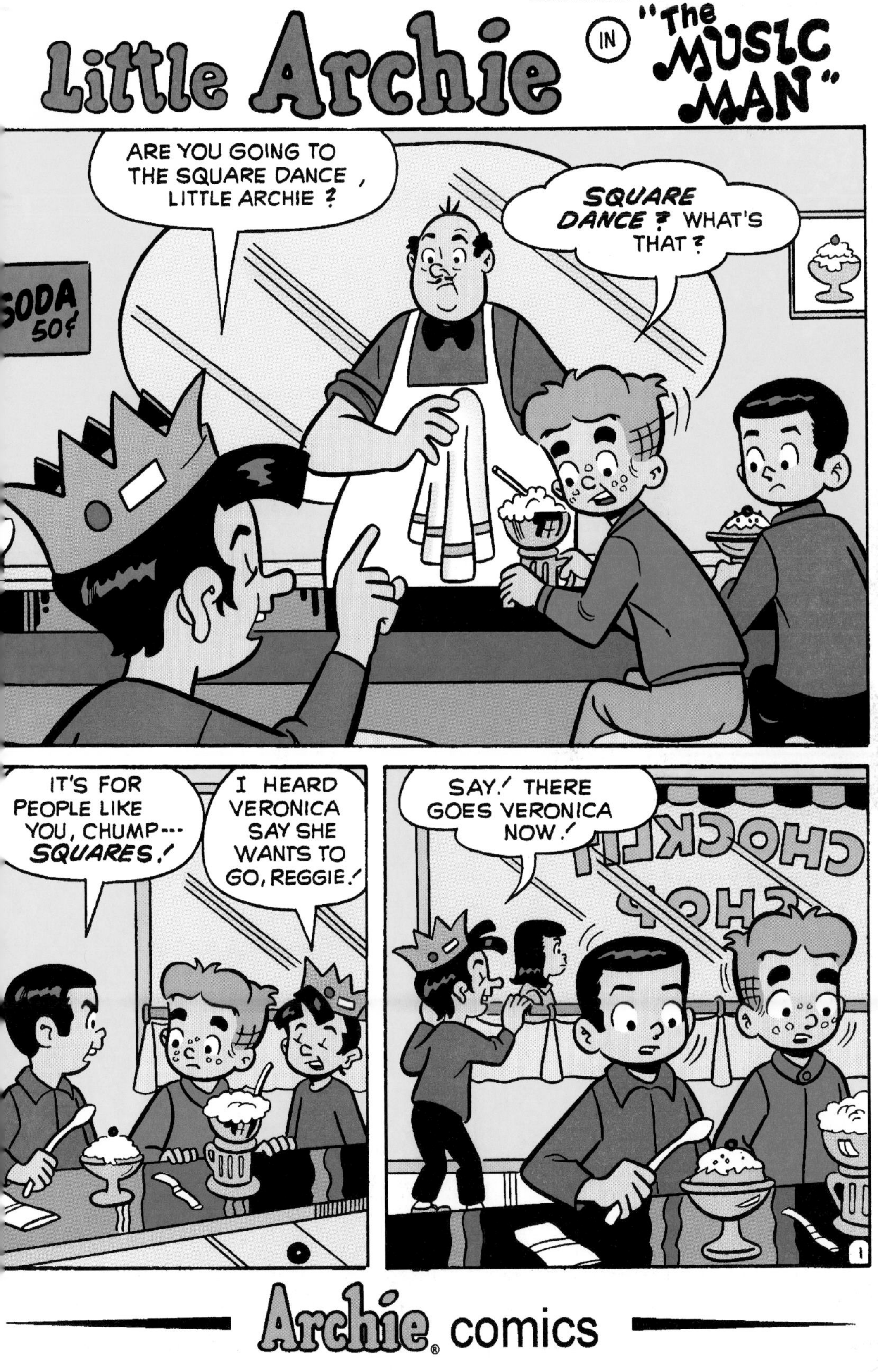
Little Archie IN "The MUSIC MAN"
ARE YOU GOING TO THE SQUARE DANCE, LITTLE ARCHIE?
SQUARE DANCE? WHAT'S THAT?
SODA 50¢
IT'S FOR PEOPLE LIKE YOU, CHUMP--- SQUARES!
I HEARD VERONICA SAY SHE WANTS TO GO, REGGIE!
SAY! THERE GOES VERONICA NOW!
1
Archie comics

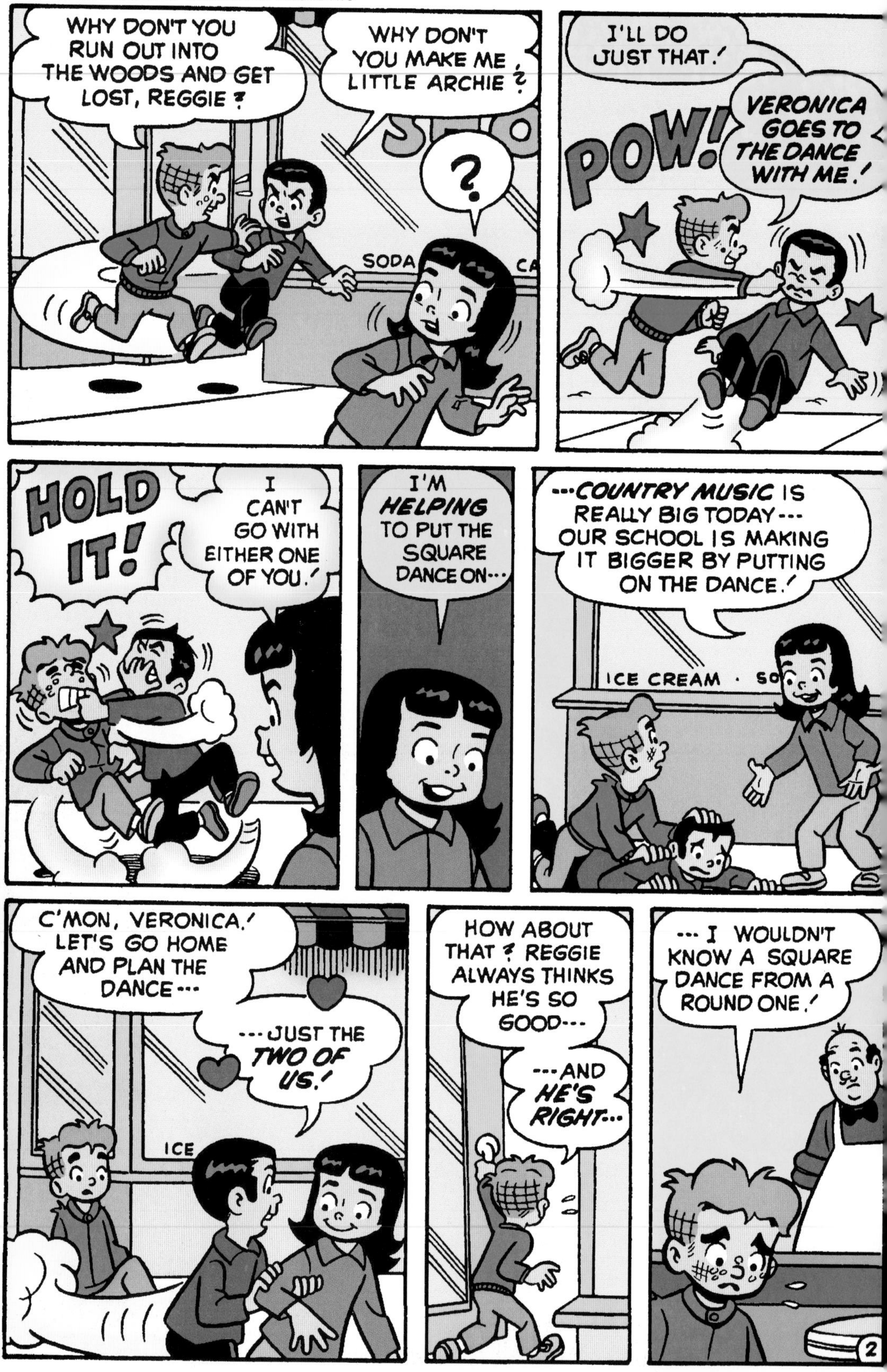
WHY DON'T YOU RUN OUT INTO THE WOODS AND GET LOST, REGGIE ?
WHY DON'T YOU MAKE ME, LITTLE ARCHIE ?
?
SODA
I'LL DO JUST THAT.!
POW!
VERONICA GOES TO THE DANCE WITH ME.!
HOLD IT!
I CAN'T GO WITH EITHER ONE OF YOU.!
I'M *HELPING* TO PUT THE SQUARE DANCE ON---
---*COUNTRY MUSIC* IS REALLY BIG TODAY--- OUR SCHOOL IS MAKING IT BIGGER BY PUTTING ON THE DANCE.!
ICE CREAM · SO
C'MON, VERONICA.! LET'S GO HOME AND PLAN THE DANCE---
---JUST THE *TWO OF US.!*
ICE
HOW ABOUT THAT ? REGGIE ALWAYS THINKS HE'S SO GOOD---
---AND *HE'S RIGHT*---
--- I WOULDN'T KNOW A SQUARE DANCE FROM A ROUND ONE.!
2

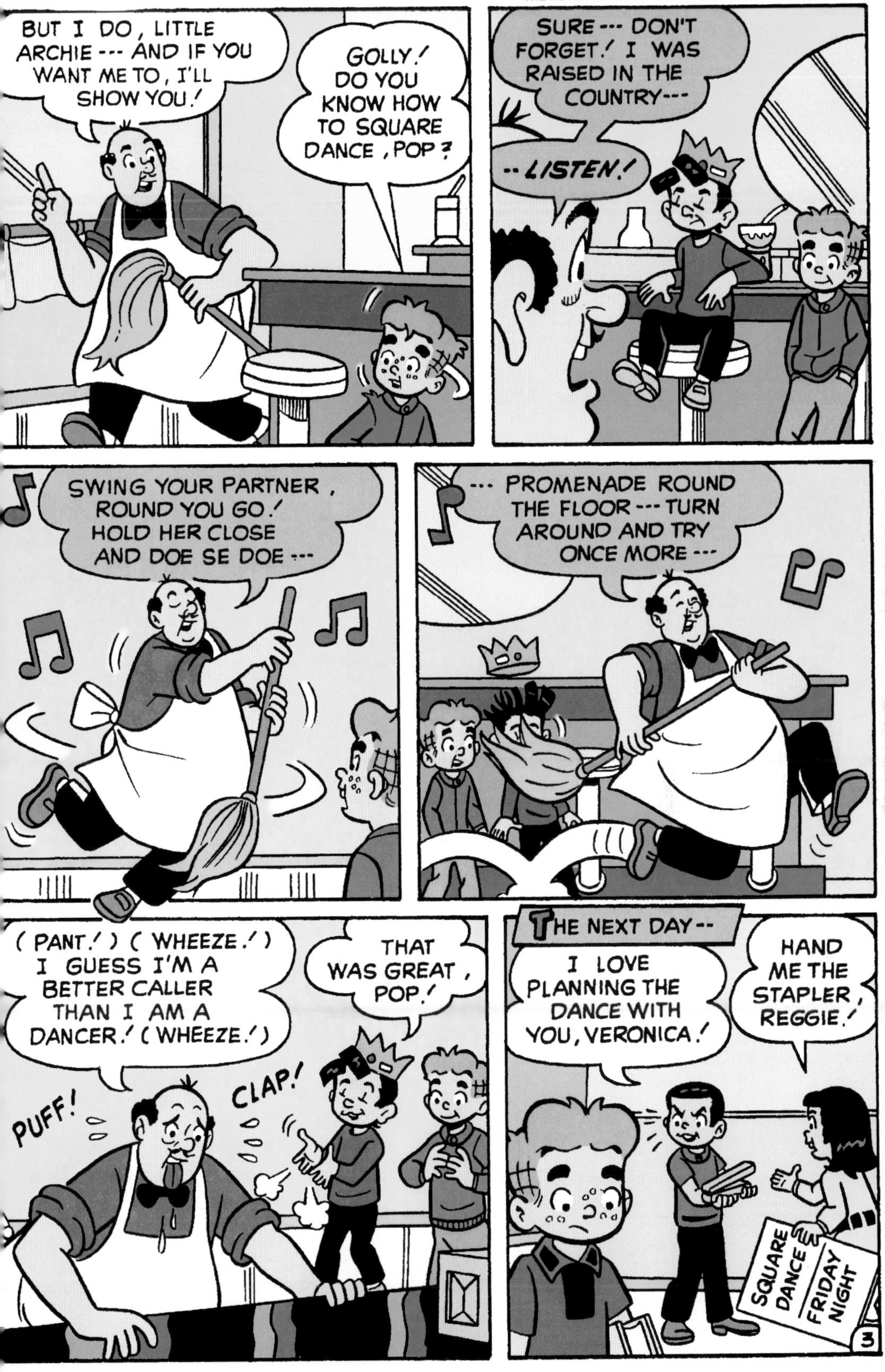
GOLLY! DO YOU KNOW HOW TO SQUARE DANCE, POP?
BUT I DO, LITTLE ARCHIE --- AND IF YOU WANT ME TO, I'LL SHOW YOU!
SURE --- DON'T FORGET! I WAS RAISED IN THE COUNTRY---
--LISTEN!
SWING YOUR PARTNER, ROUND YOU GO! HOLD HER CLOSE AND DOE SE DOE ---
--- PROMENADE ROUND THE FLOOR --- TURN AROUND AND TRY ONCE MORE ---
(PANT!) (WHEEZE!) I GUESS I'M A BETTER CALLER THAN I AM A DANCER! (WHEEZE!)
PUFF!
CLAP!
THAT WAS GREAT, POP!
THE NEXT DAY--
I LOVE PLANNING THE DANCE WITH YOU, VERONICA!
HAND ME THE STAPLER, REGGIE!
SQUARE DANCE
FRIDAY NIGHT
3

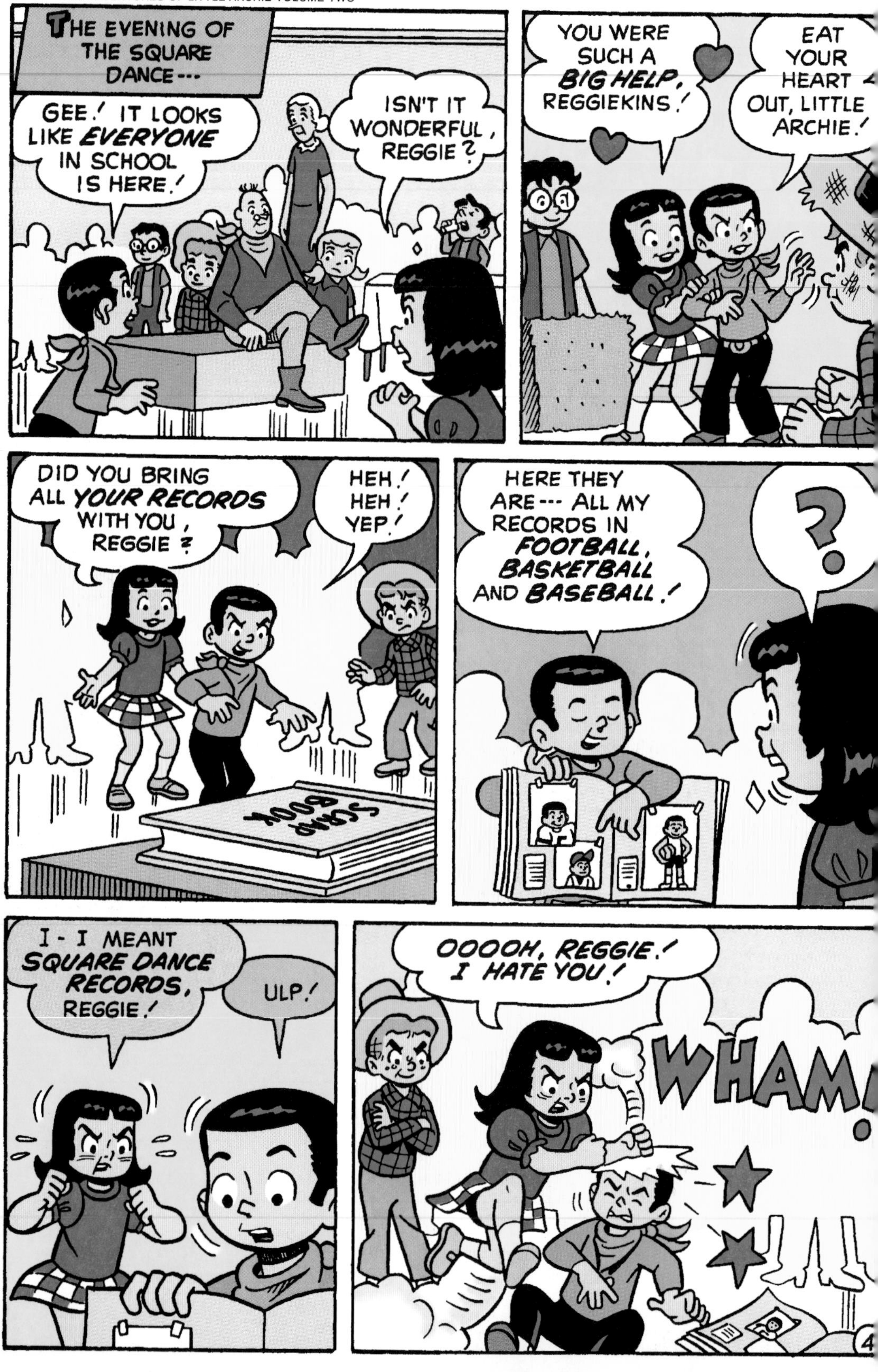
THE EVENING OF THE SQUARE DANCE---
GEE! IT LOOKS LIKE EVERYONE IN SCHOOL IS HERE!
ISN'T IT WONDERFUL, REGGIE?
YOU WERE SUCH A BIG HELP, REGGIEKINS!
EAT YOUR HEART OUT, LITTLE ARCHIE!
DID YOU BRING ALL YOUR RECORDS WITH YOU, REGGIE?
HEH! HEH! YEP!
SCRAP BOOK
HERE THEY ARE--- ALL MY RECORDS IN FOOTBALL, BASKETBALL AND BASEBALL!
?
I - I MEANT SQUARE DANCE RECORDS, REGGIE!
ULP!
OOOOH, REGGIE! I HATE YOU!
WHAM

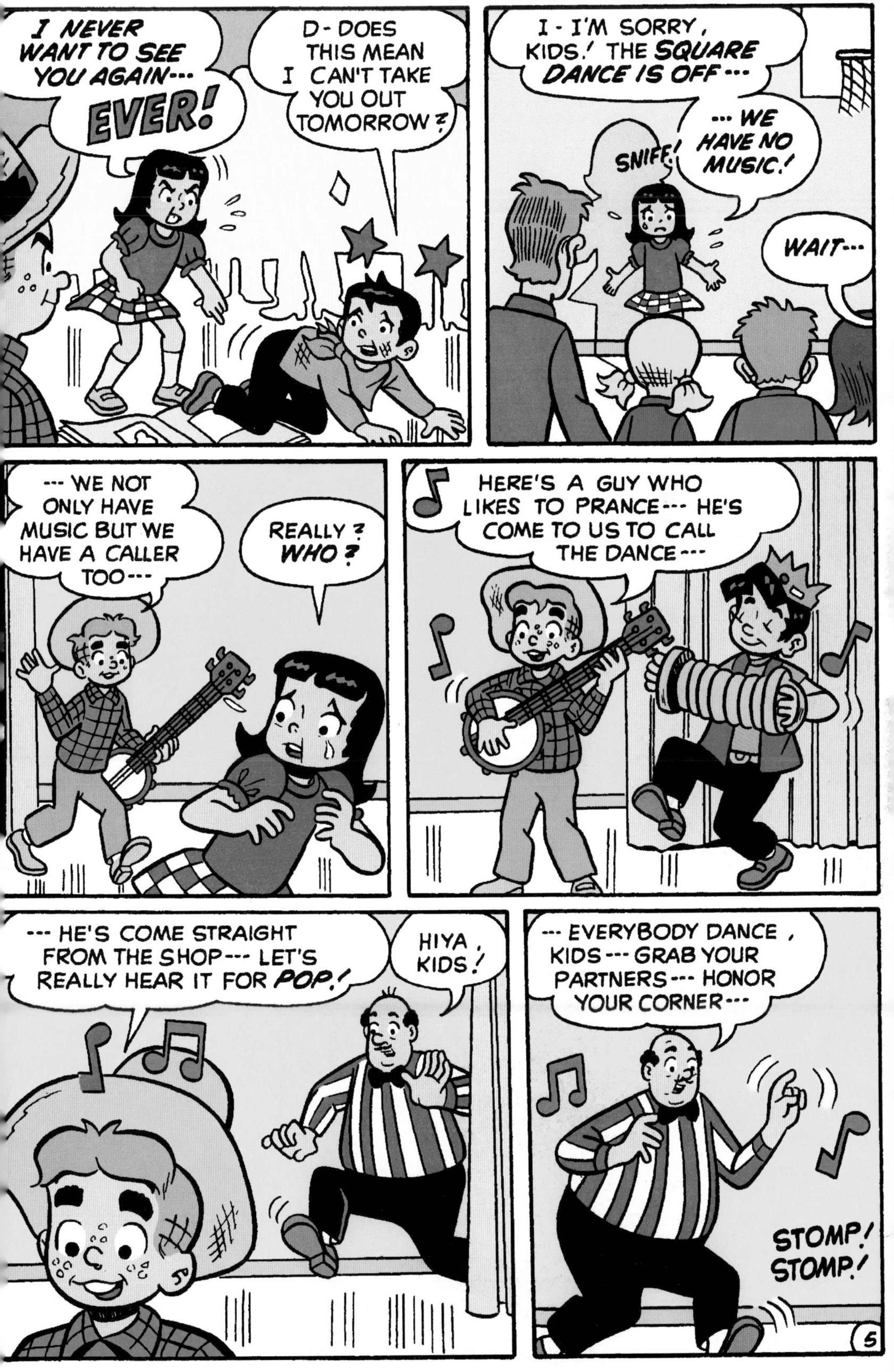
I NEVER WANT TO SEE YOU AGAIN--- EVER!
D-DOES THIS MEAN I CAN'T TAKE YOU OUT TOMORROW?
I-I'M SORRY, KIDS! THE SQUARE DANCE IS OFF---
SNIFF!
--- WE HAVE NO MUSIC!
WAIT---
--- WE NOT ONLY HAVE MUSIC BUT WE HAVE A CALLER TOO---
REALLY? WHO?
HERE'S A GUY WHO LIKES TO PRANCE--- HE'S COME TO US TO CALL THE DANCE---
--- HE'S COME STRAIGHT FROM THE SHOP--- LET'S REALLY HEAR IT FOR POP!
HIYA, KIDS!
--- EVERYBODY DANCE, KIDS--- GRAB YOUR PARTNERS--- HONOR YOUR CORNER---
STOMP! STOMP!
5

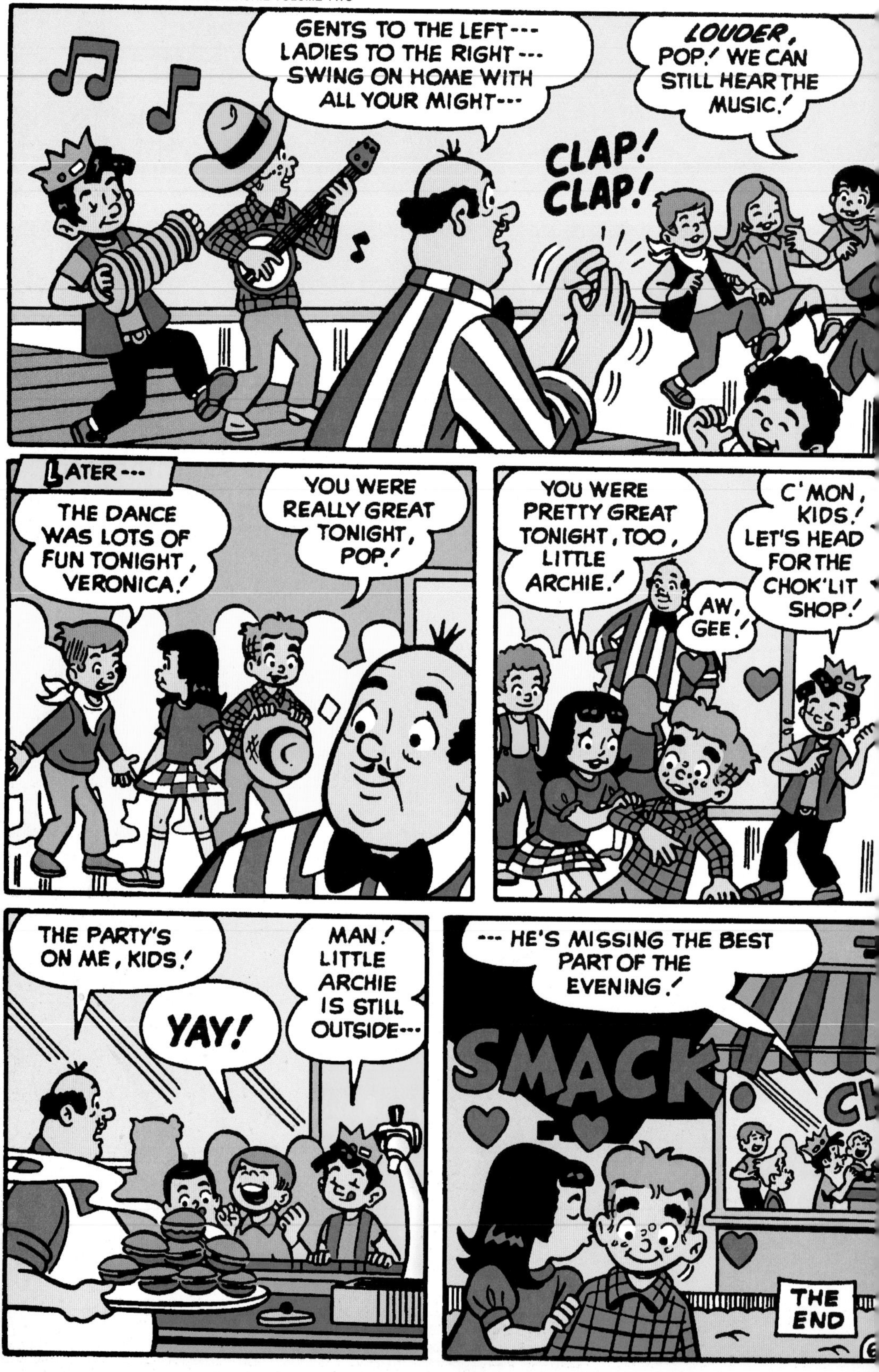
GENTS TO THE LEFT--- LADIES TO THE RIGHT--- SWING ON HOME WITH ALL YOUR MIGHT---
LOUDER, POP! WE CAN STILL HEAR THE MUSIC!
CLAP! CLAP!
LATER---
THE DANCE WAS LOTS OF FUN TONIGHT, VERONICA!
YOU WERE REALLY GREAT TONIGHT, POP!
YOU WERE PRETTY GREAT TONIGHT, TOO, LITTLE ARCHIE!
AW, GEE!
C'MON, KIDS! LET'S HEAD FOR THE CHOK'LIT SHOP!
THE PARTY'S ON ME, KIDS!
YAY!
MAN! LITTLE ARCHIE IS STILL OUTSIDE---
--- HE'S MISSING THE BEST PART OF THE EVENING!
SMACK!
THE END

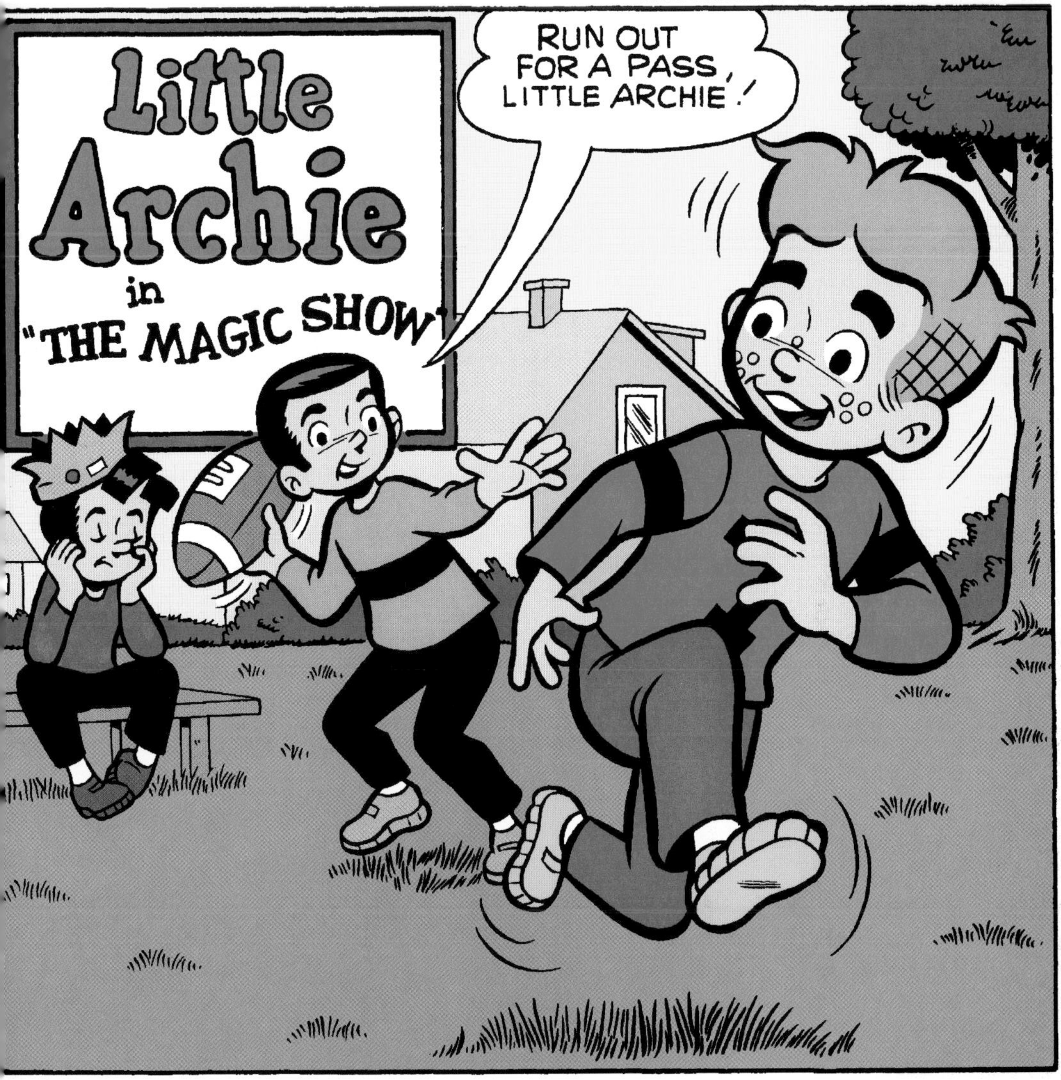
Little Archie
in
"THE MAGIC SHOW"
RUN OUT FOR A PASS, LITTLE ARCHIE!

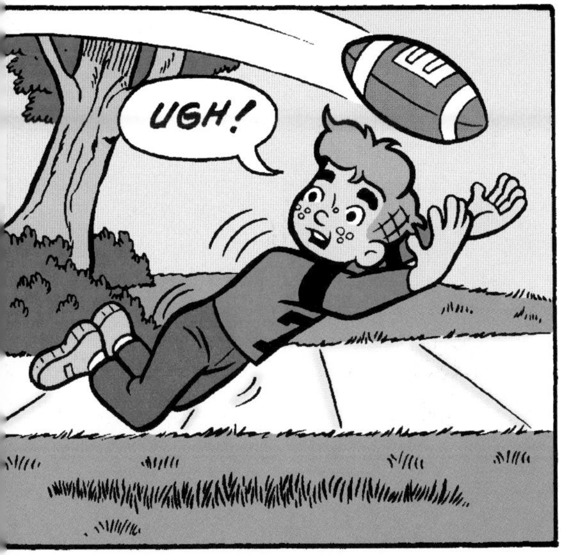
UGH!

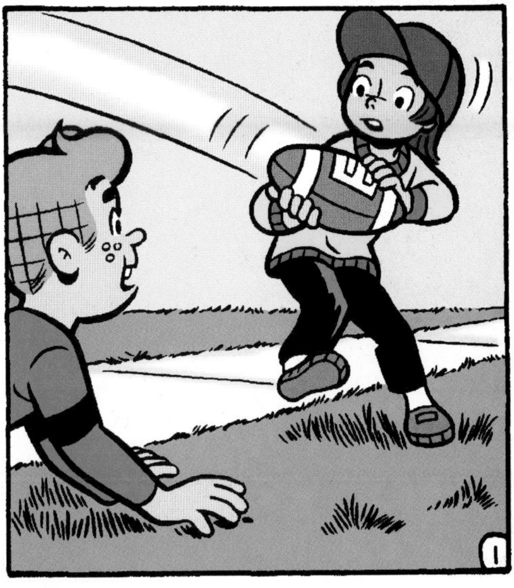
1

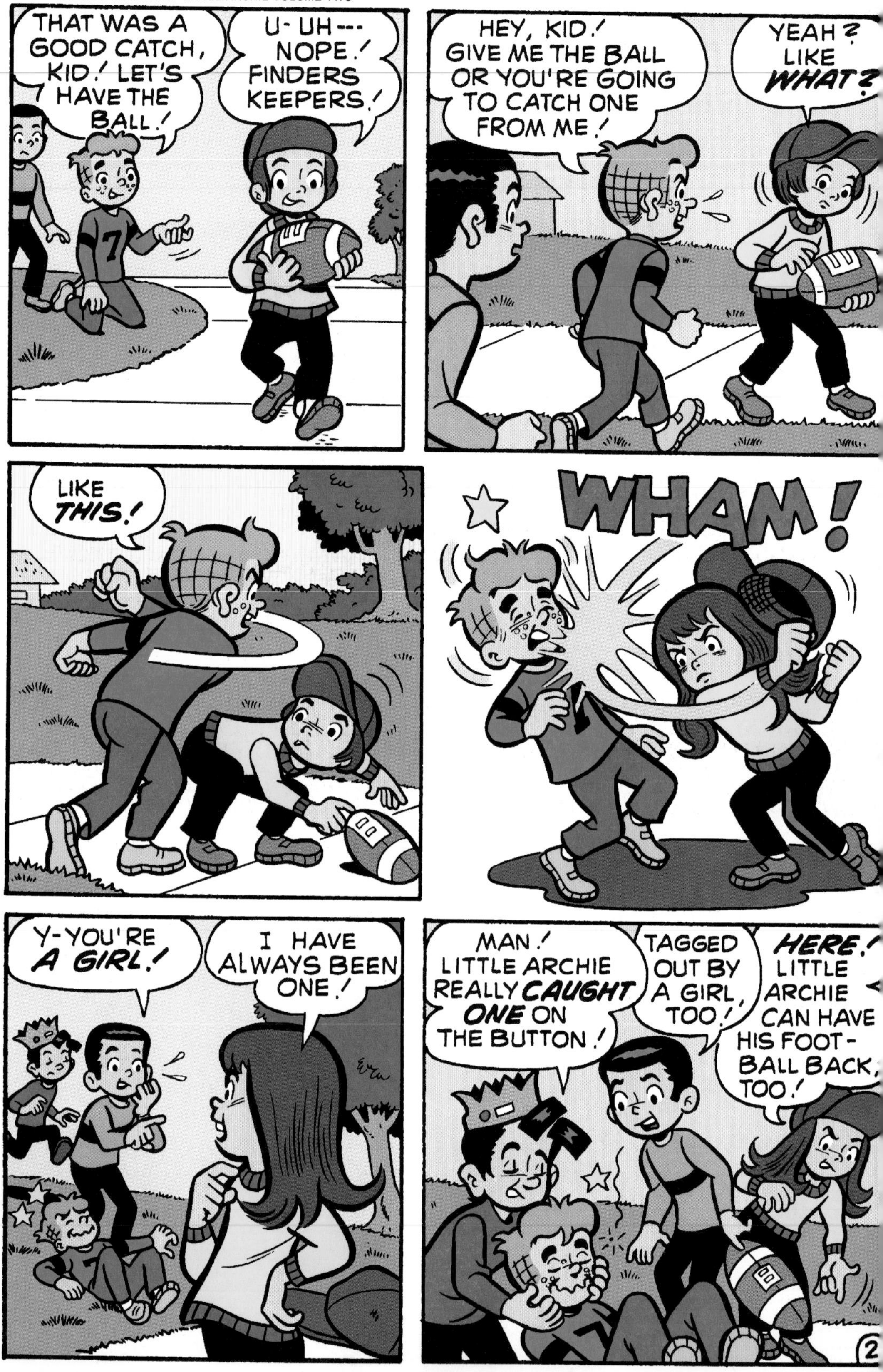
THAT WAS A GOOD CATCH, KID! LET'S HAVE THE BALL!
U-UH--- NOPE! FINDERS KEEPERS!
HEY, KID! GIVE ME THE BALL OR YOU'RE GOING TO CATCH ONE FROM ME!
YEAH? LIKE WHAT?
LIKE THIS!
WHAM!
Y-YOU'RE A GIRL!
I HAVE ALWAYS BEEN ONE!
MAN! LITTLE ARCHIE REALLY CAUGHT ONE ON THE BUTTON!
TAGGED OUT BY A GIRL, TOO!
HERE! LITTLE ARCHIE CAN HAVE HIS FOOT-BALL BACK, TOO!
2

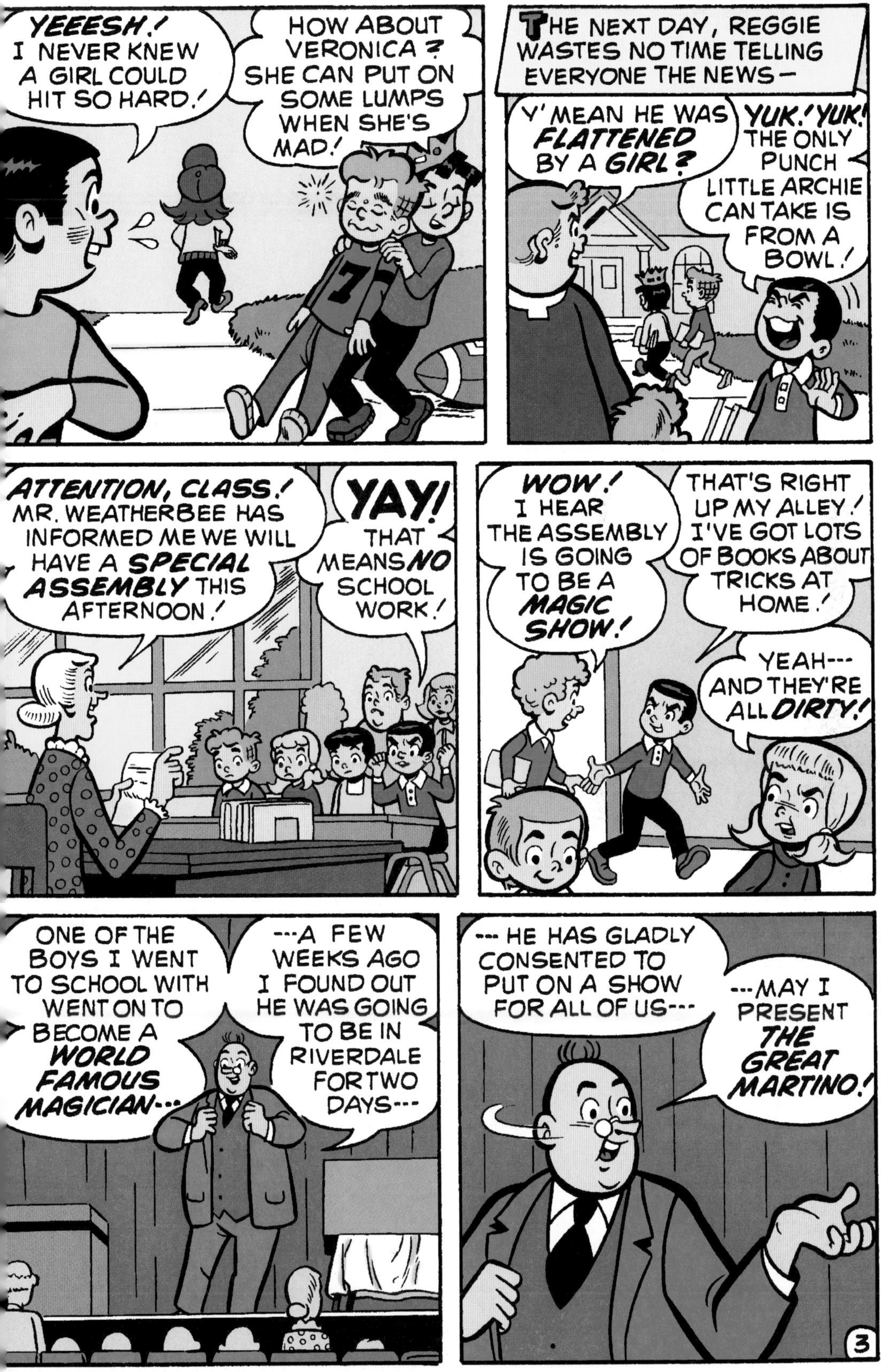
YEEESH! I NEVER KNEW A GIRL COULD HIT SO HARD!
HOW ABOUT VERONICA? SHE CAN PUT ON SOME LUMPS WHEN SHE'S MAD!
THE NEXT DAY, REGGIE WASTES NO TIME TELLING EVERYONE THE NEWS—
Y' MEAN HE WAS FLATTENED BY A GIRL?
YUK! YUK! THE ONLY PUNCH LITTLE ARCHIE CAN TAKE IS FROM A BOWL!
ATTENTION, CLASS! MR. WEATHERBEE HAS INFORMED ME WE WILL HAVE A SPECIAL ASSEMBLY THIS AFTERNOON!
YAY! THAT MEANS NO SCHOOL WORK!
WOW! I HEAR THE ASSEMBLY IS GOING TO BE A MAGIC SHOW!
THAT'S RIGHT UP MY ALLEY! I'VE GOT LOTS OF BOOKS ABOUT TRICKS AT HOME!
YEAH--- AND THEY'RE ALL DIRTY!
ONE OF THE BOYS I WENT TO SCHOOL WITH WENT ON TO BECOME A WORLD FAMOUS MAGICIAN---
---A FEW WEEKS AGO I FOUND OUT HE WAS GOING TO BE IN RIVERDALE FOR TWO DAYS---
--- HE HAS GLADLY CONSENTED TO PUT ON A SHOW FOR ALL OF US---
---MAY I PRESENT THE GREAT MARTINO!
3

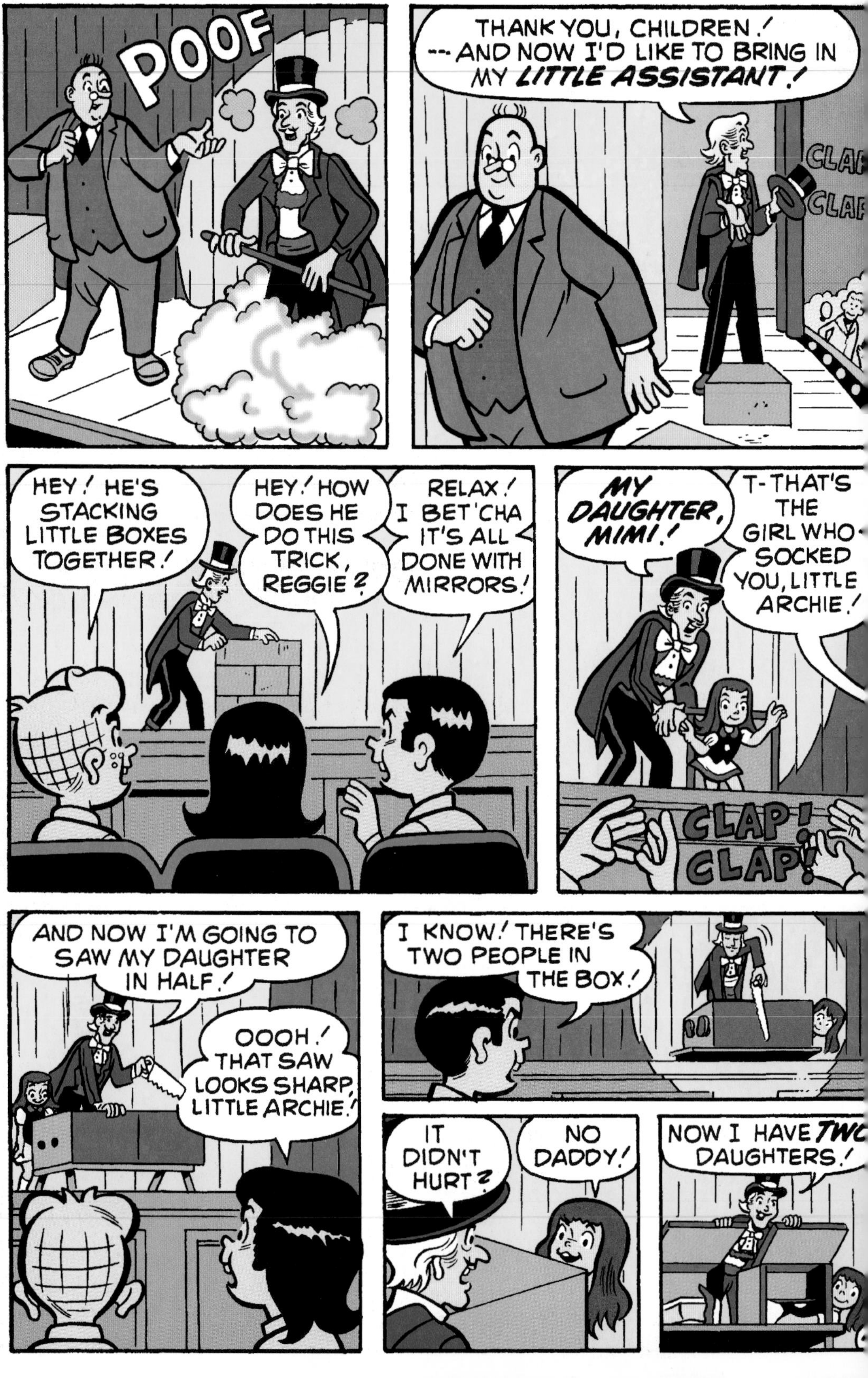
POOF
THANK YOU, CHILDREN! --- AND NOW I'D LIKE TO BRING IN MY LITTLE ASSISTANT!
HEY! HE'S STACKING LITTLE BOXES TOGETHER!
HEY! HOW DOES HE DO THIS TRICK, REGGIE?
RELAX! I BET'CHA IT'S ALL DONE WITH MIRRORS!
MY DAUGHTER, MIMI!
T-THAT'S THE GIRL WHO SOCKED YOU, LITTLE ARCHIE!
CLAP! CLAP!
AND NOW I'M GOING TO SAW MY DAUGHTER IN HALF!
OOOH! THAT SAW LOOKS SHARP, LITTLE ARCHIE!
I KNOW! THERE'S TWO PEOPLE IN THE BOX!
IT DIDN'T HURT?
NO DADDY!
NOW I HAVE TWO DAUGHTERS!

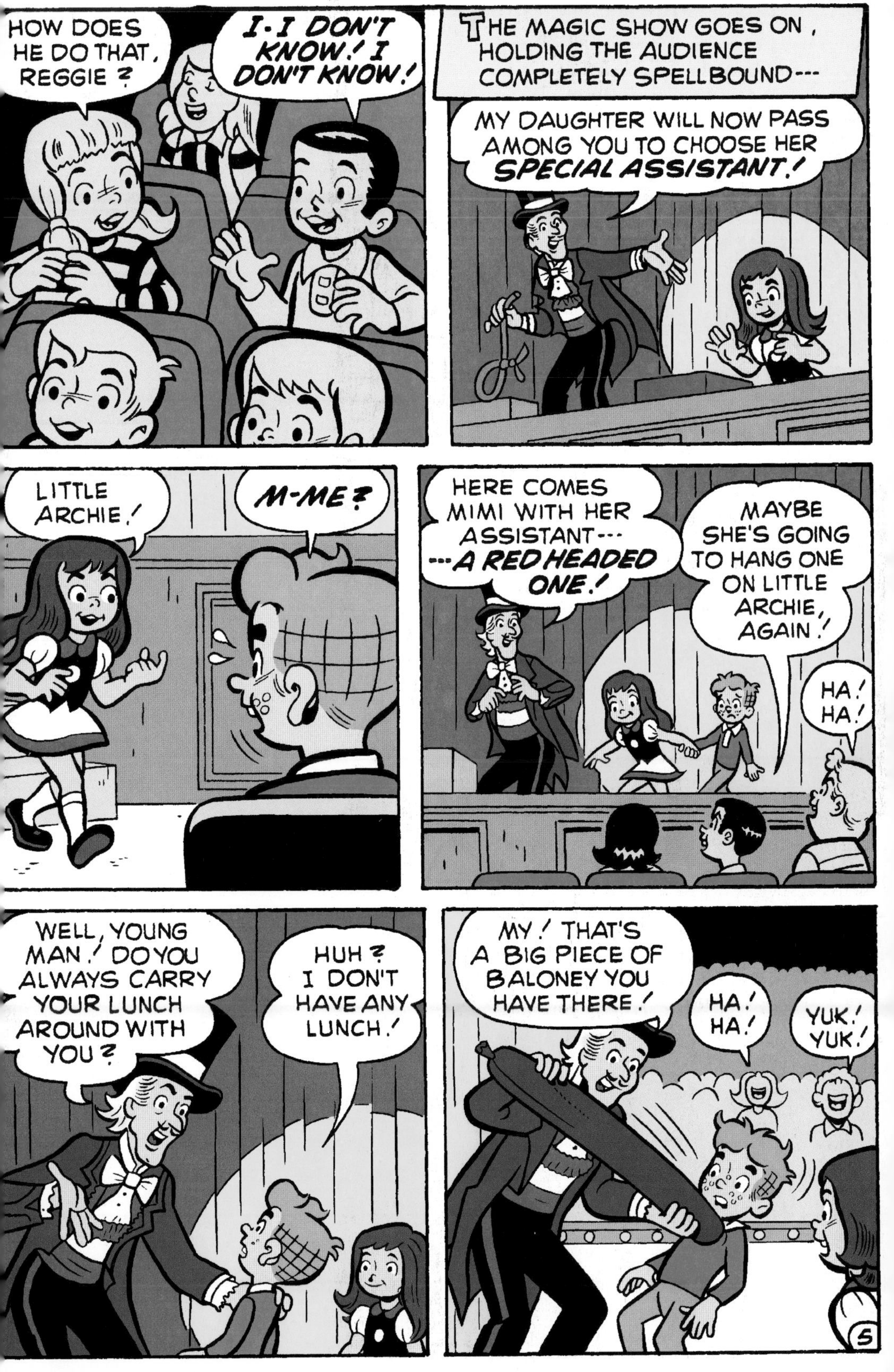
HOW DOES HE DO THAT, REGGIE ?
I-I DON'T KNOW! I DON'T KNOW!
THE MAGIC SHOW GOES ON, HOLDING THE AUDIENCE COMPLETELY SPELLBOUND---
MY DAUGHTER WILL NOW PASS AMONG YOU TO CHOOSE HER SPECIAL ASSISTANT!
LITTLE ARCHIE!
M-ME?
HERE COMES MIMI WITH HER ASSISTANT--- ---A RED HEADED ONE!
MAYBE SHE'S GOING TO HANG ONE ON LITTLE ARCHIE, AGAIN!
HA! HA!
WELL, YOUNG MAN! DO YOU ALWAYS CARRY YOUR LUNCH AROUND WITH YOU?
HUH? I DON'T HAVE ANY LUNCH!
MY! THAT'S A BIG PIECE OF BALONEY YOU HAVE THERE!
HA! HA!
YUK! YUK!
5

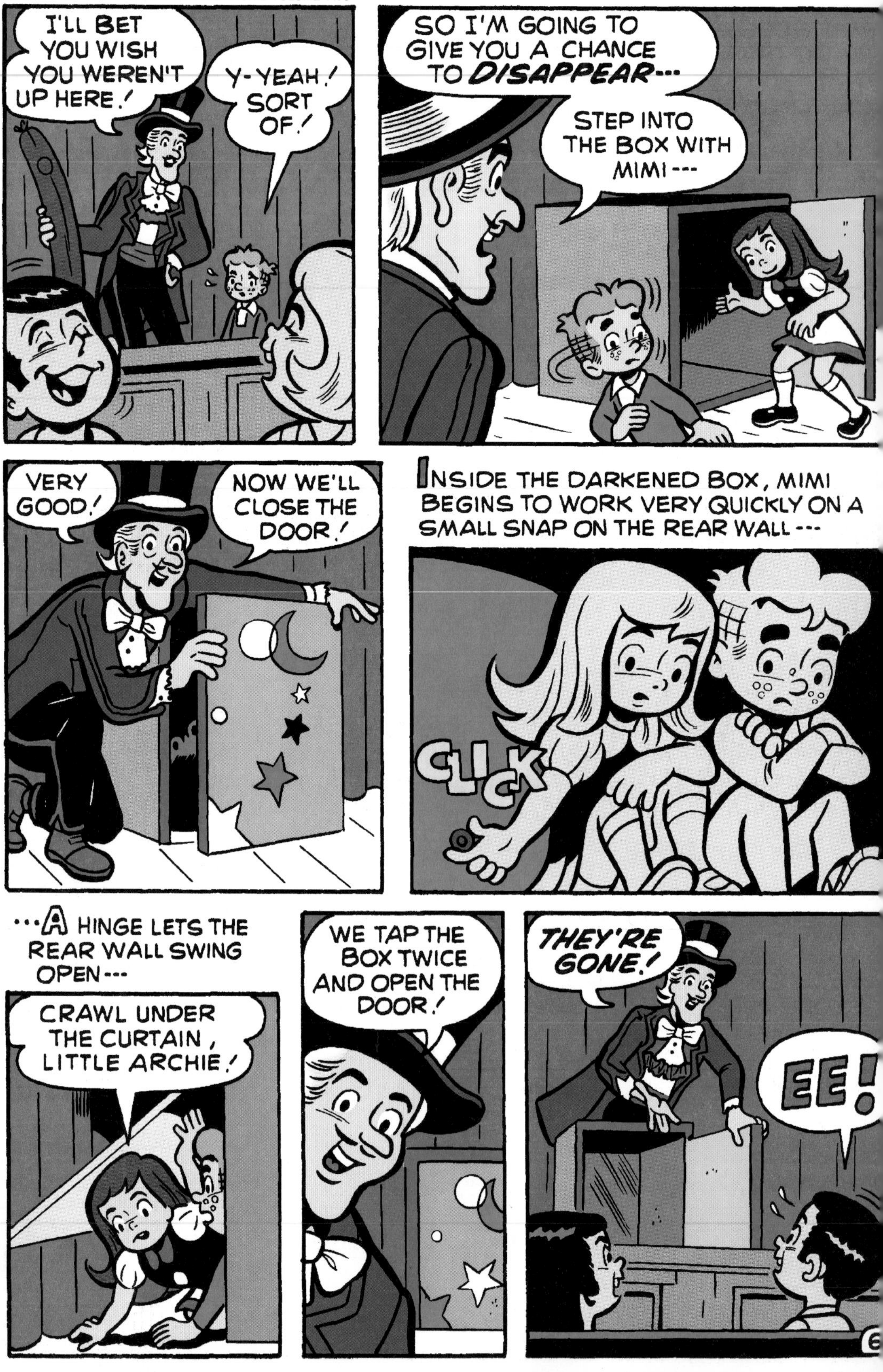
I'LL BET YOU WISH YOU WEREN'T UP HERE!
Y-YEAH! SORT OF!
SO I'M GOING TO GIVE YOU A CHANCE TO DISAPPEAR---
STEP INTO THE BOX WITH MIMI---
VERY GOOD!
NOW WE'LL CLOSE THE DOOR!
INSIDE THE DARKENED BOX, MIMI BEGINS TO WORK VERY QUICKLY ON A SMALL SNAP ON THE REAR WALL---
CLICK
---A HINGE LETS THE REAR WALL SWING OPEN---
CRAWL UNDER THE CURTAIN, LITTLE ARCHIE!
WE TAP THE BOX TWICE AND OPEN THE DOOR!
THEY'RE GONE!
EE!

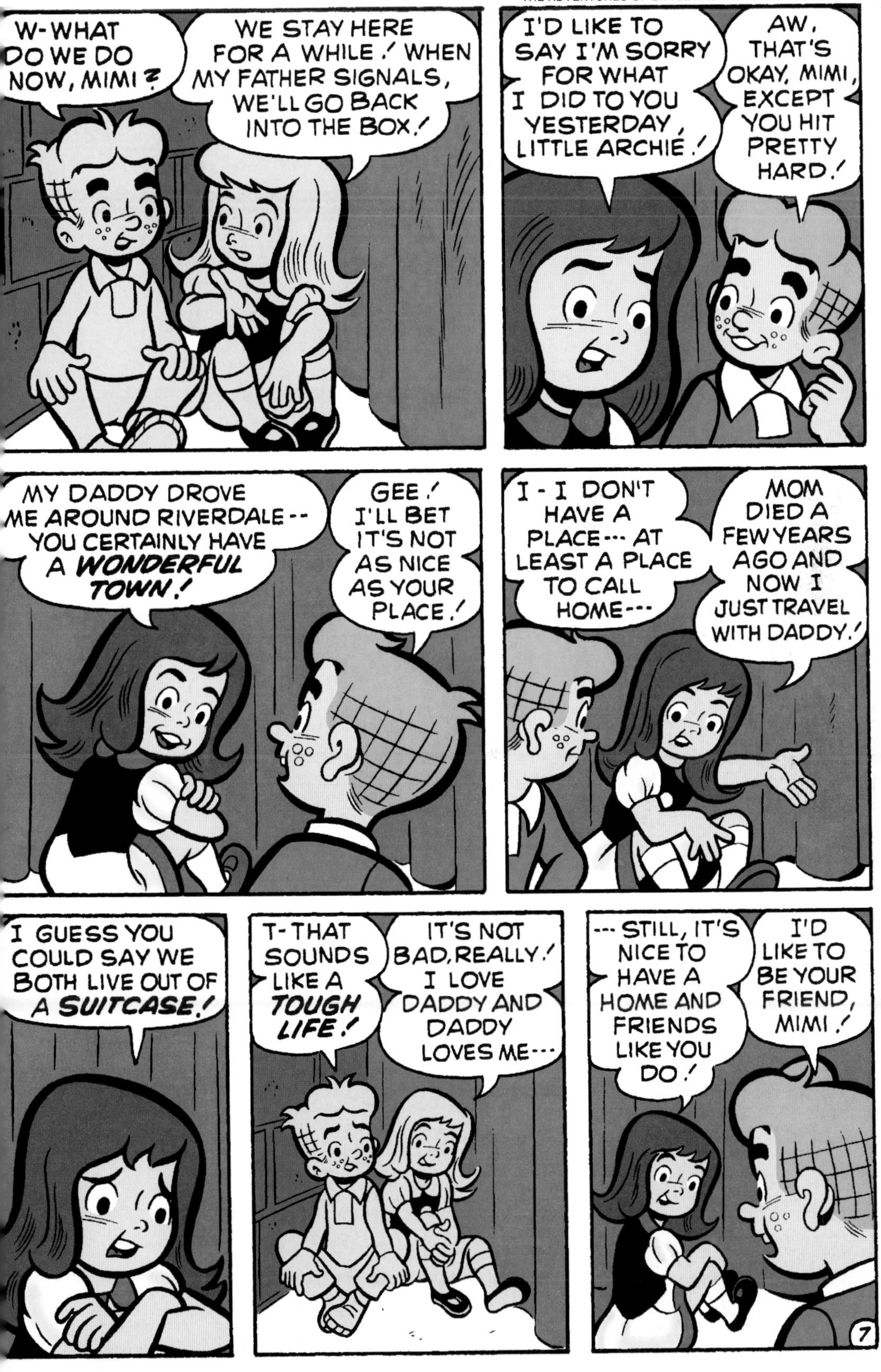
W-WHAT DO WE DO NOW, MIMI?
WE STAY HERE FOR A WHILE! WHEN MY FATHER SIGNALS, WE'LL GO BACK INTO THE BOX!
I'D LIKE TO SAY I'M SORRY FOR WHAT I DID TO YOU YESTERDAY, LITTLE ARCHIE!
AW, THAT'S OKAY, MIMI, EXCEPT YOU HIT PRETTY HARD!
MY DADDY DROVE ME AROUND RIVERDALE-- YOU CERTAINLY HAVE A **WONDERFUL TOWN**!
GEE! I'LL BET IT'S NOT AS NICE AS YOUR PLACE!
I-I DON'T HAVE A PLACE--- AT LEAST A PLACE TO CALL HOME---
MOM DIED A FEW YEARS AGO AND NOW I JUST TRAVEL WITH DADDY!
I GUESS YOU COULD SAY WE BOTH LIVE OUT OF A **SUITCASE**!
T-THAT SOUNDS LIKE A **TOUGH LIFE**!
IT'S NOT BAD, REALLY! I LOVE DADDY AND DADDY LOVES ME---
---STILL, IT'S NICE TO HAVE A HOME AND FRIENDS LIKE YOU DO!
I'D LIKE TO BE YOUR FRIEND, MIMI!
7

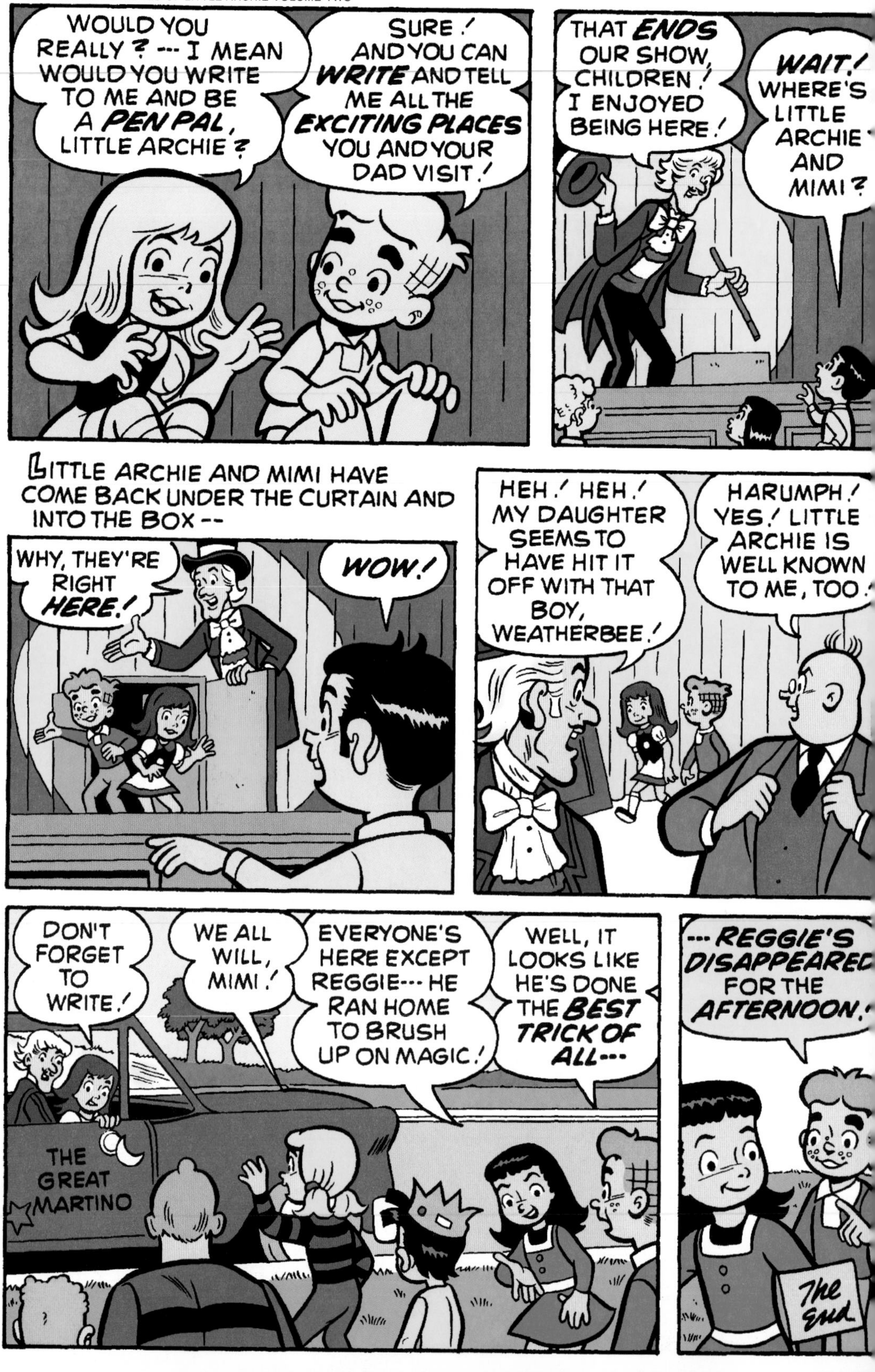
WOULD YOU REALLY ? --- I MEAN WOULD YOU WRITE TO ME AND BE A PEN PAL, LITTLE ARCHIE ?
SURE! AND YOU CAN WRITE AND TELL ME ALL THE EXCITING PLACES YOU AND YOUR DAD VISIT!
THAT ENDS OUR SHOW, CHILDREN! I ENJOYED BEING HERE!
WAIT! WHERE'S LITTLE ARCHIE AND MIMI ?
LITTLE ARCHIE AND MIMI HAVE COME BACK UNDER THE CURTAIN AND INTO THE BOX --
WHY, THEY'RE RIGHT HERE!
WOW!
HEH! HEH! MY DAUGHTER SEEMS TO HAVE HIT IT OFF WITH THAT BOY, WEATHERBEE!
HARUMPH! YES! LITTLE ARCHIE IS WELL KNOWN TO ME, TOO!
DON'T FORGET TO WRITE!
WE ALL WILL, MIMI!
EVERYONE'S HERE EXCEPT REGGIE--- HE RAN HOME TO BRUSH UP ON MAGIC!
WELL, IT LOOKS LIKE HE'S DONE THE BEST TRICK OF ALL---
THE GREAT MARTINO
--- REGGIE'S DISAPPEARED FOR THE AFTERNOON!
The End

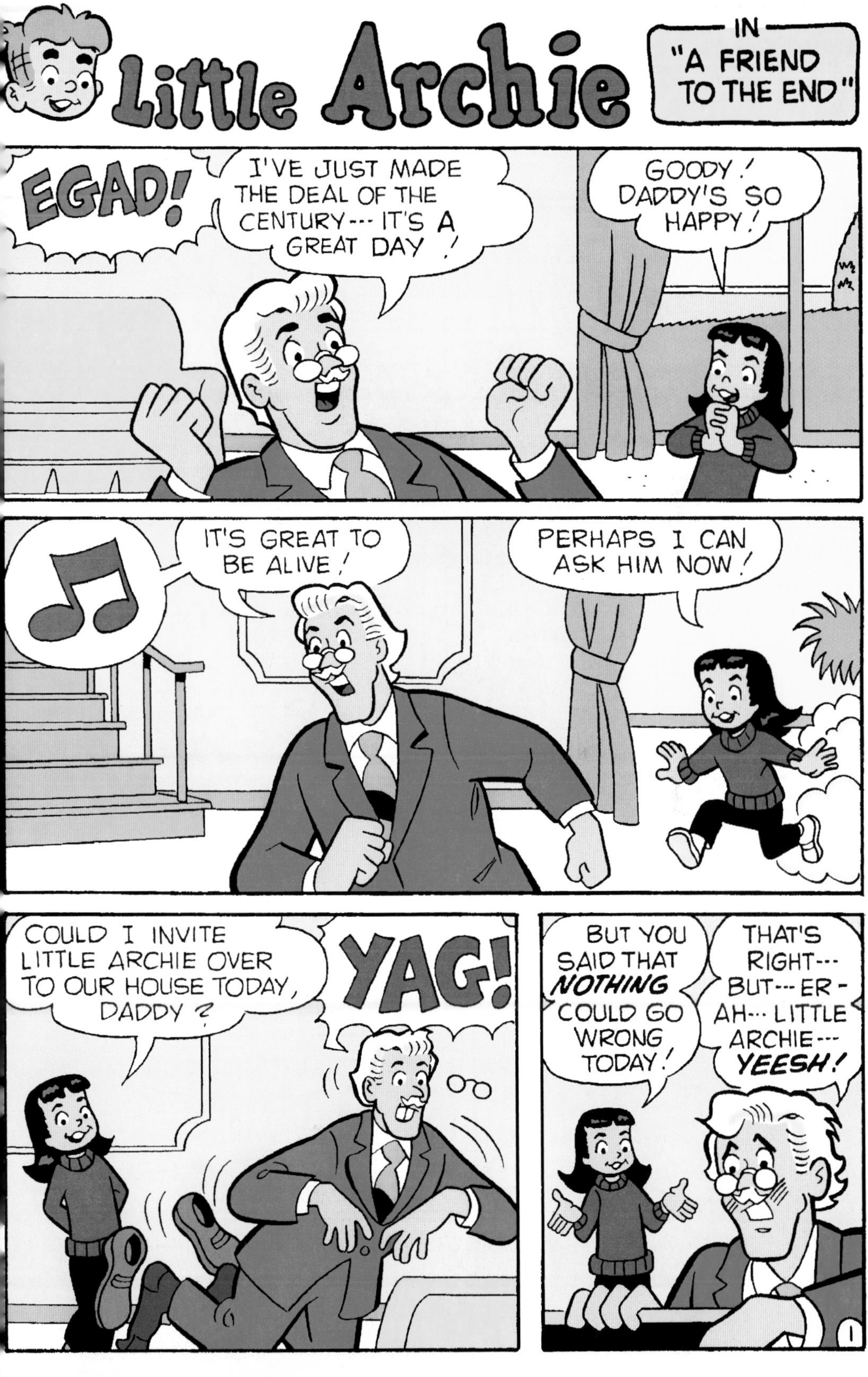
Little Archie
IN "A FRIEND TO THE END"
EGAD!
I'VE JUST MADE THE DEAL OF THE CENTURY--- IT'S A GREAT DAY!
GOODY! DADDY'S SO HAPPY!
IT'S GREAT TO BE ALIVE!
PERHAPS I CAN ASK HIM NOW!
COULD I INVITE LITTLE ARCHIE OVER TO OUR HOUSE TODAY, DADDY?
YAG!
BUT YOU SAID THAT NOTHING COULD GO WRONG TODAY!
THAT'S RIGHT--- BUT--- ER- AH--- LITTLE ARCHIE--- YEESH!
1

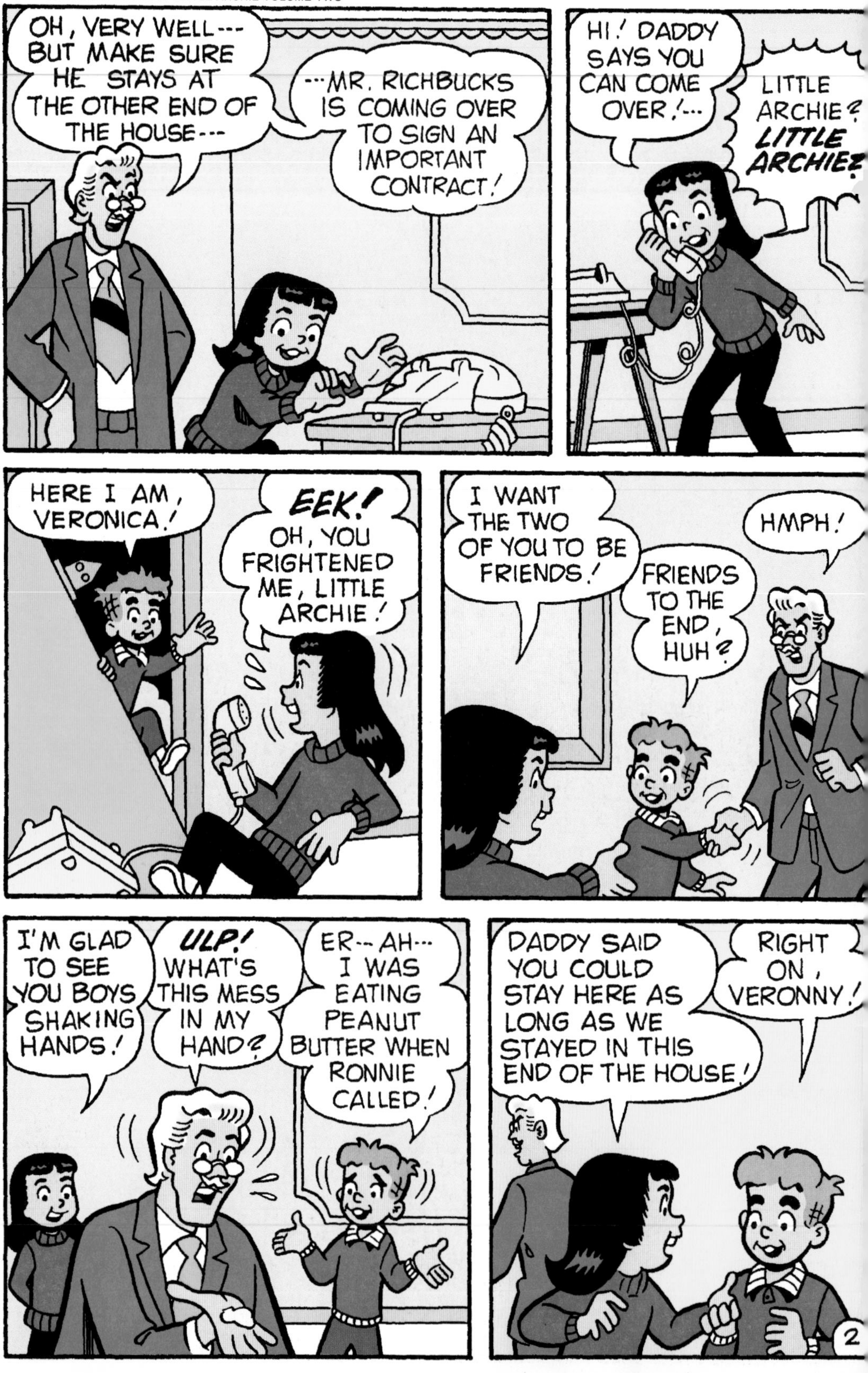
OH, VERY WELL--- BUT MAKE SURE HE STAYS AT THE OTHER END OF THE HOUSE---
---MR. RICHBUCKS IS COMING OVER TO SIGN AN IMPORTANT CONTRACT!
HI! DADDY SAYS YOU CAN COME OVER!...
LITTLE ARCHIE? LITTLE ARCHIE?
HERE I AM, VERONICA!
EEK! OH, YOU FRIGHTENED ME, LITTLE ARCHIE!
I WANT THE TWO OF YOU TO BE FRIENDS!
HMPH!
FRIENDS TO THE END, HUH?
I'M GLAD TO SEE YOU BOYS SHAKING HANDS!
ULP! WHAT'S THIS MESS IN MY HAND?
ER-- AH--- I WAS EATING PEANUT BUTTER WHEN RONNIE CALLED!
DADDY SAID YOU COULD STAY HERE AS LONG AS WE STAYED IN THIS END OF THE HOUSE!
RIGHT ON, VERONNY!
2

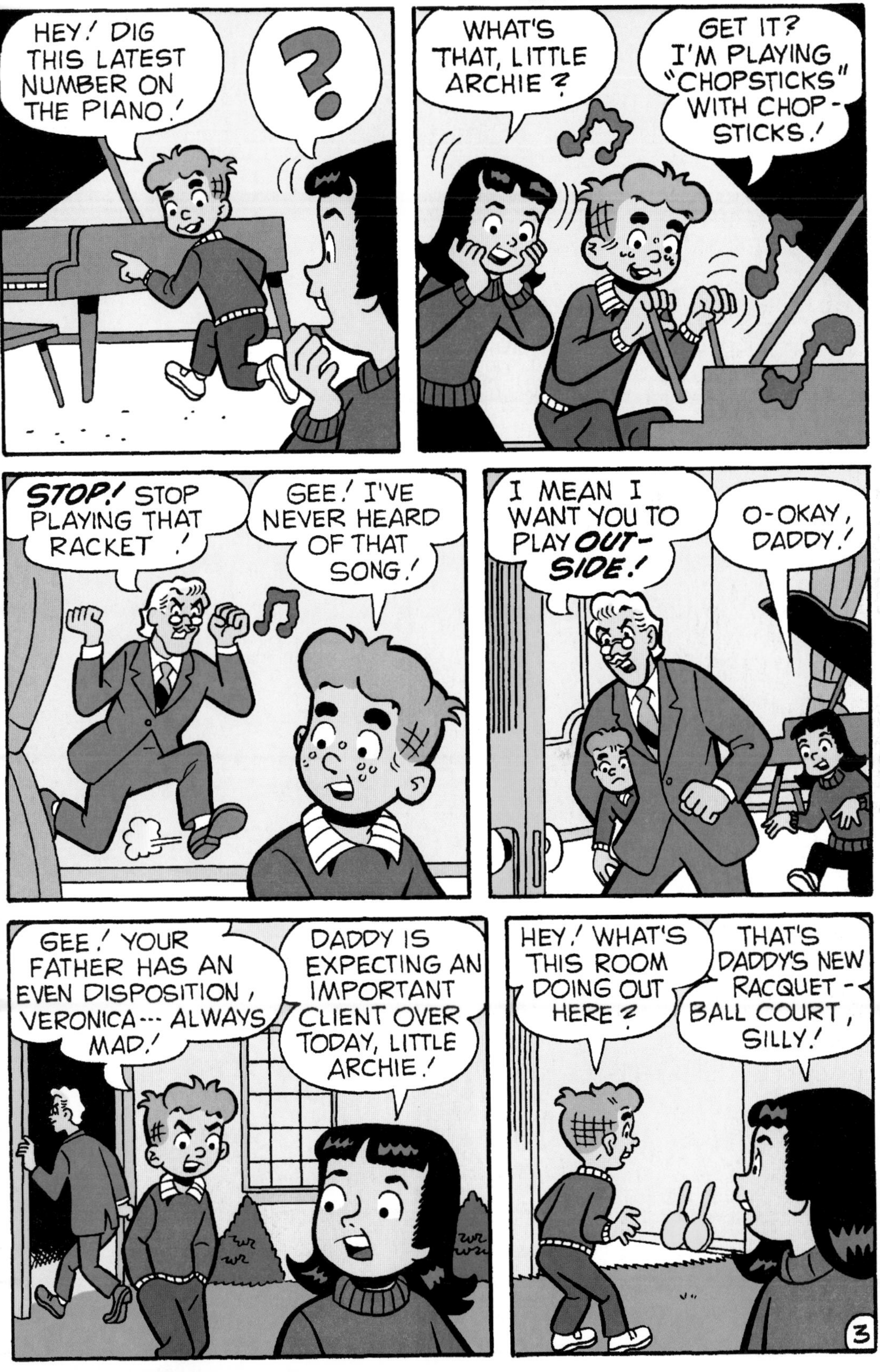
HEY! DIG THIS LATEST NUMBER ON THE PIANO!
?
WHAT'S THAT, LITTLE ARCHIE?
GET IT? I'M PLAYING "CHOPSTICKS" WITH CHOP-STICKS!
STOP! STOP PLAYING THAT RACKET!
GEE! I'VE NEVER HEARD OF THAT SONG!
I MEAN I WANT YOU TO PLAY OUT-SIDE!
O-OKAY, DADDY!
GEE! YOUR FATHER HAS AN EVEN DISPOSITION, VERONICA--- ALWAYS MAD!
DADDY IS EXPECTING AN IMPORTANT CLIENT OVER TODAY, LITTLE ARCHIE!
HEY! WHAT'S THIS ROOM DOING OUT HERE?
THAT'S DADDY'S NEW RACQUET-BALL COURT, SILLY!
3

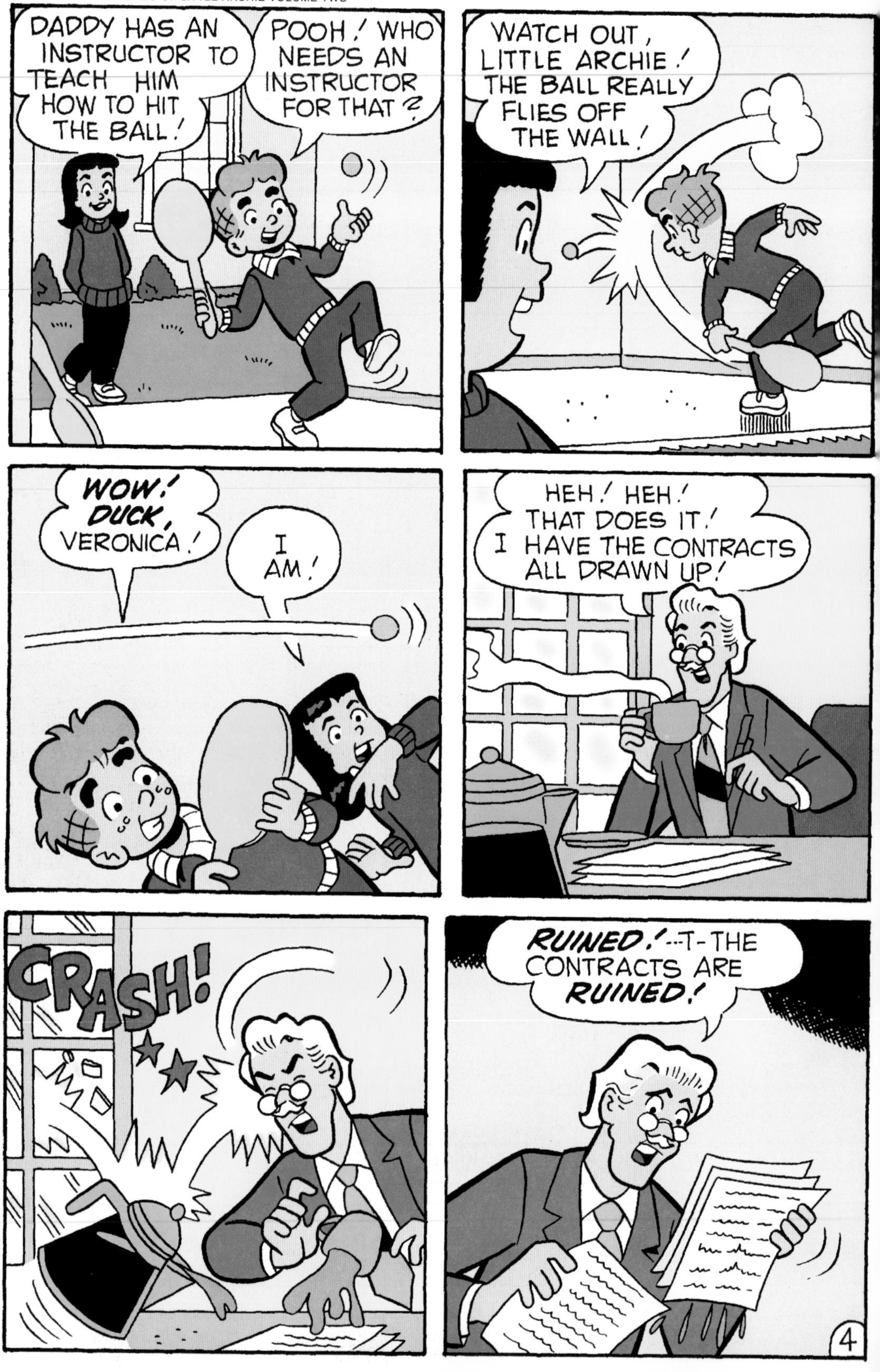
DADDY HAS AN INSTRUCTOR TO TEACH HIM HOW TO HIT THE BALL!
POOH! WHO NEEDS AN INSTRUCTOR FOR THAT?
WATCH OUT, LITTLE ARCHIE! THE BALL REALLY FLIES OFF THE WALL!
WOW! DUCK, VERONICA!
I AM!
HEH! HEH! THAT DOES IT! I HAVE THE CONTRACTS ALL DRAWN UP!
CRASH!
RUINED!--T-THE CONTRACTS ARE RUINED!
4

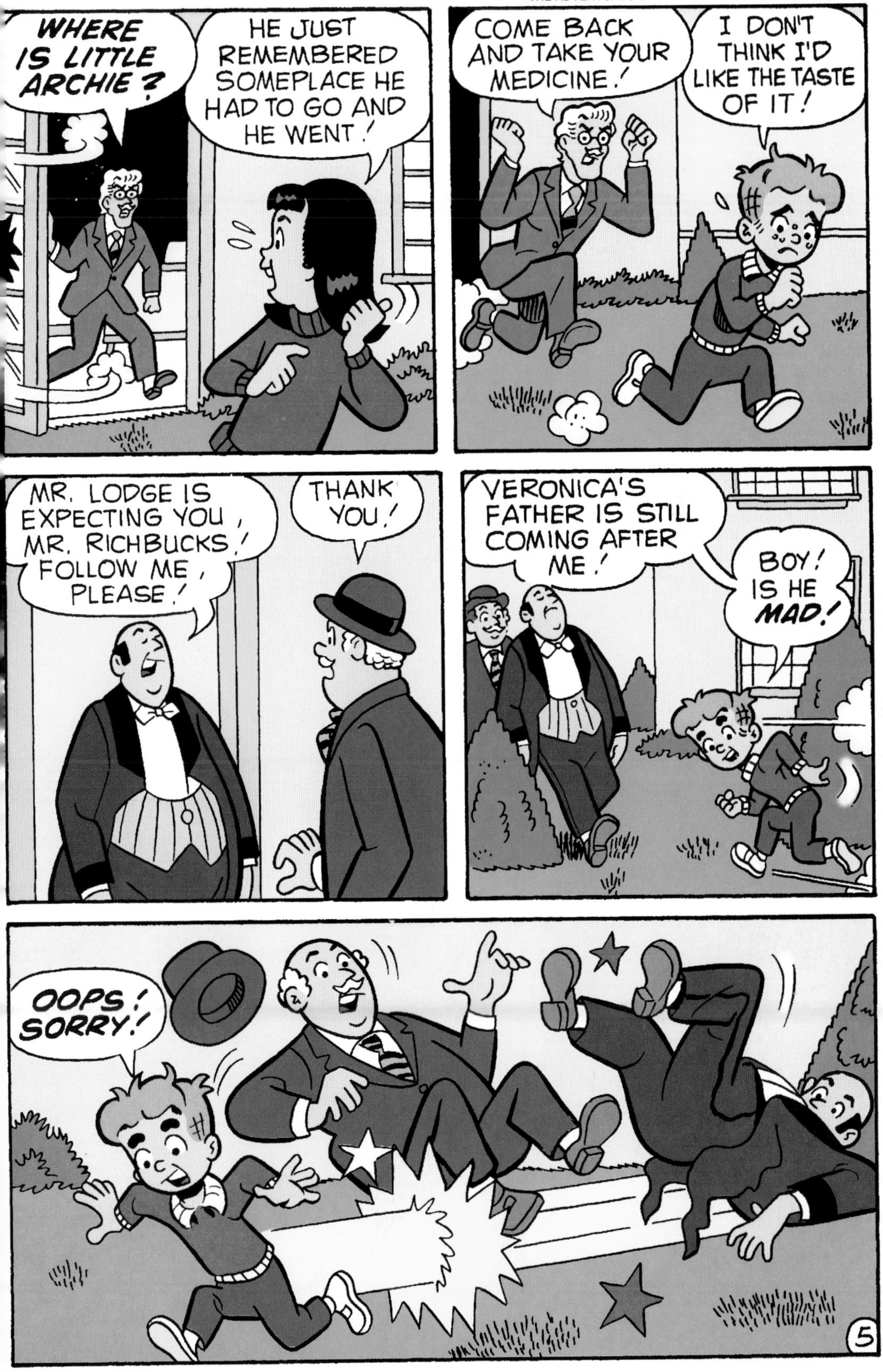
WHERE IS LITTLE ARCHIE?
HE JUST REMEMBERED SOMEPLACE HE HAD TO GO AND HE WENT!
COME BACK AND TAKE YOUR MEDICINE!
I DON'T THINK I'D LIKE THE TASTE OF IT!
MR. LODGE IS EXPECTING YOU, MR. RICHBUCKS! FOLLOW ME, PLEASE!
THANK YOU!
VERONICA'S FATHER IS STILL COMING AFTER ME!
BOY! IS HE MAD!
OOPS! SORRY!
5

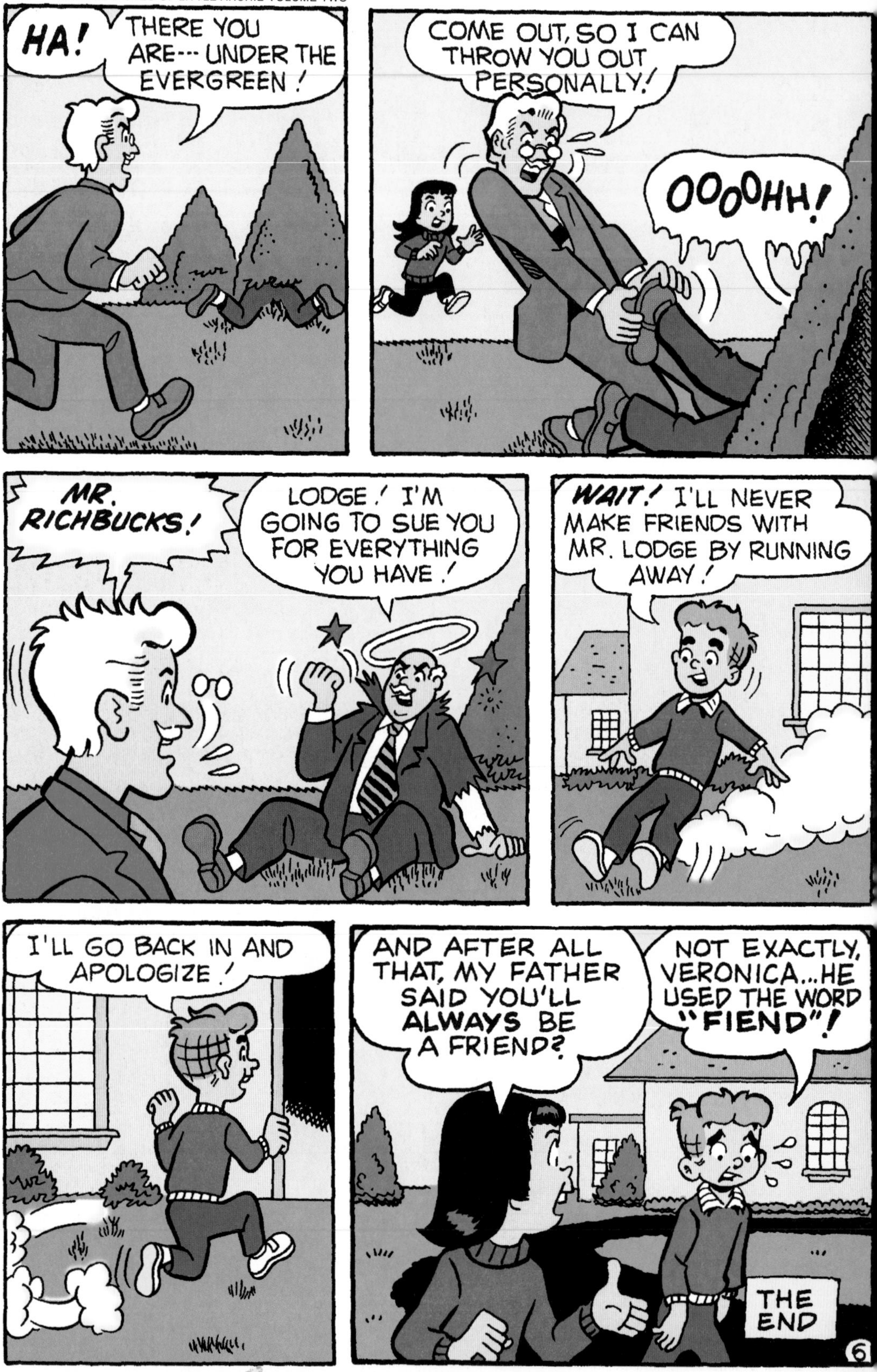
HA!
THERE YOU ARE--- UNDER THE EVERGREEN!
COME OUT, SO I CAN THROW YOU OUT PERSONALLY!
OOOOHH!
MR. RICHBUCKS!
LODGE! I'M GOING TO SUE YOU FOR EVERYTHING YOU HAVE!
WAIT! I'LL NEVER MAKE FRIENDS WITH MR. LODGE BY RUNNING AWAY!
I'LL GO BACK IN AND APOLOGIZE!
AND AFTER ALL THAT, MY FATHER SAID YOU'LL ALWAYS BE A FRIEND?
NOT EXACTLY, VERONICA...HE USED THE WORD "FIEND"!
THE END
6

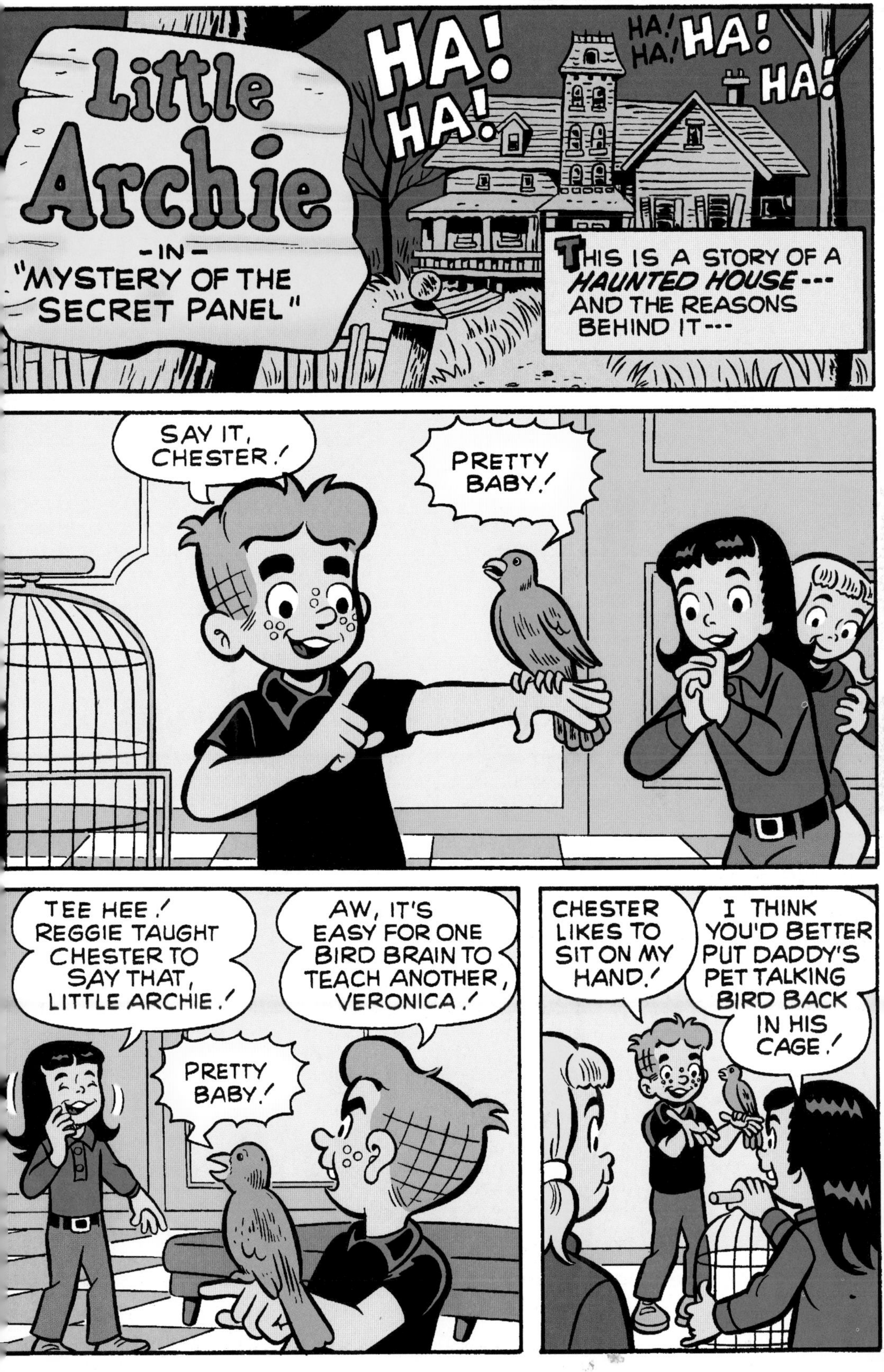
Little Archie
-IN-
"MYSTERY OF THE SECRET PANEL"
HA! HA!
HA! HA! HA! HA!
THIS IS A STORY OF A HAUNTED HOUSE--- AND THE REASONS BEHIND IT---
SAY IT, CHESTER!
PRETTY BABY!
TEE HEE! REGGIE TAUGHT CHESTER TO SAY THAT, LITTLE ARCHIE!
AW, IT'S EASY FOR ONE BIRD BRAIN TO TEACH ANOTHER, VERONICA!
PRETTY BABY!
CHESTER LIKES TO SIT ON MY HAND!
I THINK YOU'D BETTER PUT DADDY'S PET TALKING BIRD BACK IN HIS CAGE!

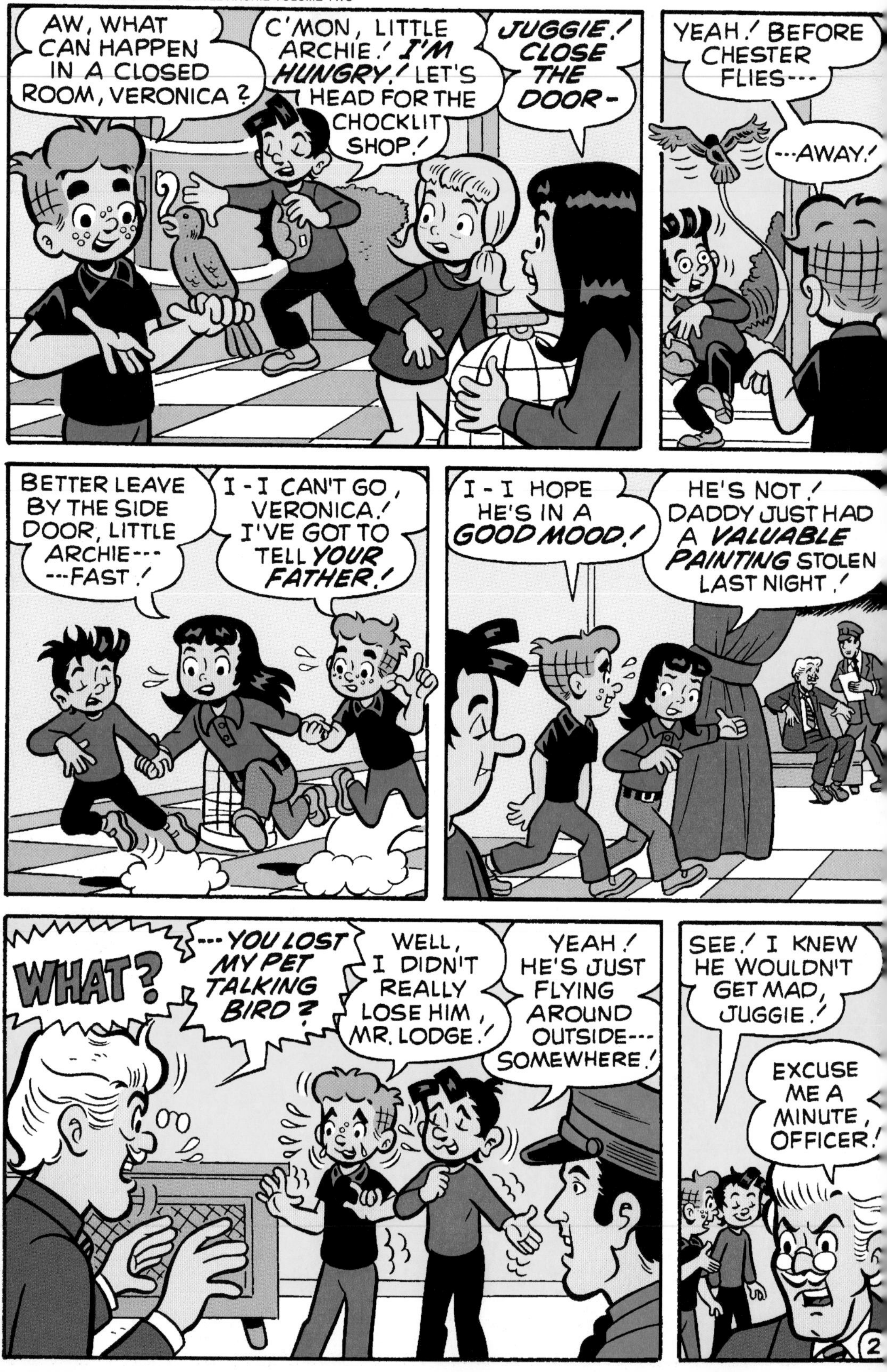
AW, WHAT CAN HAPPEN IN A CLOSED ROOM, VERONICA?
C'MON, LITTLE ARCHIE! I'M HUNGRY! LET'S HEAD FOR THE CHOCKLIT SHOP!
JUGGIE! CLOSE THE DOOR-
YEAH! BEFORE CHESTER FLIES---
---AWAY!
BETTER LEAVE BY THE SIDE DOOR, LITTLE ARCHIE--- ---FAST!
I-I CAN'T GO, VERONICA! I'VE GOT TO TELL YOUR FATHER!
I-I HOPE HE'S IN A GOOD MOOD!
HE'S NOT! DADDY JUST HAD A VALUABLE PAINTING STOLEN LAST NIGHT!
WHAT?
---YOU LOST MY PET TALKING BIRD?
WELL, I DIDN'T REALLY LOSE HIM, MR. LODGE!
YEAH! HE'S JUST FLYING AROUND OUTSIDE--- SOMEWHERE!
SEE! I KNEW HE WOULDN'T GET MAD, JUGGIE!
EXCUSE ME A MINUTE, OFFICER!
2

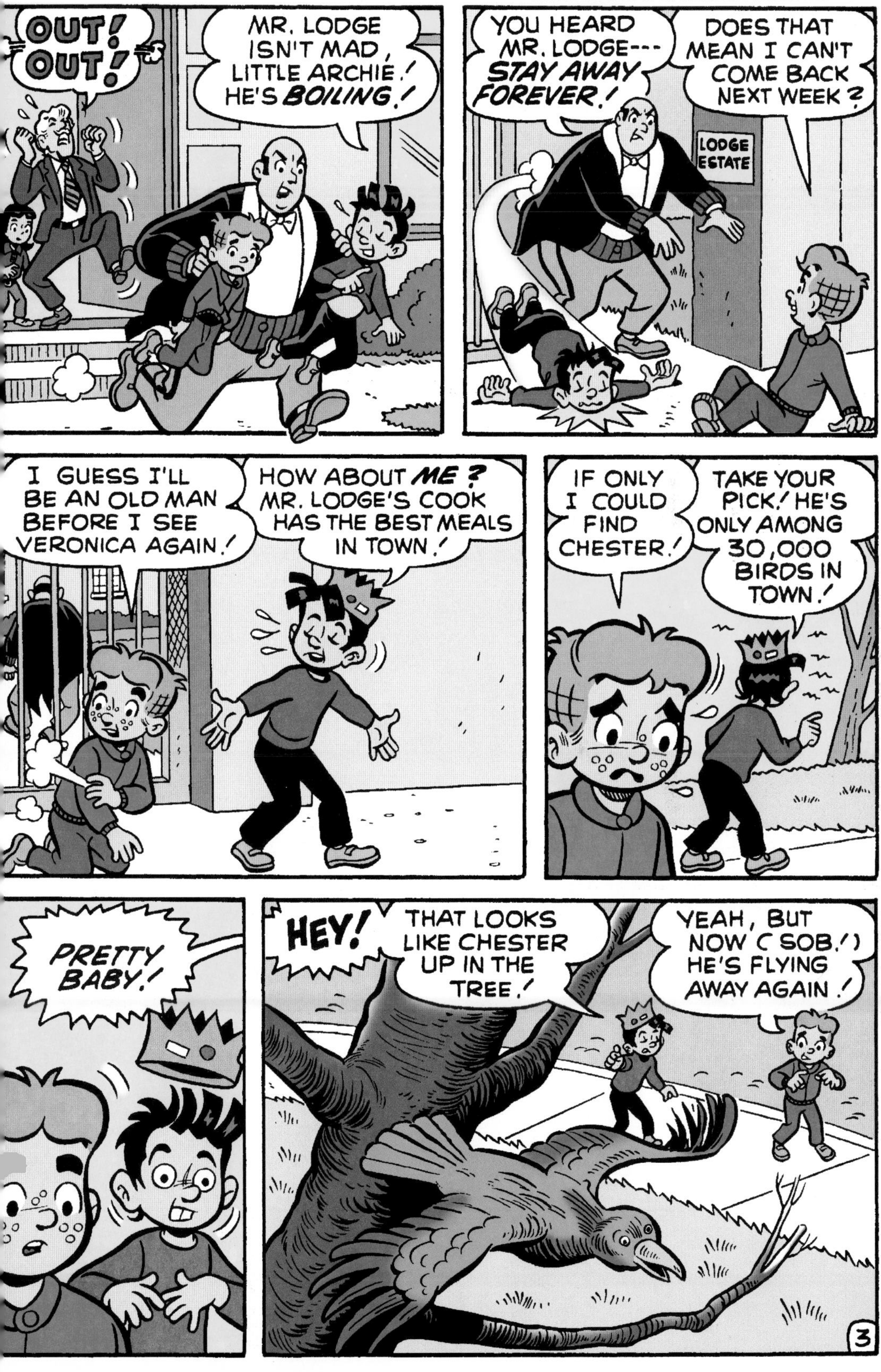
OUT! OUT!
MR. LODGE ISN'T MAD, LITTLE ARCHIE! HE'S BOILING!
YOU HEARD MR. LODGE--- STAY AWAY FOREVER!
DOES THAT MEAN I CAN'T COME BACK NEXT WEEK?
LODGE ESTATE
I GUESS I'LL BE AN OLD MAN BEFORE I SEE VERONICA AGAIN!
HOW ABOUT ME? MR. LODGE'S COOK HAS THE BEST MEALS IN TOWN!
IF ONLY I COULD FIND CHESTER!
TAKE YOUR PICK! HE'S ONLY AMONG 30,000 BIRDS IN TOWN!
PRETTY BABY!
HEY!
THAT LOOKS LIKE CHESTER UP IN THE TREE!
YEAH, BUT NOW (SOB!) HE'S FLYING AWAY AGAIN!
3

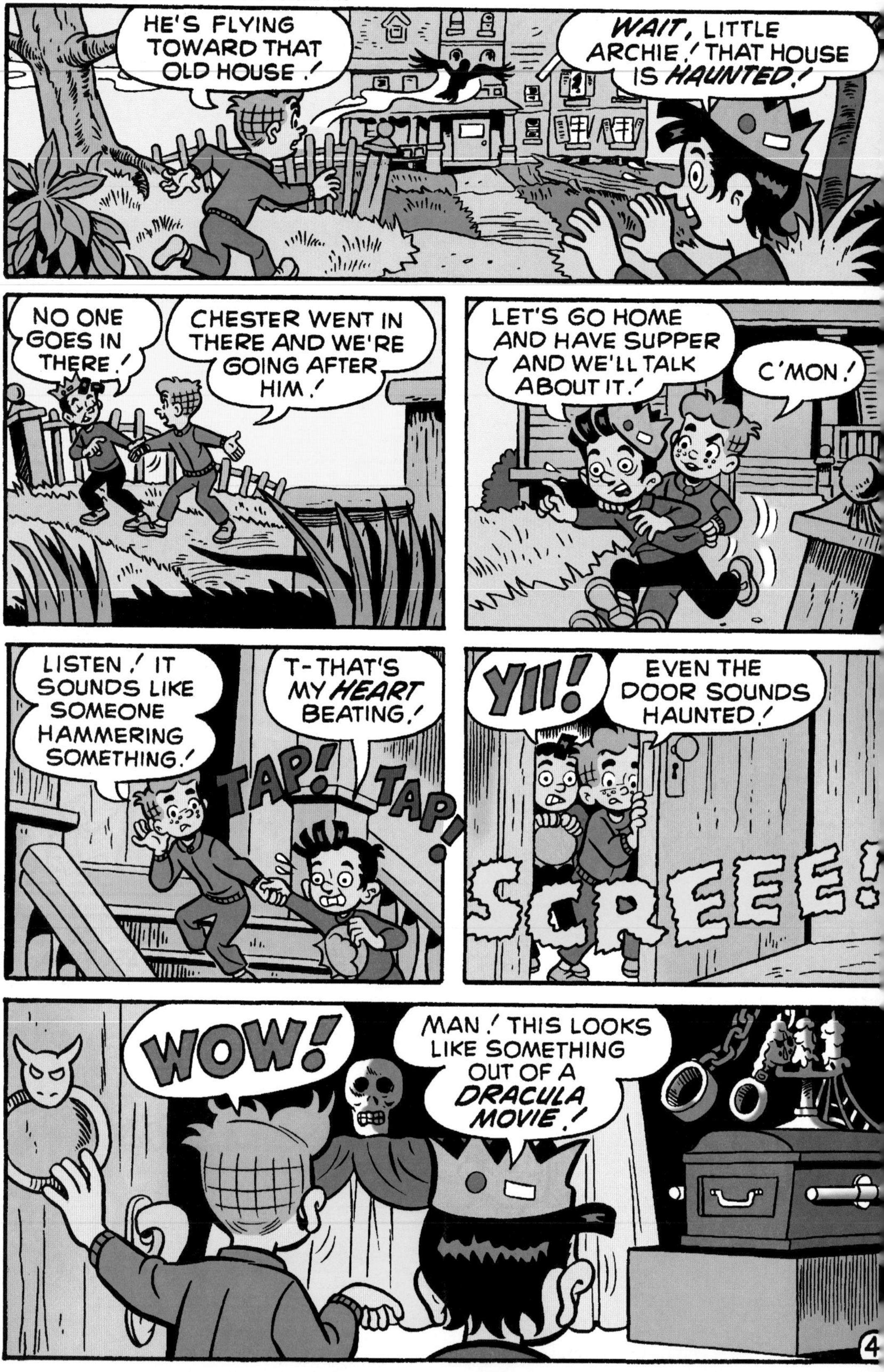
HE'S FLYING TOWARD THAT OLD HOUSE!
WAIT, LITTLE ARCHIE! THAT HOUSE IS HAUNTED!
NO ONE GOES IN THERE!
CHESTER WENT IN THERE AND WE'RE GOING AFTER HIM!
LET'S GO HOME AND HAVE SUPPER AND WE'LL TALK ABOUT IT!
C'MON!
LISTEN! IT SOUNDS LIKE SOMEONE HAMMERING SOMETHING!
T-THAT'S MY HEART BEATING!
TAP! TAP!
YII!
EVEN THE DOOR SOUNDS HAUNTED!
SCREEE!
WOW!
MAN! THIS LOOKS LIKE SOMETHING OUT OF A DRACULA MOVIE!
4

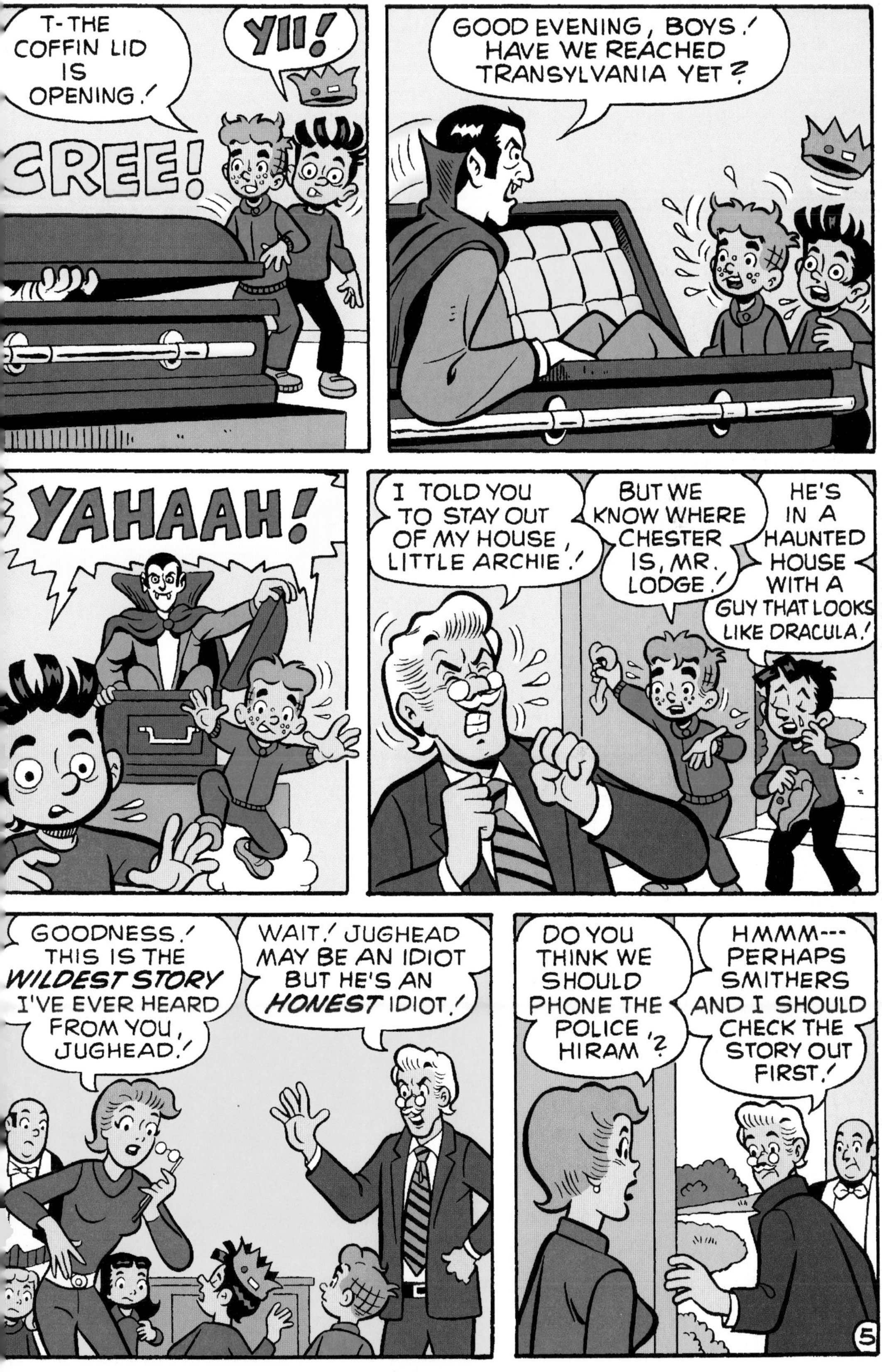
T-THE COFFIN LID IS OPENING!
YII!
CREE!
GOOD EVENING, BOYS! HAVE WE REACHED TRANSYLVANIA YET?
YAHAAH!
I TOLD YOU TO STAY OUT OF MY HOUSE, LITTLE ARCHIE!!
BUT WE KNOW WHERE CHESTER IS, MR. LODGE!
HE'S IN A HAUNTED HOUSE WITH A GUY THAT LOOKS LIKE DRACULA!
GOODNESS! THIS IS THE *WILDEST STORY* I'VE EVER HEARD FROM YOU, JUGHEAD!
WAIT! JUGHEAD MAY BE AN IDIOT BUT HE'S AN *HONEST* IDIOT!
DO YOU THINK WE SHOULD PHONE THE POLICE, HIRAM?
HMMM--- PERHAPS SMITHERS AND I SHOULD CHECK THE STORY OUT FIRST!
5

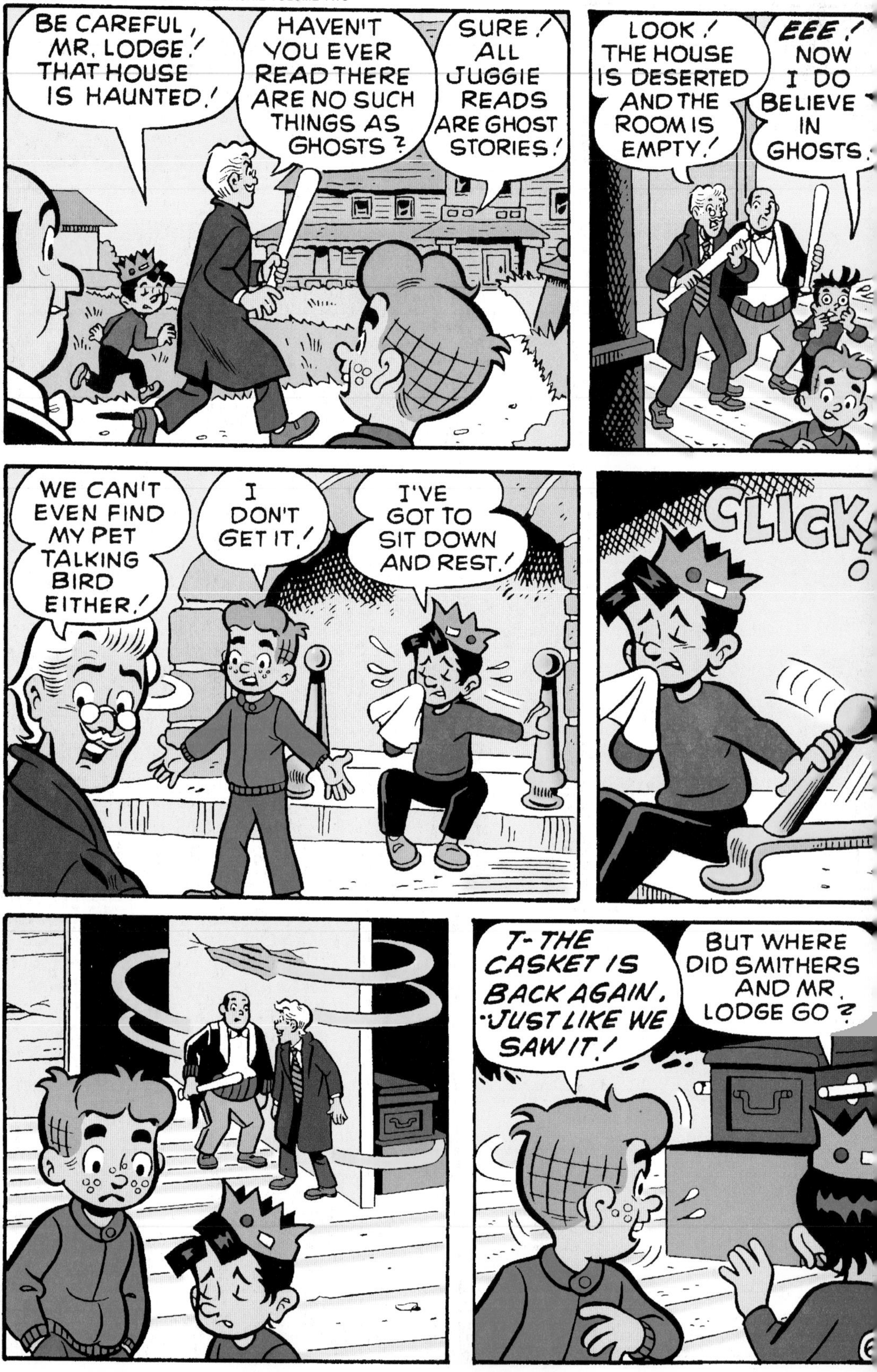
BE CAREFUL, MR. LODGE! THAT HOUSE IS HAUNTED!
HAVEN'T YOU EVER READ THERE ARE NO SUCH THINGS AS GHOSTS?
SURE! ALL JUGGIE READS ARE GHOST STORIES!
LOOK! THE HOUSE IS DESERTED AND THE ROOM IS EMPTY!
EEE! NOW I DO BELIEVE IN GHOSTS
WE CAN'T EVEN FIND MY PET TALKING BIRD EITHER!
I DON'T GET IT!
I'VE GOT TO SIT DOWN AND REST!
CLICK
T-THE CASKET IS BACK AGAIN, JUST LIKE WE SAW IT!
BUT WHERE DID SMITHERS AND MR. LODGE GO?

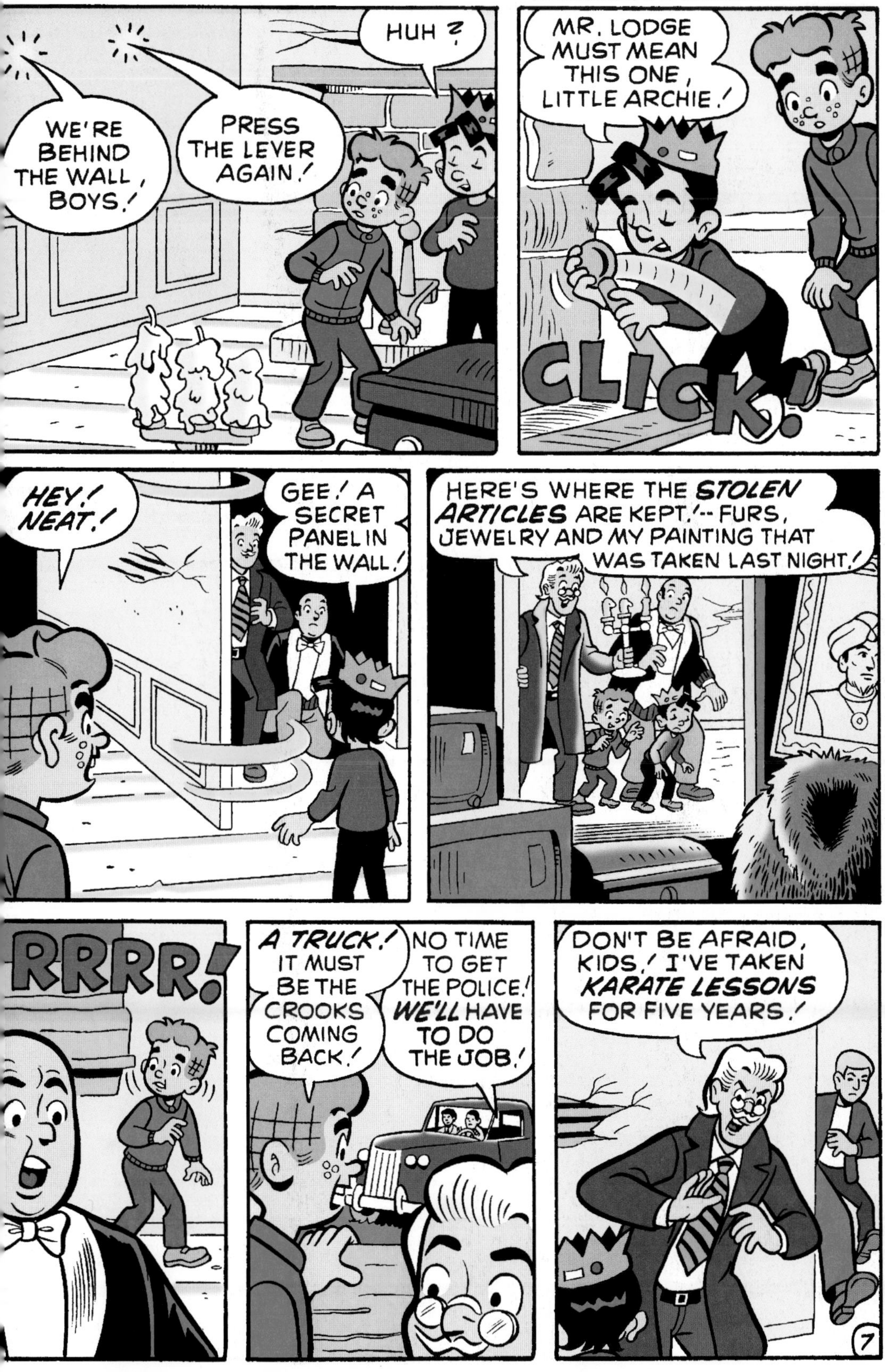
WE'RE BEHIND THE WALL, BOYS!
PRESS THE LEVER AGAIN!
HUH ?
MR. LODGE MUST MEAN THIS ONE, LITTLE ARCHIE!
CLICK!
HEY! NEAT!
GEE! A SECRET PANEL IN THE WALL!
HERE'S WHERE THE STOLEN ARTICLES ARE KEPT!-- FURS, JEWELRY AND MY PAINTING THAT WAS TAKEN LAST NIGHT!
RRRR!
A TRUCK! IT MUST BE THE CROOKS COMING BACK!
NO TIME TO GET THE POLICE! WE'LL HAVE TO DO THE JOB!
DON'T BE AFRAID, KIDS! I'VE TAKEN KARATE LESSONS FOR FIVE YEARS!
7

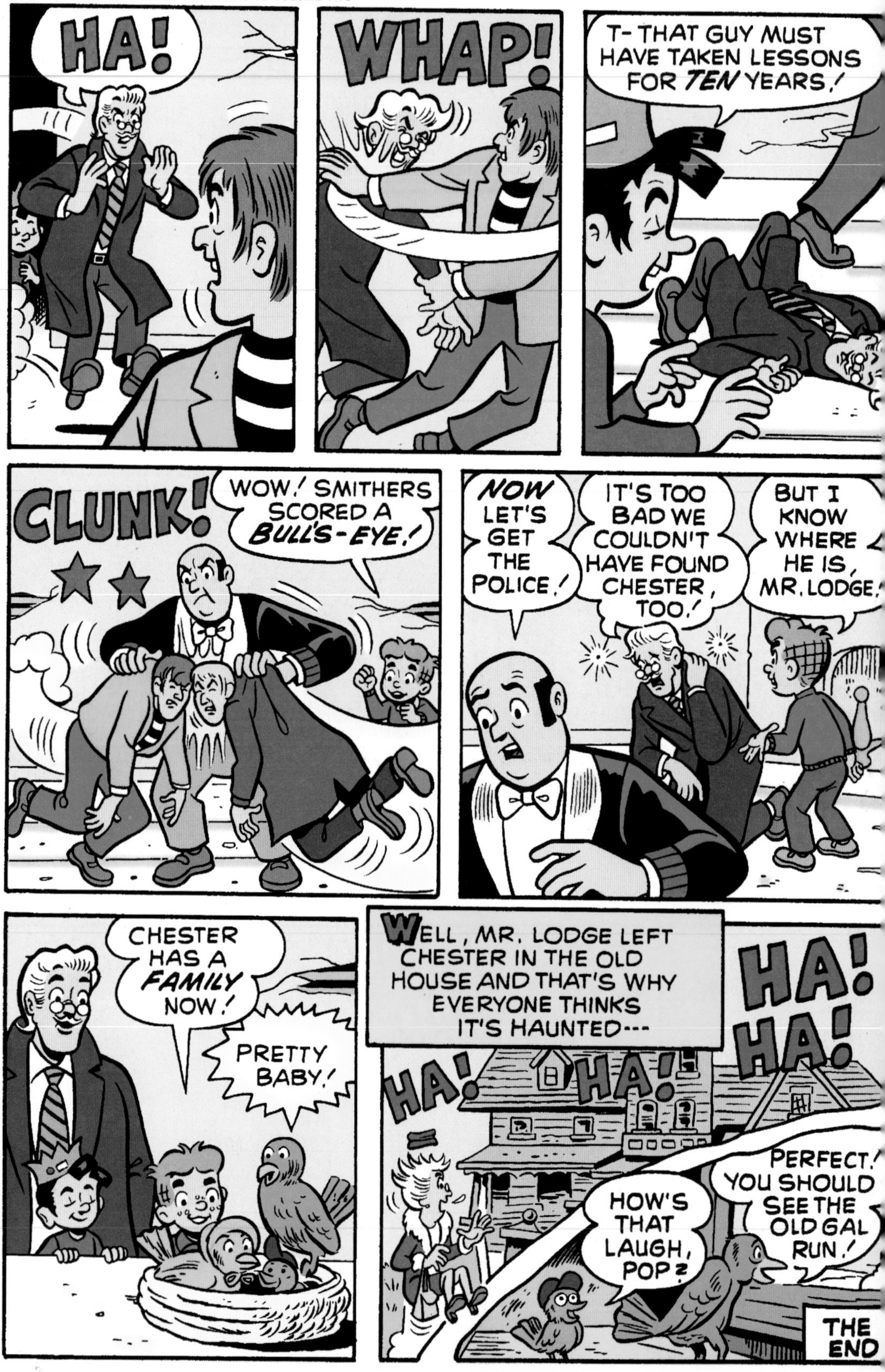
HA!
WHAP!
T-THAT GUY MUST HAVE TAKEN LESSONS FOR TEN YEARS!
CLUNK!
WOW! SMITHERS SCORED A BULL'S-EYE!
NOW LET'S GET THE POLICE!
IT'S TOO BAD WE COULDN'T HAVE FOUND CHESTER, TOO!
BUT I KNOW WHERE HE IS, MR. LODGE!
CHESTER HAS A FAMILY NOW!
PRETTY BABY!
WELL, MR. LODGE LEFT CHESTER IN THE OLD HOUSE AND THAT'S WHY EVERYONE THINKS IT'S HAUNTED---
HA! HA!
HA! HA!
HOW'S THAT LAUGH, POP?
PERFECT! YOU SHOULD SEE THE OLD GAL RUN!
THE END

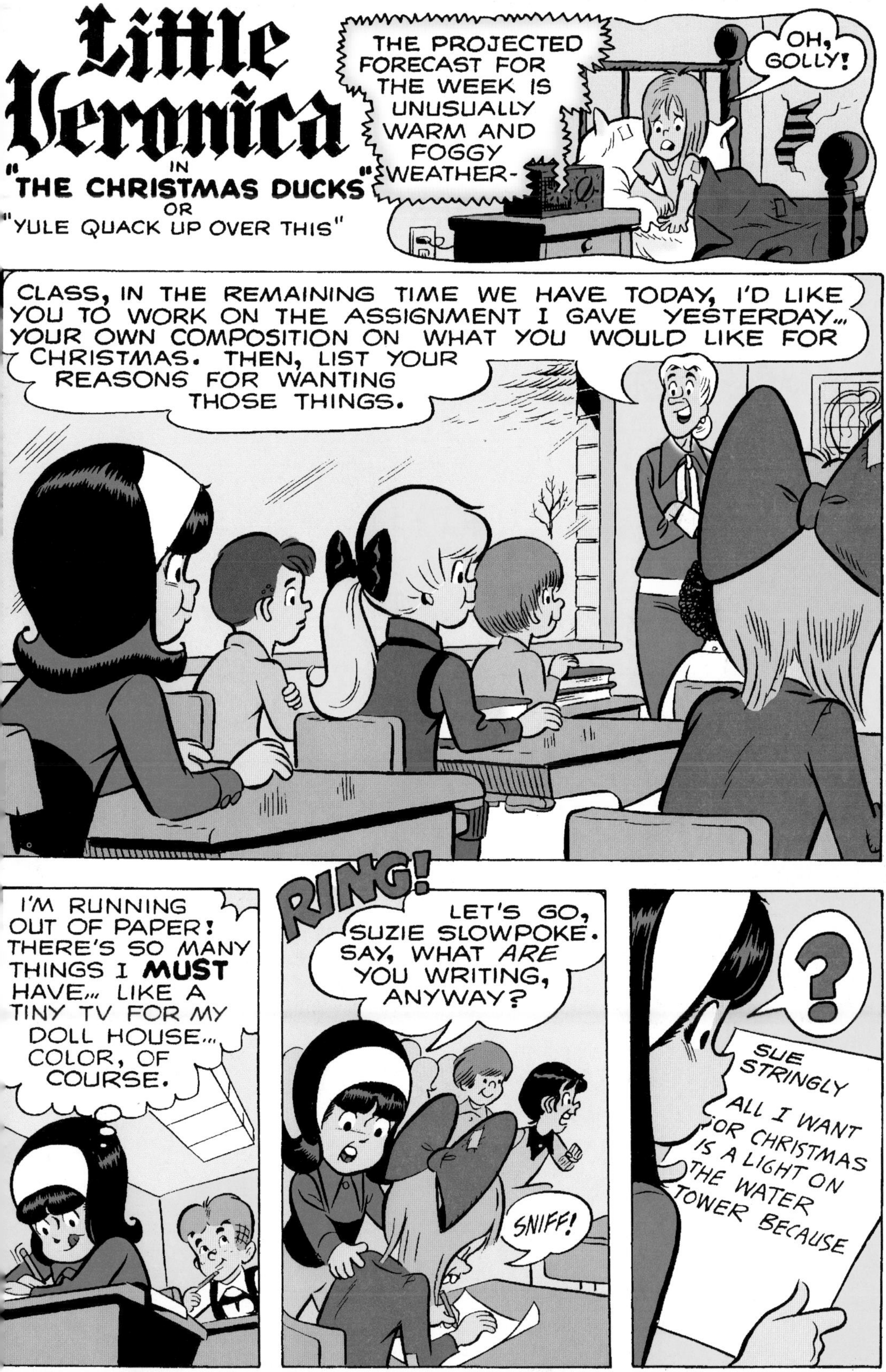
Little Veronica
IN
"THE CHRISTMAS DUCKS"
OR
"YULE QUACK UP OVER THIS"
THE PROJECTED FORECAST FOR THE WEEK IS UNUSUALLY WARM AND FOGGY WEATHER-
OH, GOLLY!
CLASS, IN THE REMAINING TIME WE HAVE TODAY, I'D LIKE YOU TO WORK ON THE ASSIGNMENT I GAVE YESTERDAY... YOUR OWN COMPOSITION ON WHAT YOU WOULD LIKE FOR CHRISTMAS. THEN, LIST YOUR REASONS FOR WANTING THOSE THINGS.
I'M RUNNING OUT OF PAPER! THERE'S SO MANY THINGS I MUST HAVE... LIKE A TINY TV FOR MY DOLL HOUSE... COLOR, OF COURSE.
RING!
LET'S GO, SUZIE SLOWPOKE. SAY, WHAT ARE YOU WRITING, ANYWAY?
SNIFF!
?
SUE STRINGLY
ALL I WANT FOR CHRISTMAS IS A LIGHT ON THE WATER TOWER BECAUSE

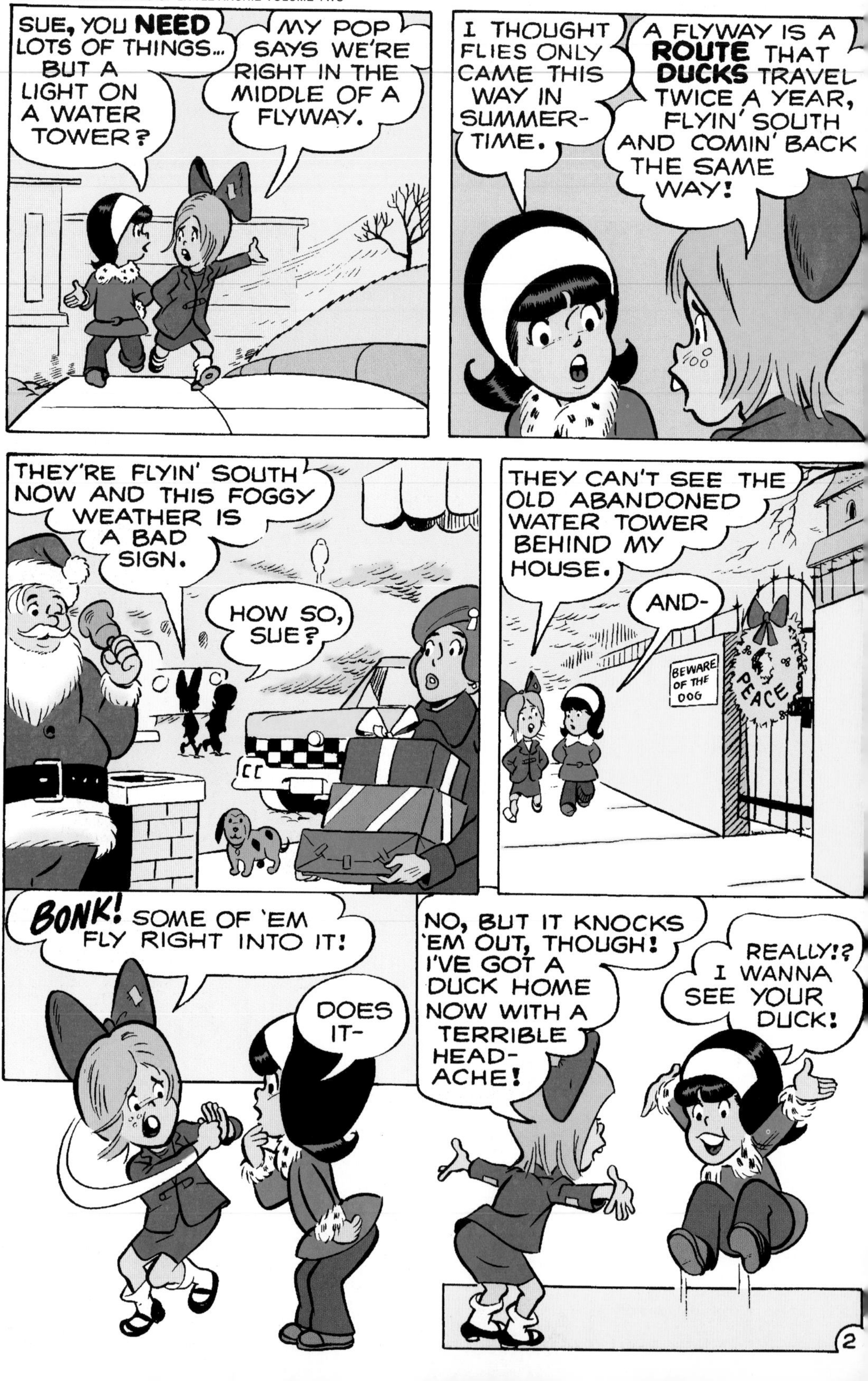
SUE, YOU NEED LOTS OF THINGS... BUT A LIGHT ON A WATER TOWER?
MY POP SAYS WE'RE RIGHT IN THE MIDDLE OF A FLYWAY.
I THOUGHT FLIES ONLY CAME THIS WAY IN SUMMER-TIME.
A FLYWAY IS A ROUTE THAT DUCKS TRAVEL TWICE A YEAR, FLYIN' SOUTH AND COMIN' BACK THE SAME WAY!
THEY'RE FLYIN' SOUTH NOW AND THIS FOGGY WEATHER IS A BAD SIGN.
HOW SO, SUE?
THEY CAN'T SEE THE OLD ABANDONED WATER TOWER BEHIND MY HOUSE.
AND-
BEWARE OF THE DOG
PEACE
BONK! SOME OF 'EM FLY RIGHT INTO IT!
DOES IT-
NO, BUT IT KNOCKS 'EM OUT, THOUGH! I'VE GOT A DUCK HOME NOW WITH A TERRIBLE HEAD-ACHE!
REALLY!? I WANNA SEE YOUR DUCK!
2

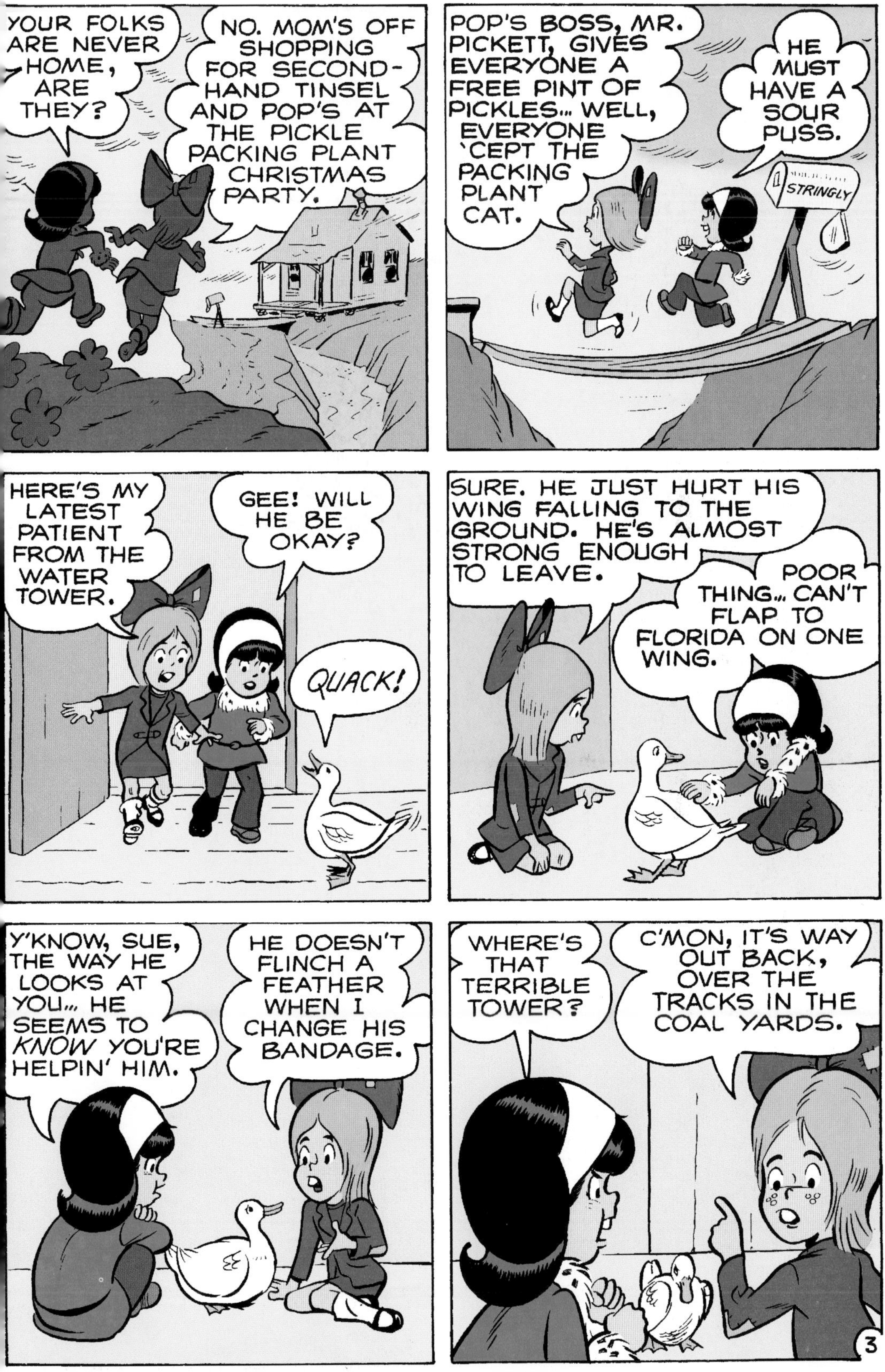
YOUR FOLKS ARE NEVER HOME, ARE THEY?
NO. MOM'S OFF SHOPPING FOR SECOND-HAND TINSEL AND POP'S AT THE PICKLE PACKING PLANT CHRISTMAS PARTY.
POP'S BOSS, MR. PICKETT, GIVES EVERYONE A FREE PINT OF PICKLES... WELL, EVERYONE 'CEPT THE PACKING PLANT CAT.
HE MUST HAVE A SOUR PUSS.
STRINGLY
HERE'S MY LATEST PATIENT FROM THE WATER TOWER.
GEE! WILL HE BE OKAY?
QUACK!
SURE. HE JUST HURT HIS WING FALLING TO THE GROUND. HE'S ALMOST STRONG ENOUGH TO LEAVE.
POOR THING... CAN'T FLAP TO FLORIDA ON ONE WING.
Y'KNOW, SUE, THE WAY HE LOOKS AT YOU... HE SEEMS TO *KNOW* YOU'RE HELPIN' HIM.
HE DOESN'T FLINCH A FEATHER WHEN I CHANGE HIS BANDAGE.
WHERE'S THAT TERRIBLE TOWER?
C'MON, IT'S WAY OUT BACK, OVER THE TRACKS IN THE COAL YARDS.
3

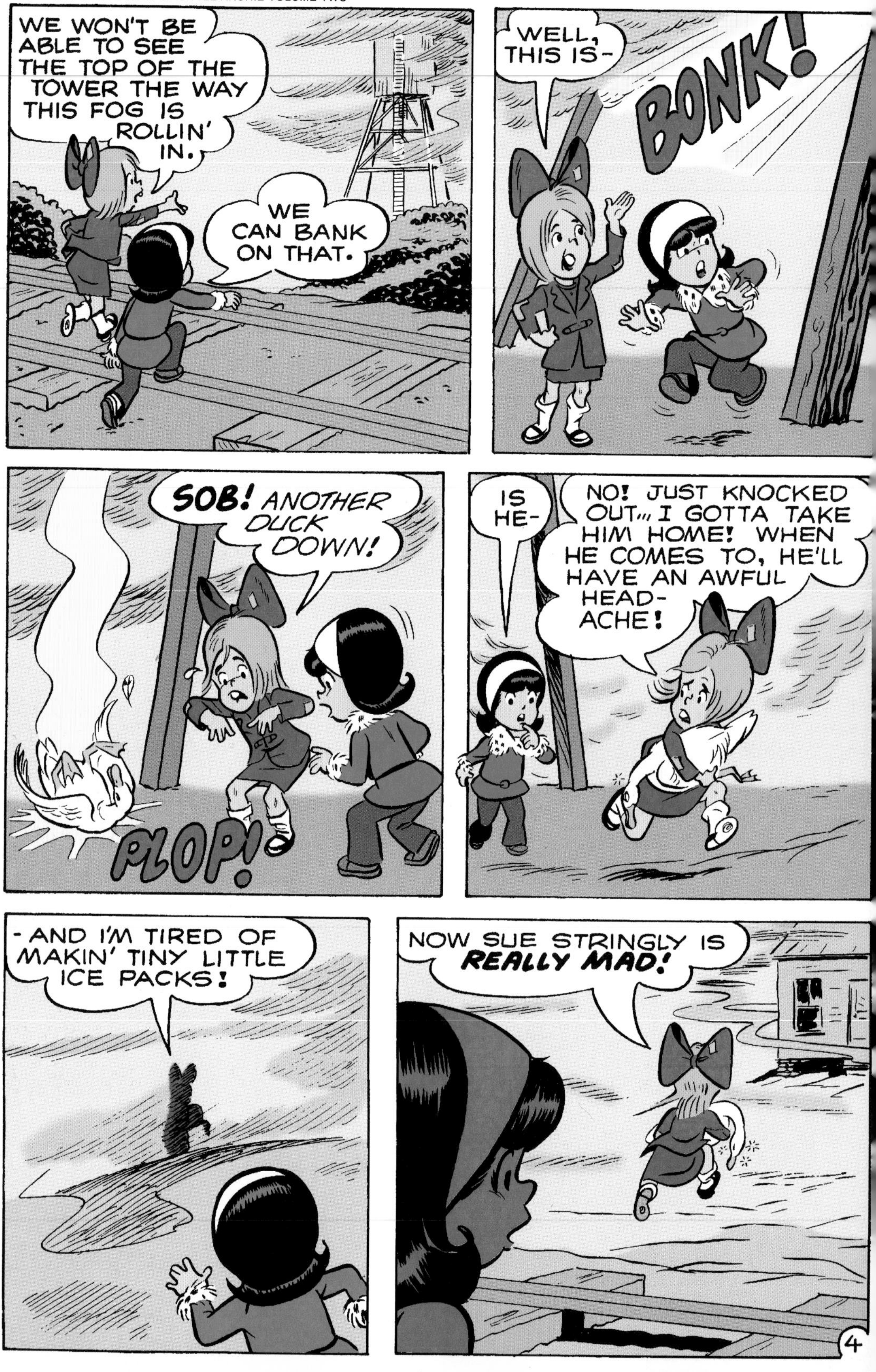
WE WON'T BE ABLE TO SEE THE TOP OF THE TOWER THE WAY THIS FOG IS ROLLIN' IN.
WE CAN BANK ON THAT.
WELL, THIS IS-
BONK!
SOB! ANOTHER DUCK DOWN!
PLOP!
IS HE-
NO! JUST KNOCKED OUT... I GOTTA TAKE HIM HOME! WHEN HE COMES TO, HE'LL HAVE AN AWFUL HEAD-ACHE!
-AND I'M TIRED OF MAKIN' TINY LITTLE ICE PACKS!
NOW SUE STRINGLY IS REALLY MAD!
4

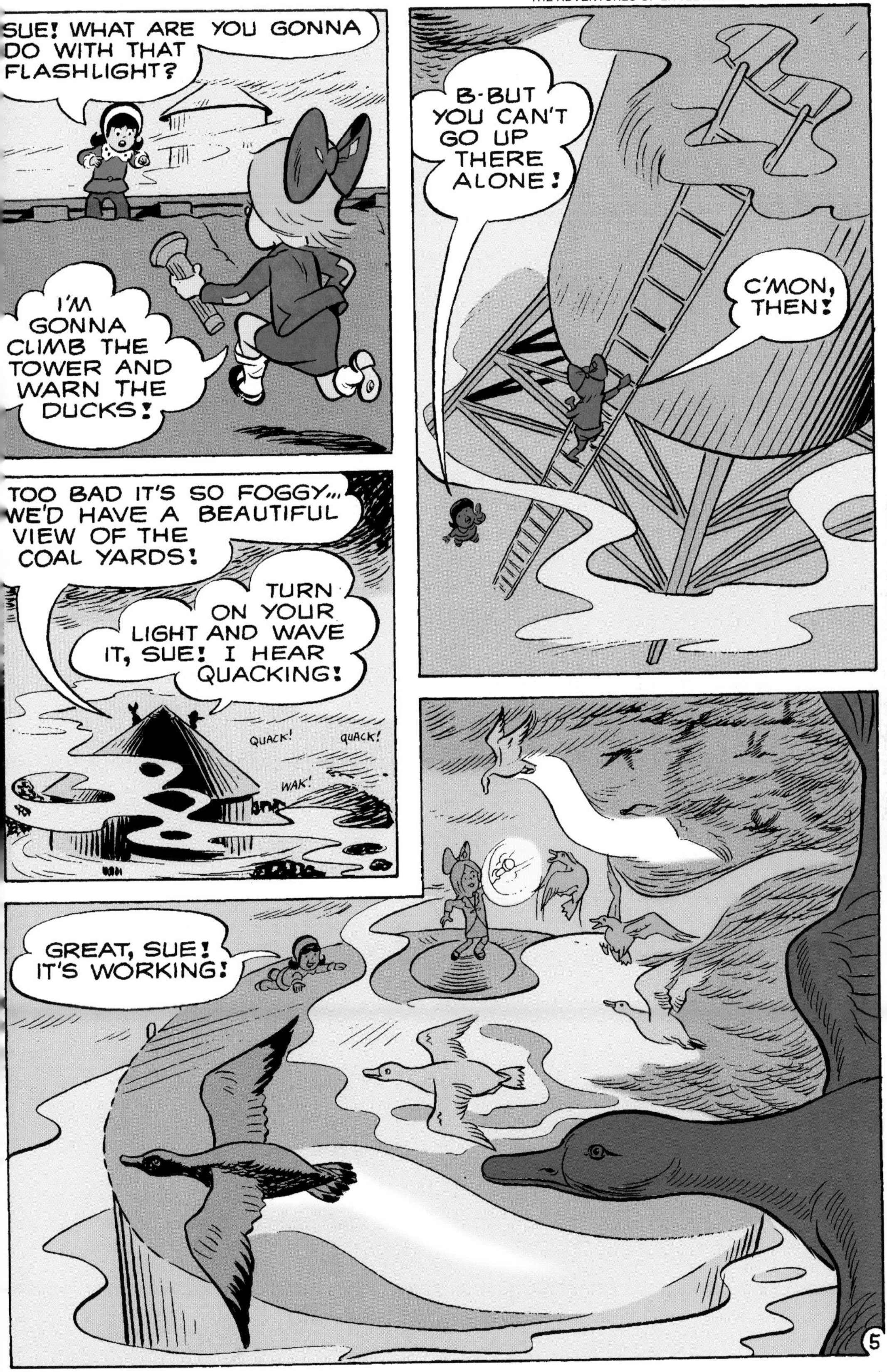
SUE! WHAT ARE YOU GONNA DO WITH THAT FLASHLIGHT?
I'M GONNA CLIMB THE TOWER AND WARN THE DUCKS!
B-BUT YOU CAN'T GO UP THERE ALONE!
C'MON, THEN!
TOO BAD IT'S SO FOGGY... WE'D HAVE A BEAUTIFUL VIEW OF THE COAL YARDS!
TURN ON YOUR LIGHT AND WAVE IT, SUE! I HEAR QUACKING!
QUACK!
QUACK!
WAK!
GREAT, SUE! IT'S WORKING!
5

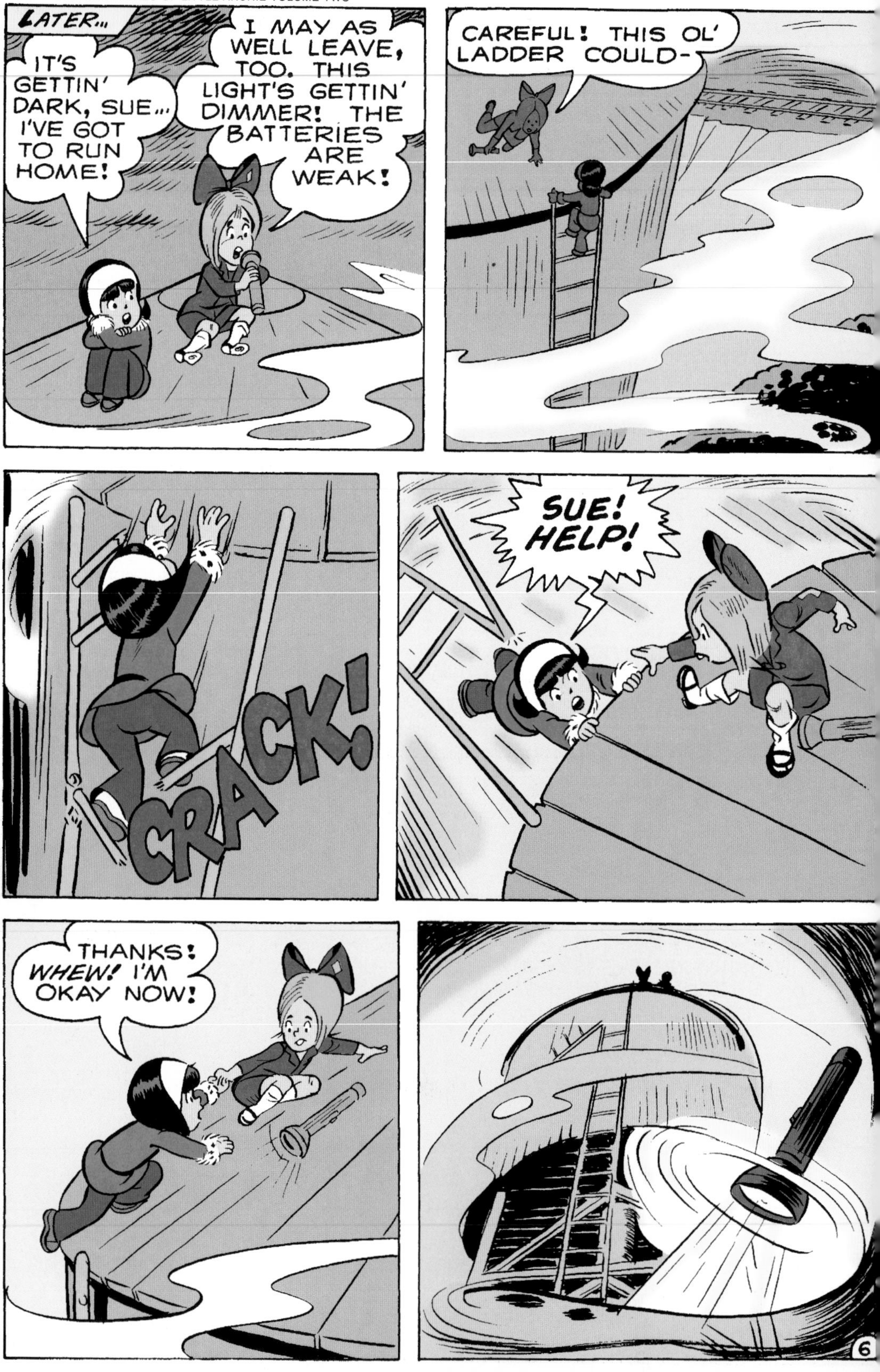
LATER...
IT'S GETTIN' DARK, SUE... I'VE GOT TO RUN HOME!
I MAY AS WELL LEAVE, TOO. THIS LIGHT'S GETTIN' DIMMER! THE BATTERIES ARE WEAK!
CAREFUL! THIS OL' LADDER COULD-
CRACK!
SUE! HELP!
THANKS! WHEW! I'M OKAY NOW!
6

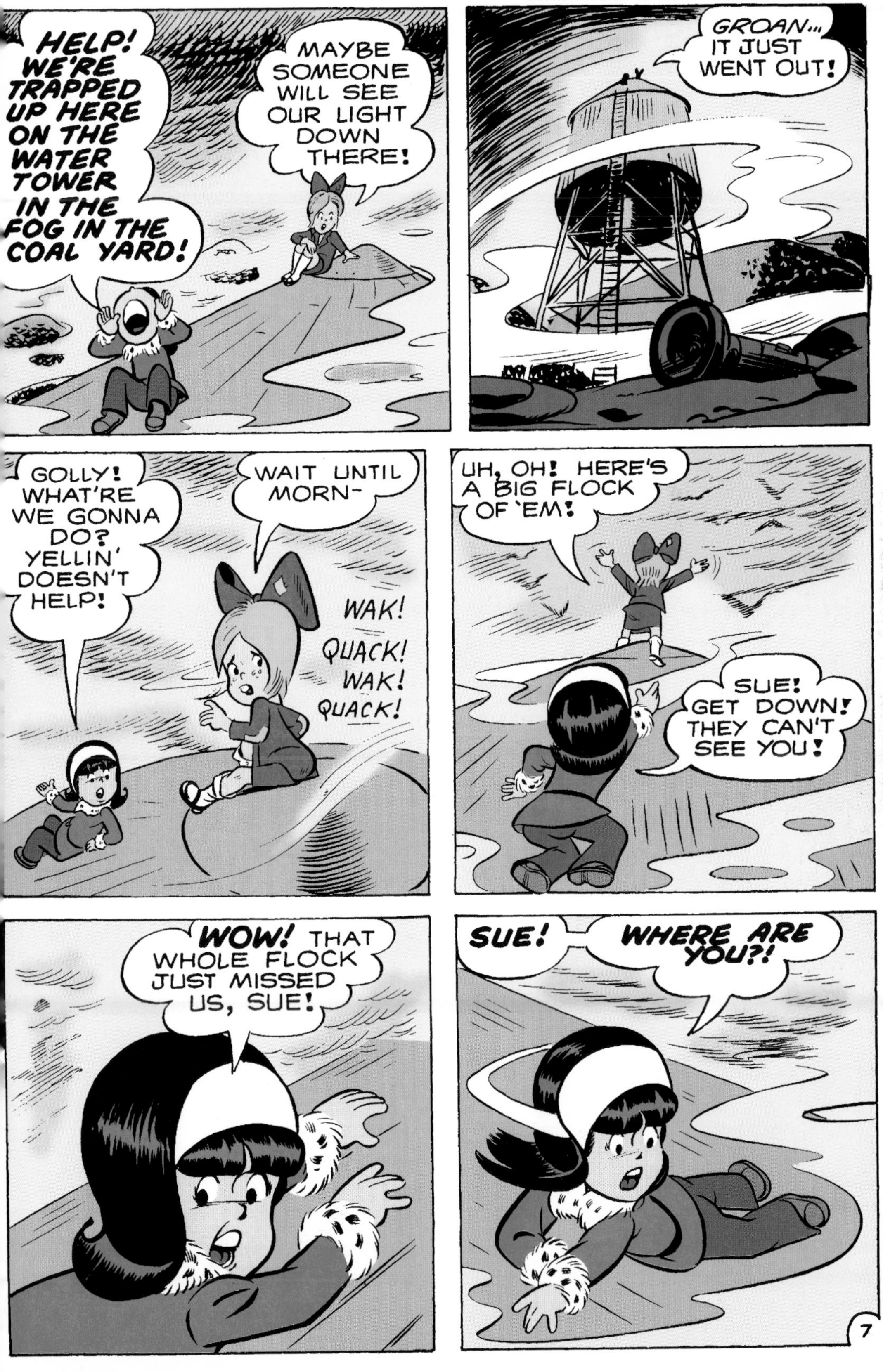
HELP! WE'RE TRAPPED UP HERE ON THE WATER TOWER IN THE FOG IN THE COAL YARD!
MAYBE SOMEONE WILL SEE OUR LIGHT DOWN THERE!
GROAN... IT JUST WENT OUT!
GOLLY! WHAT'RE WE GONNA DO? YELLIN' DOESN'T HELP!
WAIT UNTIL MORN-
WAK! QUACK! WAK! QUACK!
UH, OH! HERE'S A BIG FLOCK OF 'EM!
SUE! GET DOWN! THEY CAN'T SEE YOU!
WOW! THAT WHOLE FLOCK JUST MISSED US, SUE!
SUE!
WHERE ARE YOU?!

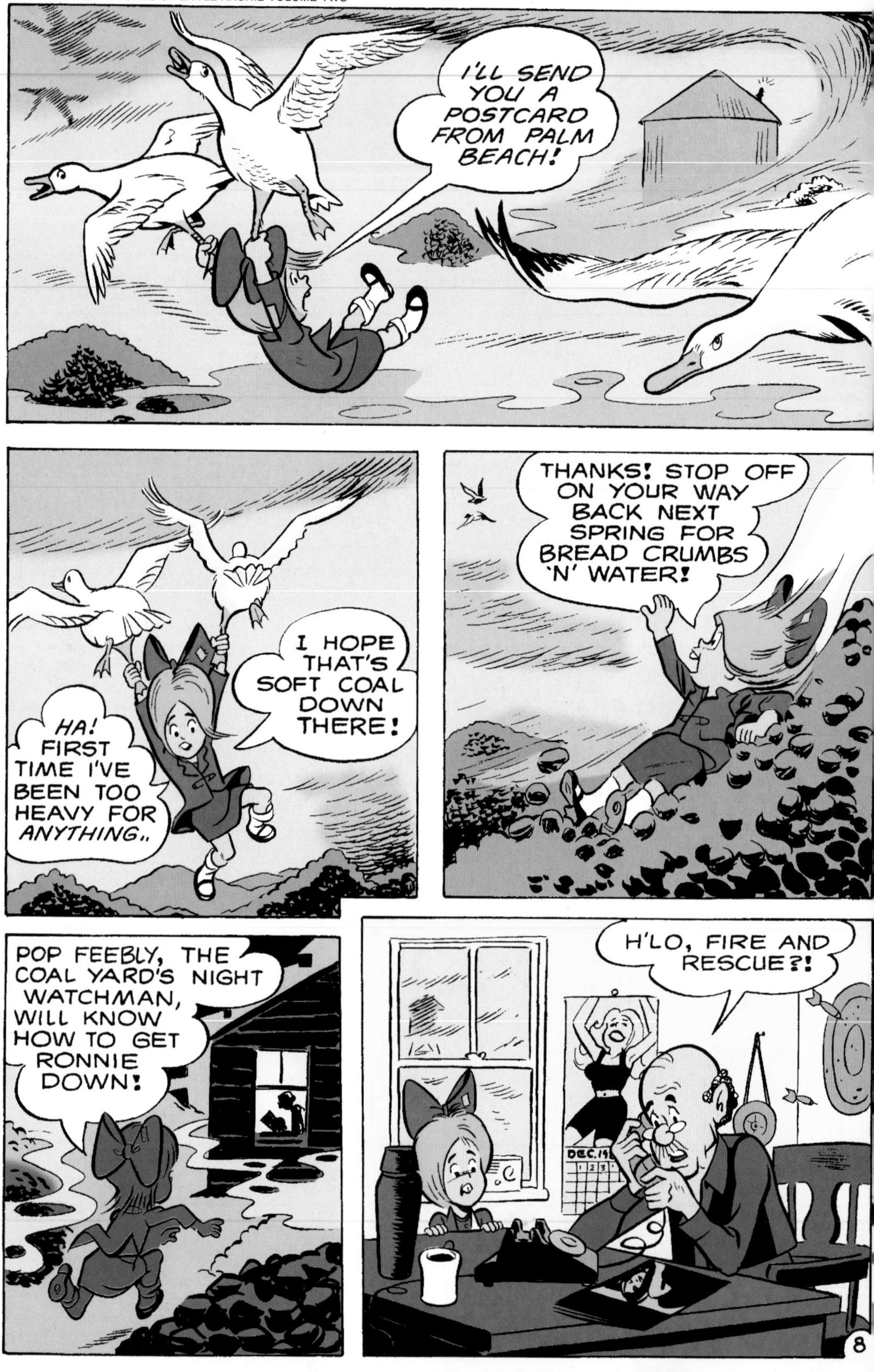
I'LL SEND YOU A POSTCARD FROM PALM BEACH!
I HOPE THAT'S SOFT COAL DOWN THERE!
HA! FIRST TIME I'VE BEEN TOO HEAVY FOR ANYTHING..
THANKS! STOP OFF ON YOUR WAY BACK NEXT SPRING FOR BREAD CRUMBS 'N' WATER!
POP FEEBLY, THE COAL YARD'S NIGHT WATCHMAN, WILL KNOW HOW TO GET RONNIE DOWN!
H'LO, FIRE AND RESCUE?!
8

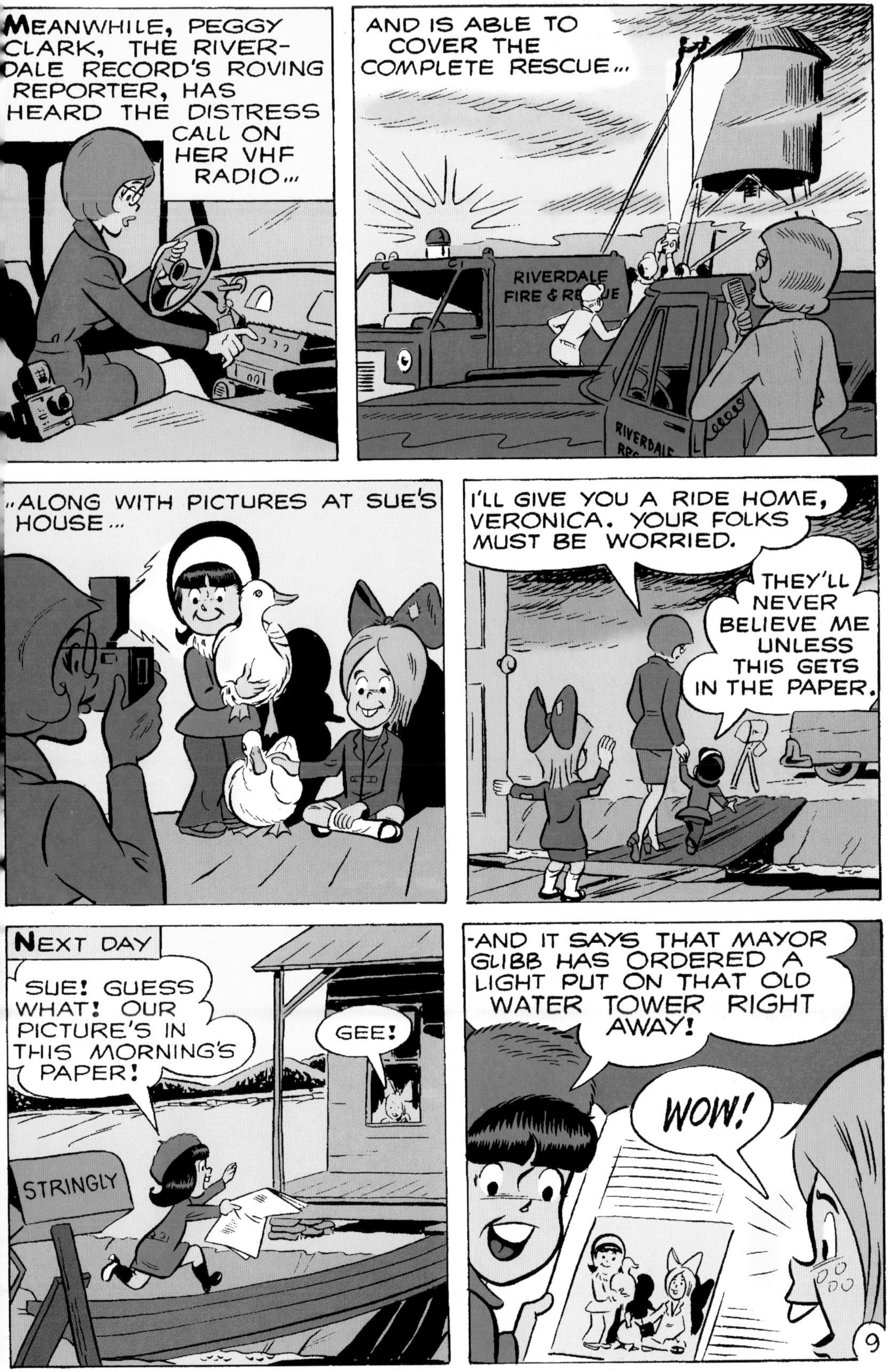
MEANWHILE, PEGGY CLARK, THE RIVERDALE RECORD'S ROVING REPORTER, HAS HEARD THE DISTRESS CALL ON HER VHF RADIO...
AND IS ABLE TO COVER THE COMPLETE RESCUE...
RIVERDALE FIRE & RESCUE
RIVERDALE REC
..ALONG WITH PICTURES AT SUE'S HOUSE...
I'LL GIVE YOU A RIDE HOME, VERONICA. YOUR FOLKS MUST BE WORRIED.
THEY'LL NEVER BELIEVE ME UNLESS THIS GETS IN THE PAPER.
NEXT DAY
SUE! GUESS WHAT! OUR PICTURE'S IN THIS MORNING'S PAPER!
GEE!
STRINGLY
-AND IT SAYS THAT MAYOR GLIBB HAS ORDERED A LIGHT PUT ON THAT OLD WATER TOWER RIGHT AWAY!
WOW!
9

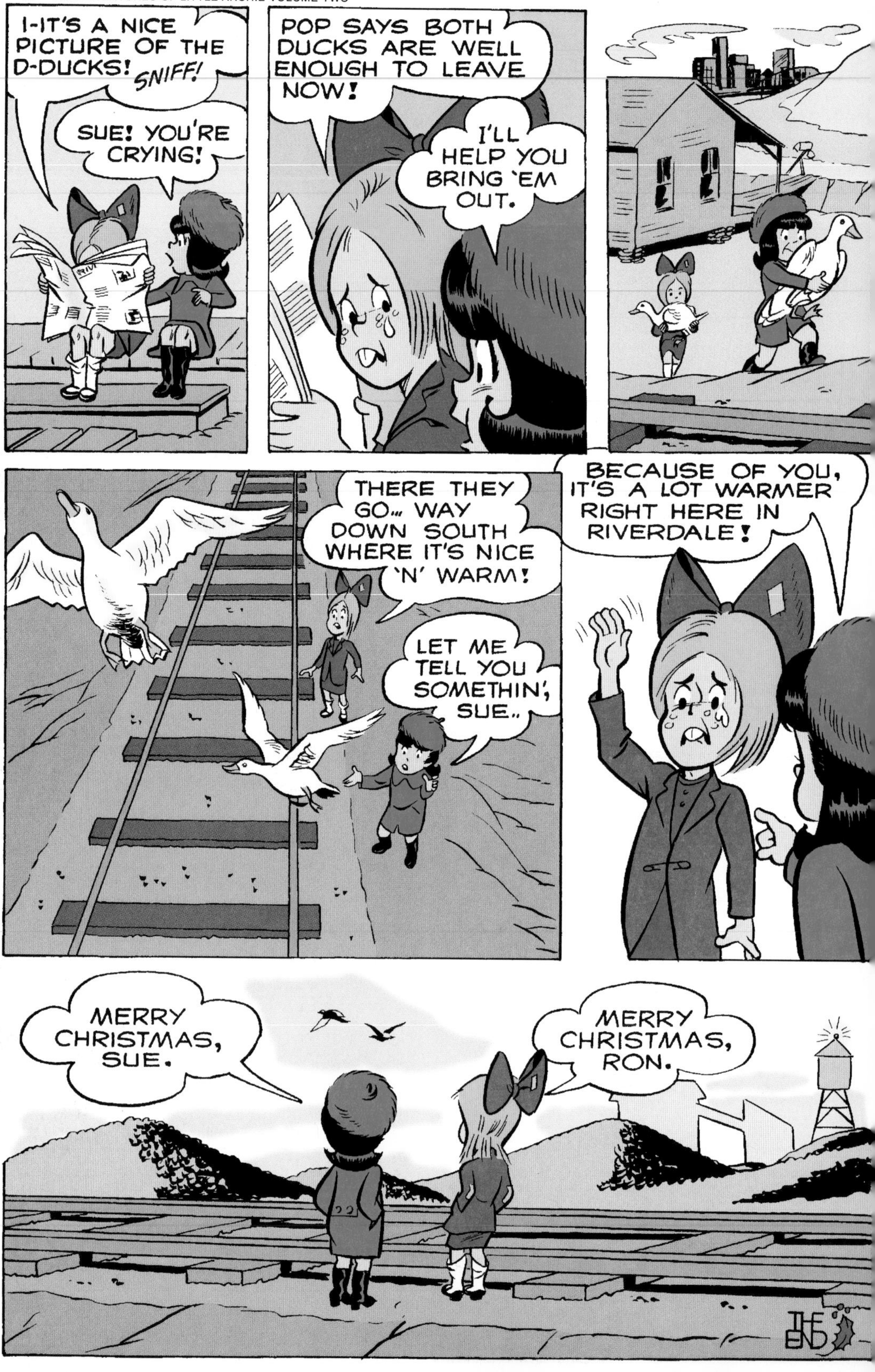
I-IT'S A NICE PICTURE OF THE D-DUCKS! SNIFF!
SUE! YOU'RE CRYING!
POP SAYS BOTH DUCKS ARE WELL ENOUGH TO LEAVE NOW!
I'LL HELP YOU BRING 'EM OUT.
THERE THEY GO... WAY DOWN SOUTH WHERE IT'S NICE 'N' WARM!
LET ME TELL YOU SOMETHIN', SUE..
BECAUSE OF YOU, IT'S A LOT WARMER RIGHT HERE IN RIVERDALE!
MERRY CHRISTMAS, SUE.
MERRY CHRISTMAS, RON.
THE END

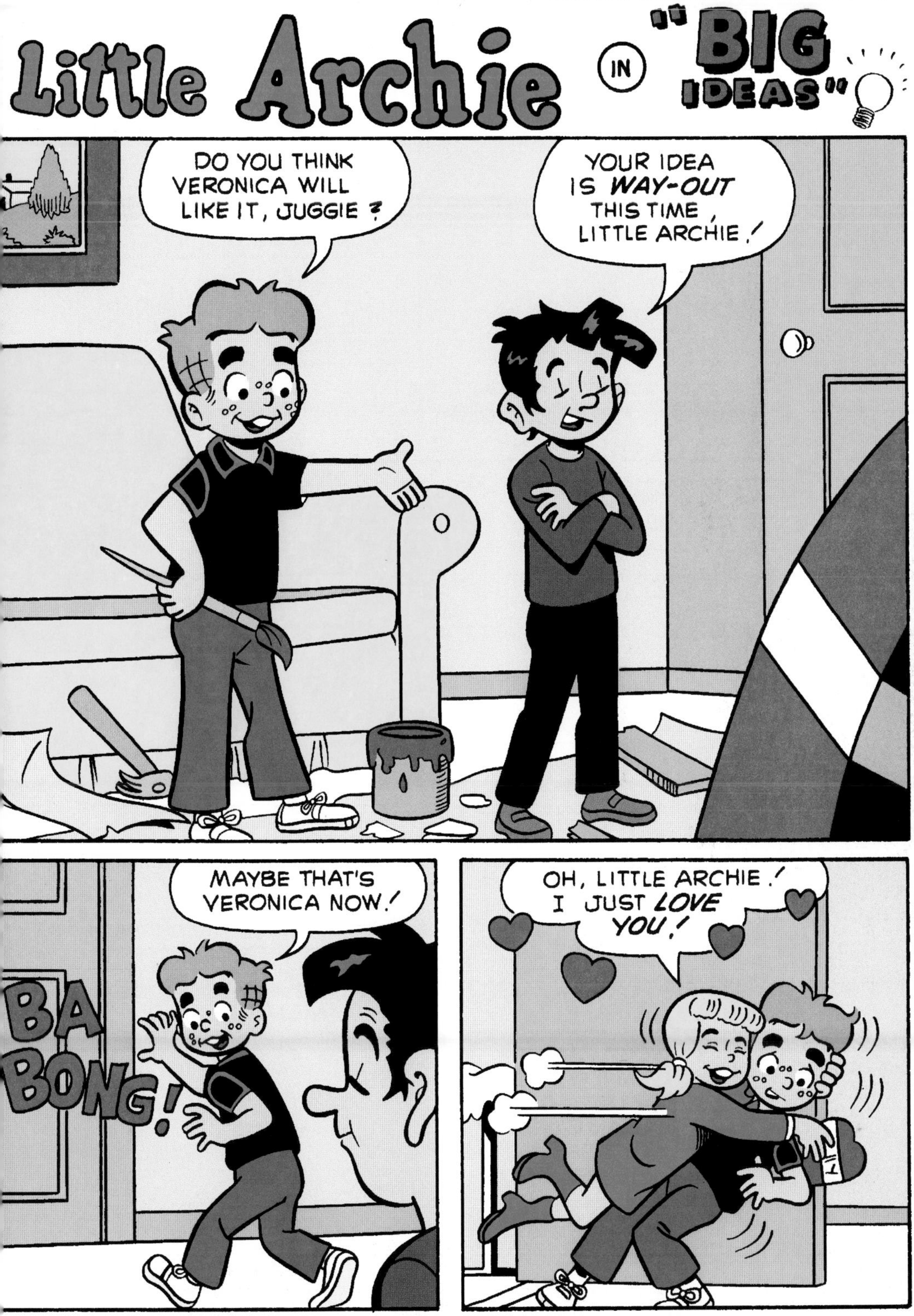
Little Archie IN "BIG IDEAS"
DO YOU THINK VERONICA WILL LIKE IT, JUGGIE ?
YOUR IDEA IS WAY-OUT THIS TIME , LITTLE ARCHIE !
BA BONG !
MAYBE THAT'S VERONICA NOW !
OH, LITTLE ARCHIE ! I JUST LOVE YOU !

Archie® comics

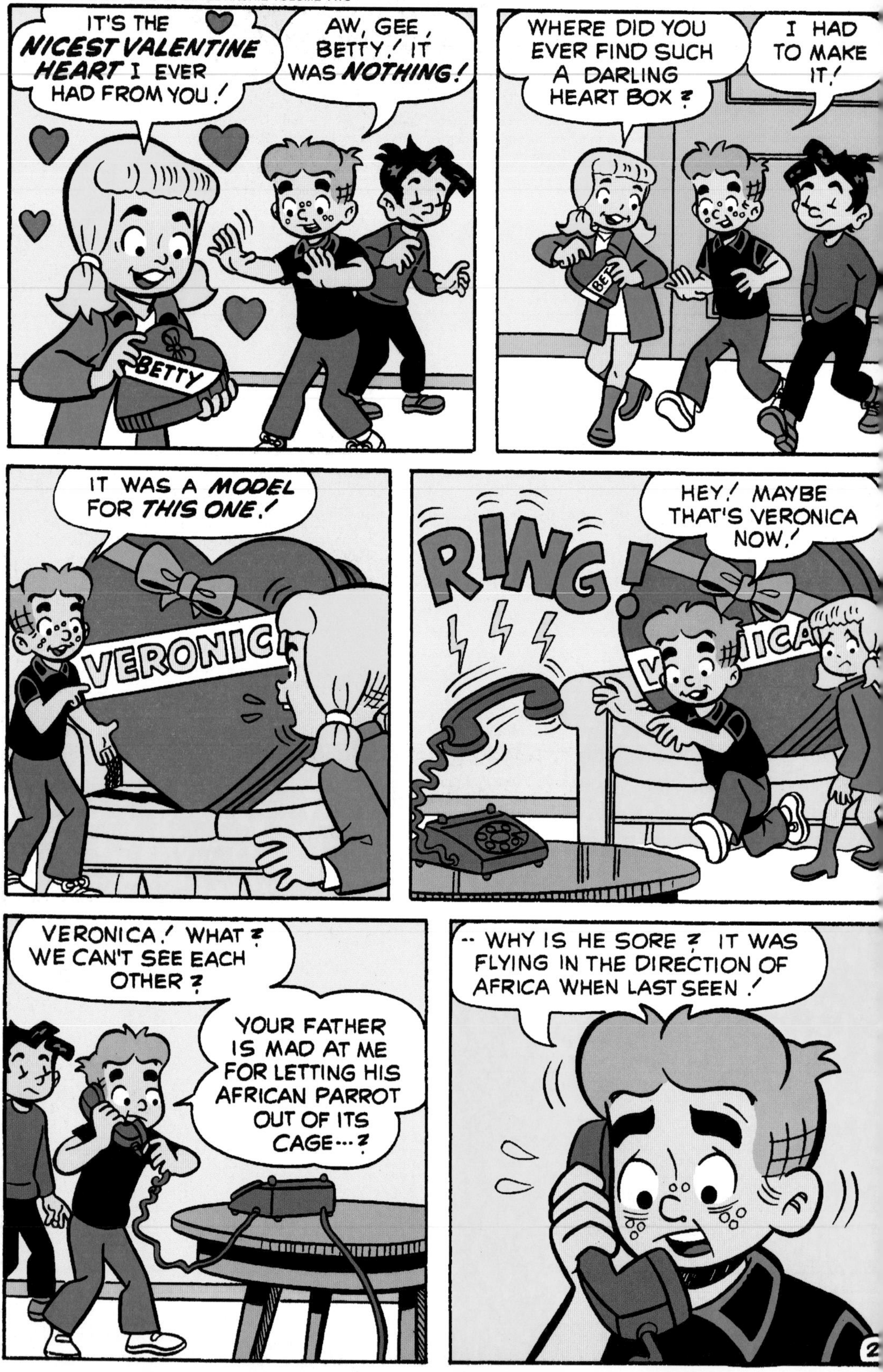
IT'S THE NICEST VALENTINE HEART I EVER HAD FROM YOU!
AW, GEE, BETTY! IT WAS NOTHING!
BETTY
WHERE DID YOU EVER FIND SUCH A DARLING HEART BOX?
I HAD TO MAKE IT!
IT WAS A MODEL FOR THIS ONE!
VERONIC
RING!
HEY! MAYBE THAT'S VERONICA NOW!
VERONICA! WHAT? WE CAN'T SEE EACH OTHER?
YOUR FATHER IS MAD AT ME FOR LETTING HIS AFRICAN PARROT OUT OF ITS CAGE...?
-- WHY IS HE SORE? IT WAS FLYING IN THE DIRECTION OF AFRICA WHEN LAST SEEN!

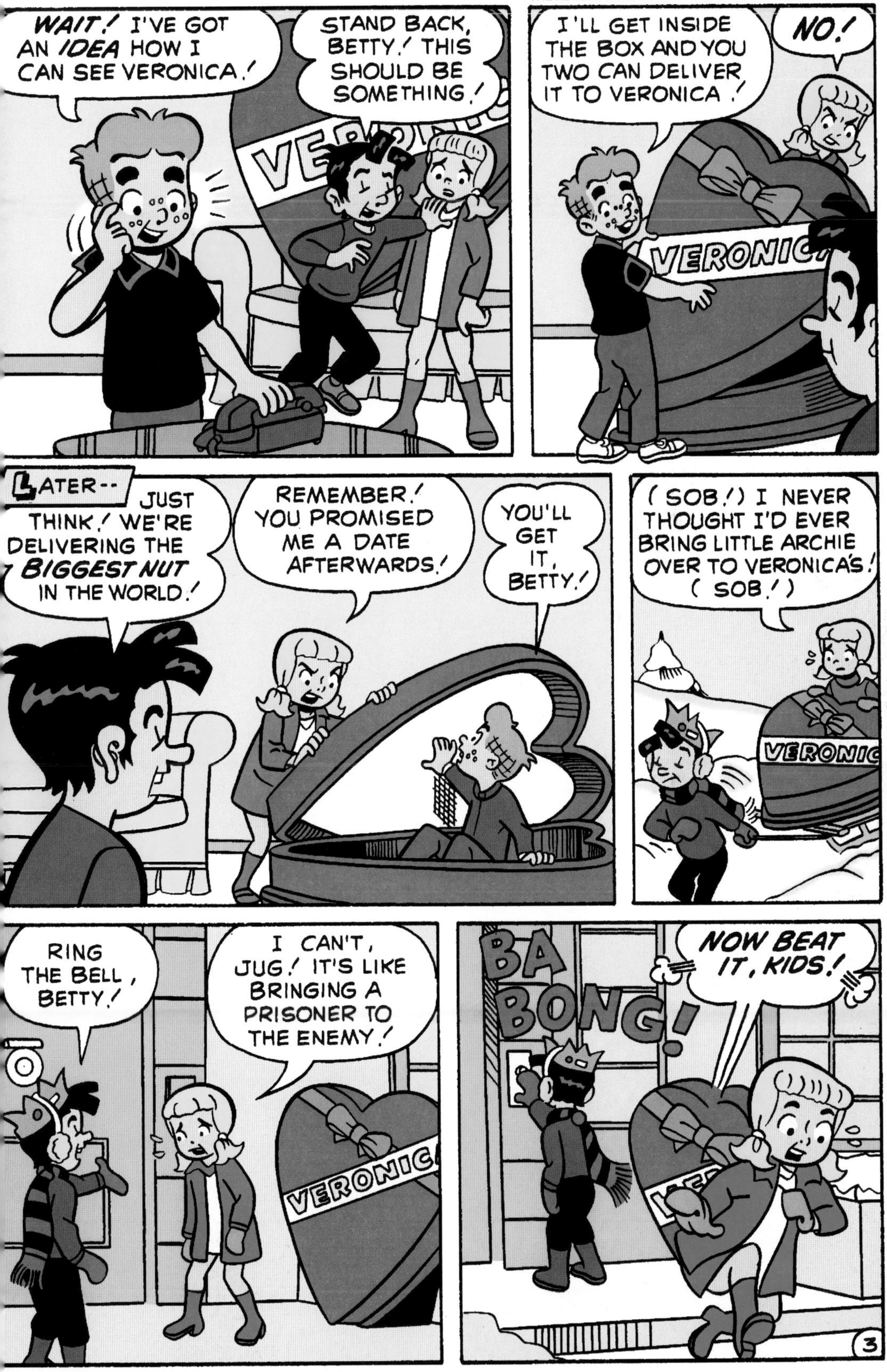
WAIT! I'VE GOT AN IDEA HOW I CAN SEE VERONICA!
STAND BACK, BETTY! THIS SHOULD BE SOMETHING!
I'LL GET INSIDE THE BOX AND YOU TWO CAN DELIVER IT TO VERONICA!
NO!
VERONICA
LATER--
JUST THINK! WE'RE DELIVERING THE BIGGEST NUT IN THE WORLD!
REMEMBER! YOU PROMISED ME A DATE AFTERWARDS!
YOU'LL GET IT, BETTY!
(SOB!) I NEVER THOUGHT I'D EVER BRING LITTLE ARCHIE OVER TO VERONICA'S! (SOB!)
VERONIC
RING THE BELL, BETTY!
I CAN'T, JUG! IT'S LIKE BRINGING A PRISONER TO THE ENEMY!
VERONIC
BA BONG!
NOW BEAT IT, KIDS!
3

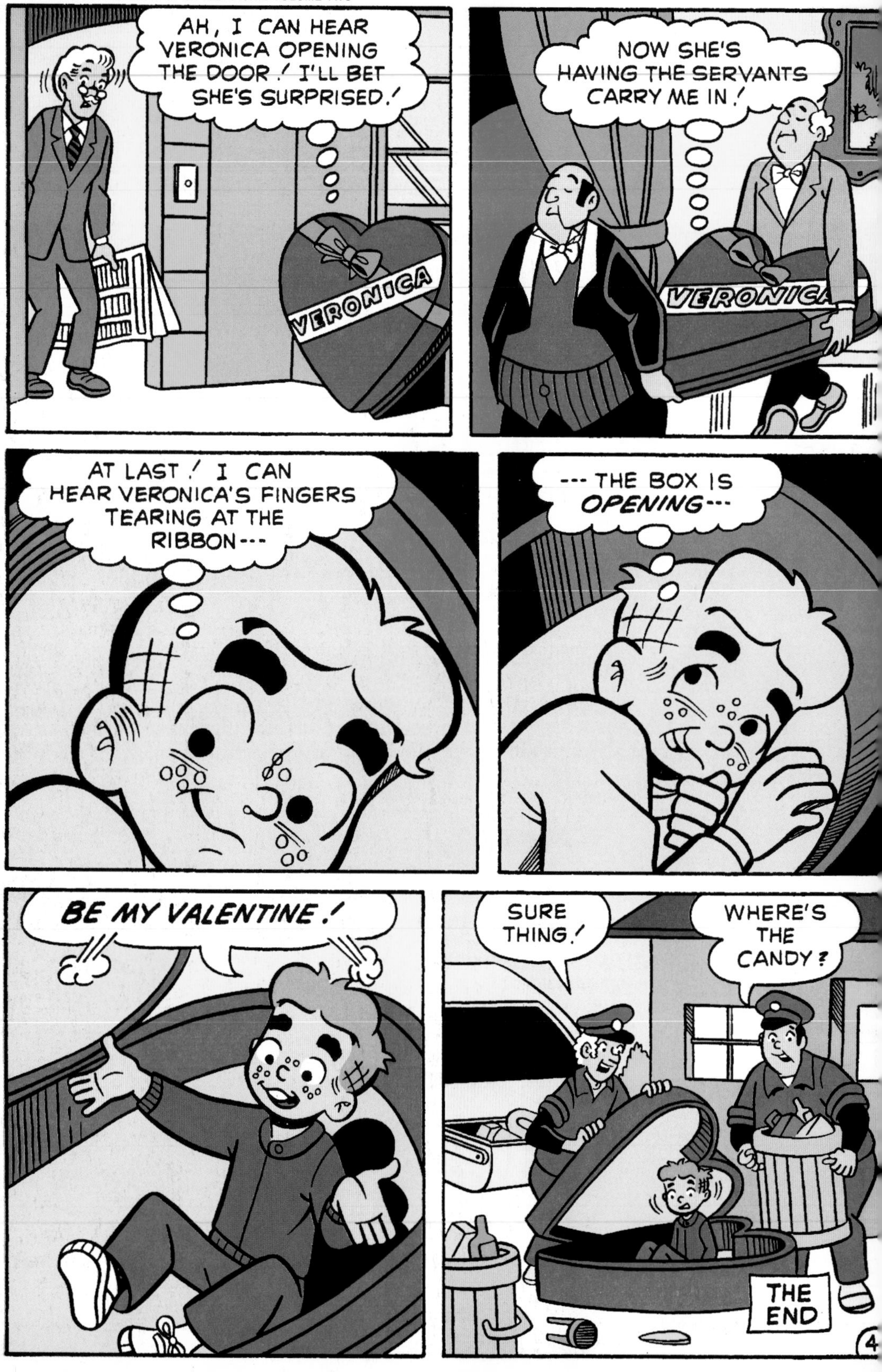
AH, I CAN HEAR VERONICA OPENING THE DOOR! I'LL BET SHE'S SURPRISED!
VERONICA
NOW SHE'S HAVING THE SERVANTS CARRY ME IN!
VERONICA
AT LAST! I CAN HEAR VERONICA'S FINGERS TEARING AT THE RIBBON---
--- THE BOX IS OPENING---
BE MY VALENTINE!
SURE THING!
WHERE'S THE CANDY?
THE END
4

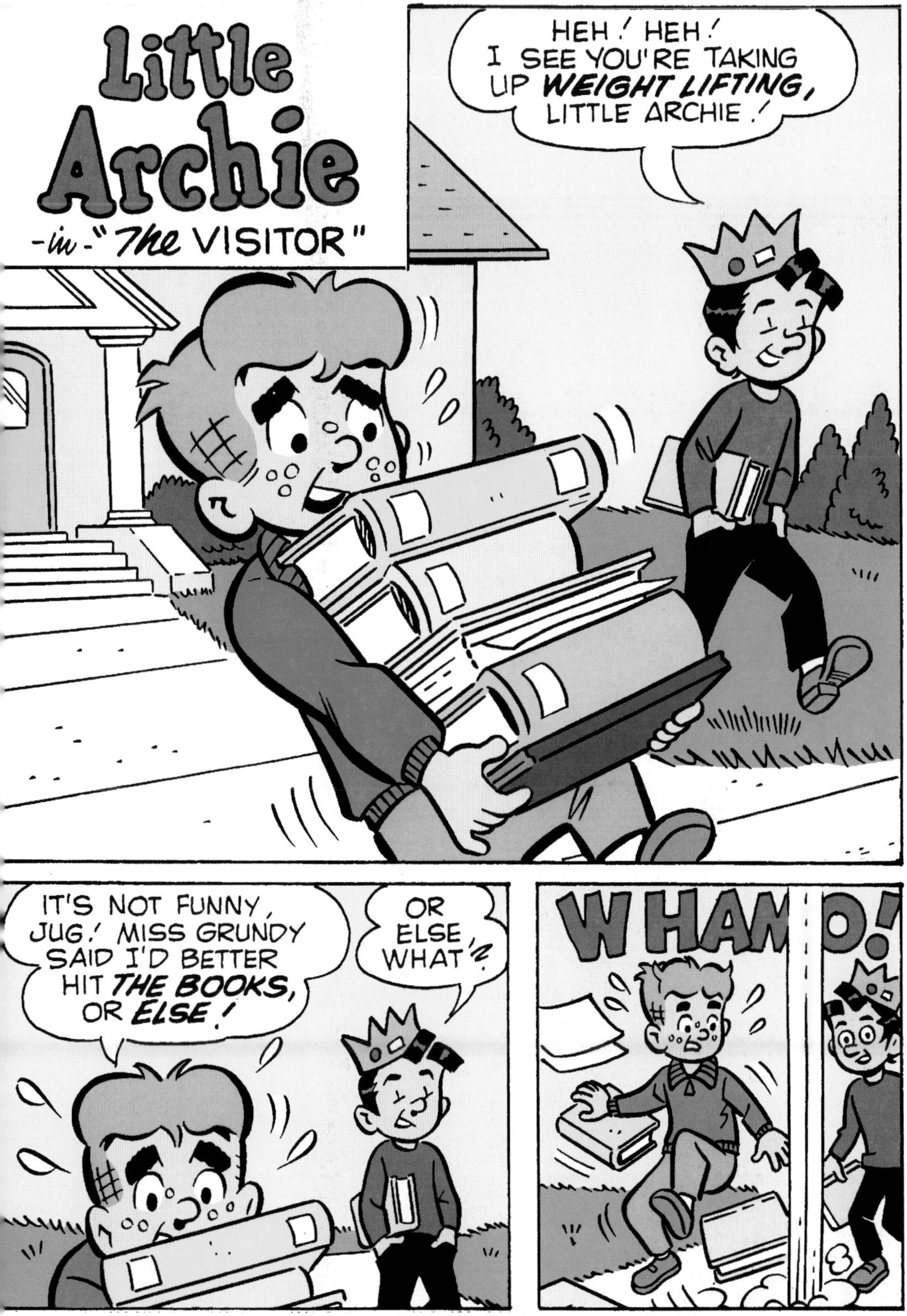
Little Archie
-in- "The VISITOR"
HEH! HEH! I SEE YOU'RE TAKING UP WEIGHT LIFTING, LITTLE ARCHIE!
IT'S NOT FUNNY, JUG! MISS GRUNDY SAID I'D BETTER HIT THE BOOKS, OR ELSE!
OR ELSE WHAT?
WHAM

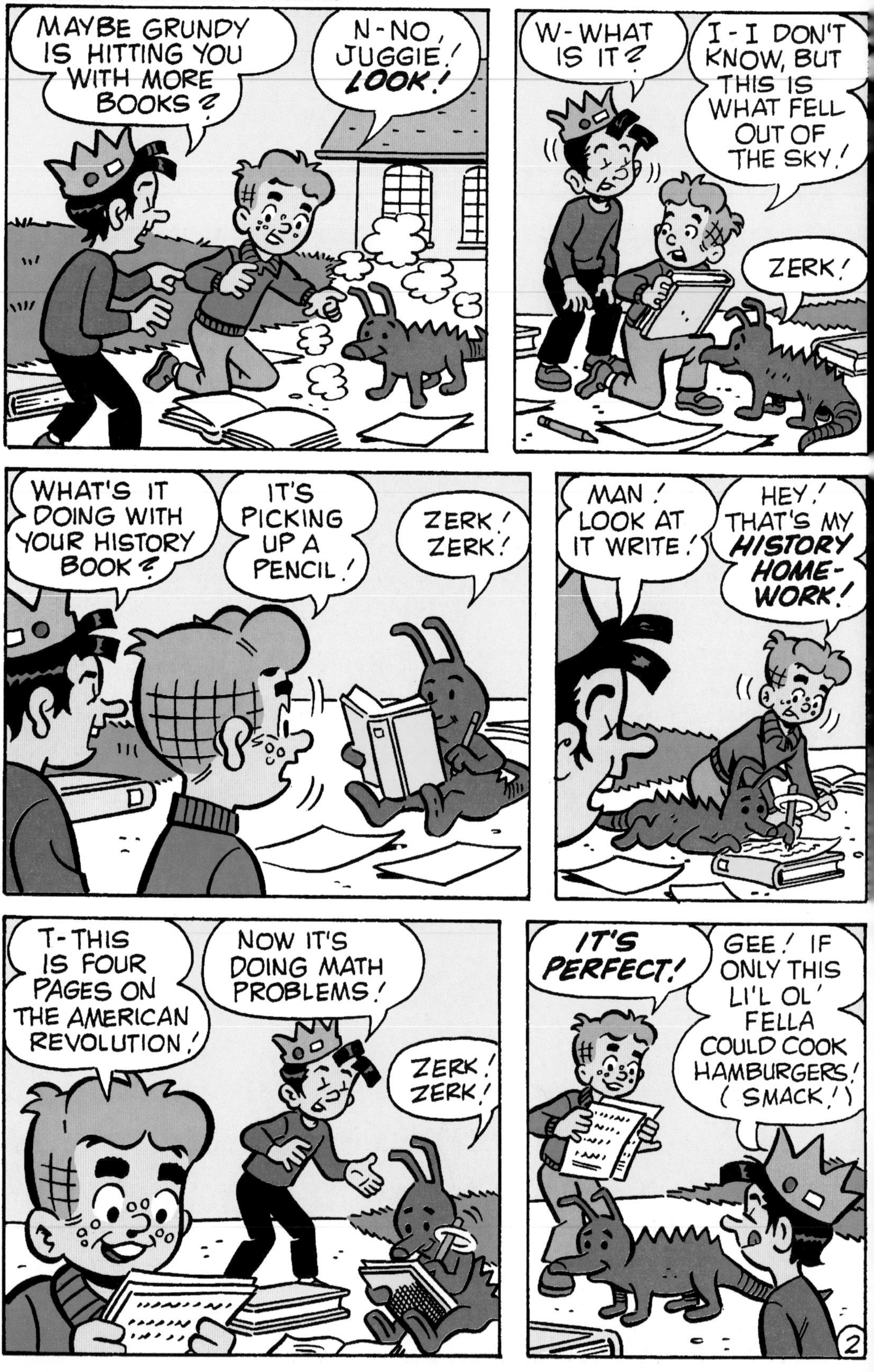
MAYBE GRUNDY IS HITTING YOU WITH MORE BOOKS?
N-NO, JUGGIE! LOOK!
W-WHAT IS IT?
I-I DON'T KNOW, BUT THIS IS WHAT FELL OUT OF THE SKY!
ZERK!
WHAT'S IT DOING WITH YOUR HISTORY BOOK?
IT'S PICKING UP A PENCIL!
ZERK! ZERK!
MAN! LOOK AT IT WRITE!
HEY! THAT'S MY HISTORY HOME-WORK!
T-THIS IS FOUR PAGES ON THE AMERICAN REVOLUTION!
NOW IT'S DOING MATH PROBLEMS!
ZERK! ZERK!
IT'S PERFECT!
GEE! IF ONLY THIS LI'L OL' FELLA COULD COOK HAMBURGERS! (SMACK!)
2

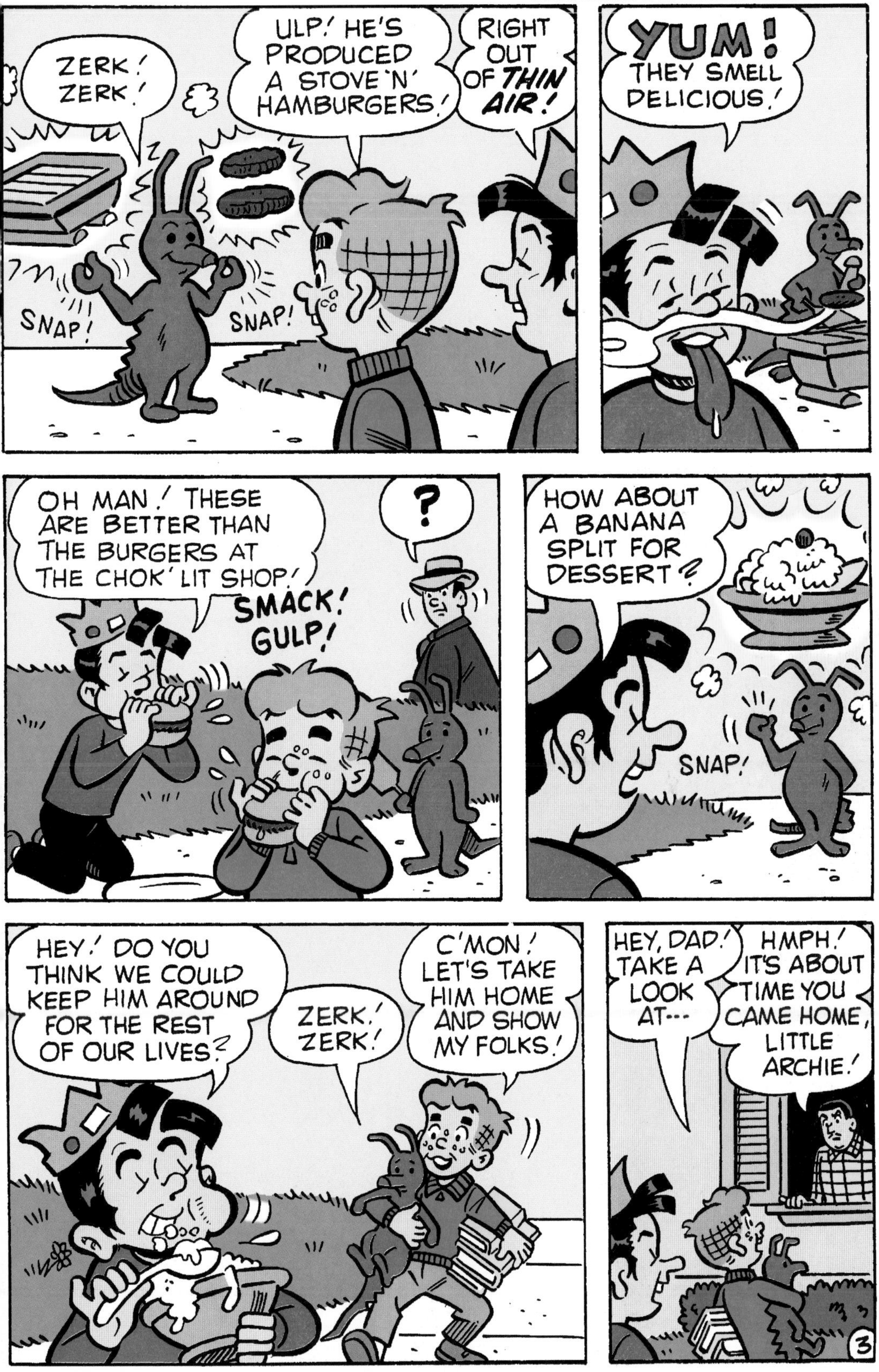
ZERK! ZERK!
ULP! HE'S PRODUCED A STOVE 'N' HAMBURGERS!
RIGHT OUT OF THIN AIR!
SNAP!
SNAP!
YUM! THEY SMELL DELICIOUS!
OH MAN! THESE ARE BETTER THAN THE BURGERS AT THE CHOK'LIT SHOP!
?
SMACK! GULP!
HOW ABOUT A BANANA SPLIT FOR DESSERT?
SNAP!
HEY! DO YOU THINK WE COULD KEEP HIM AROUND FOR THE REST OF OUR LIVES?
ZERK! ZERK!
C'MON! LET'S TAKE HIM HOME AND SHOW MY FOLKS!
HEY, DAD! TAKE A LOOK AT---
HMPH! IT'S ABOUT TIME YOU CAME HOME, LITTLE ARCHIE!
3

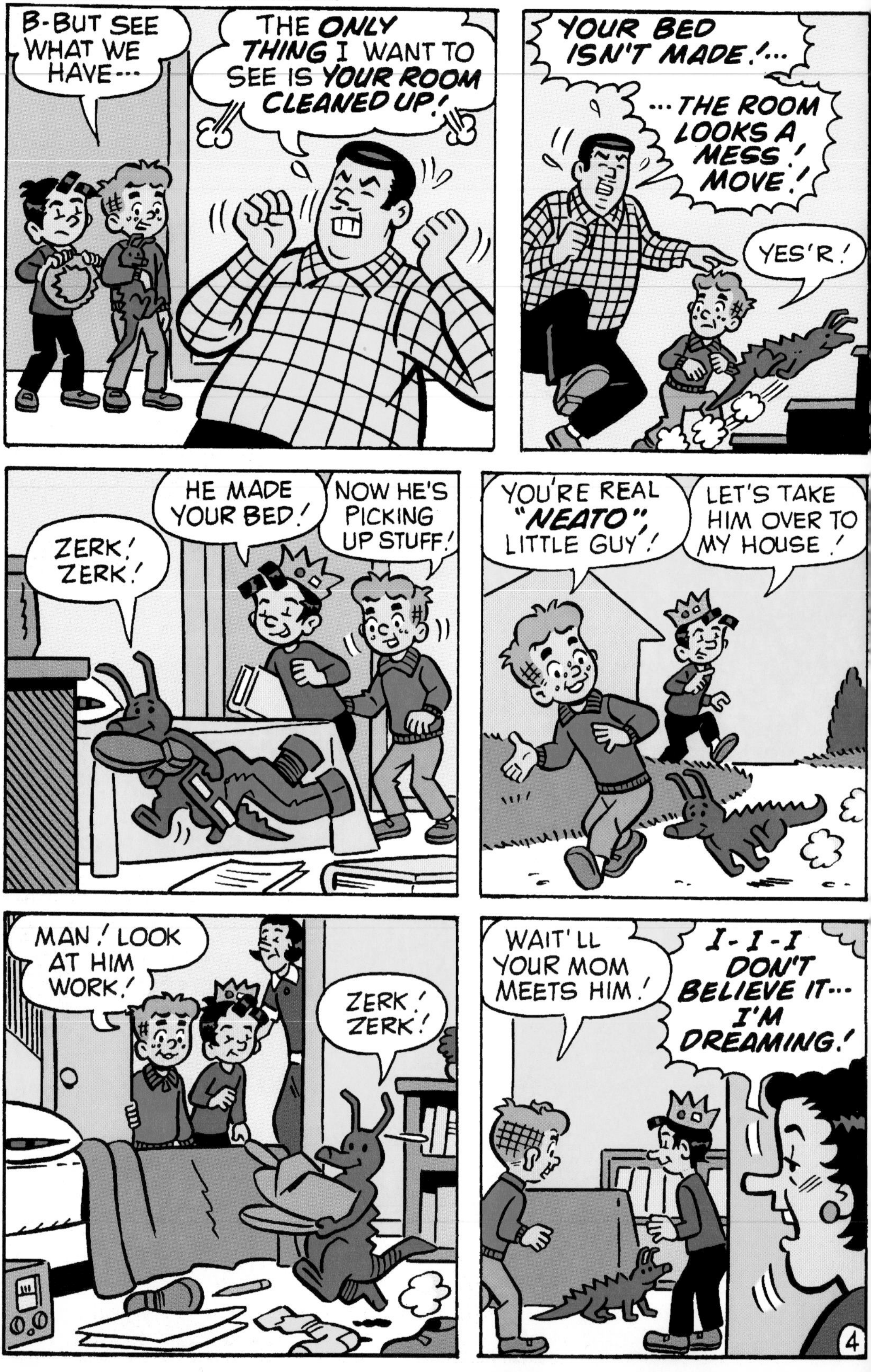
B-BUT SEE WHAT WE HAVE---
THE ONLY THING I WANT TO SEE IS YOUR ROOM CLEANED UP!
YOUR BED ISN'T MADE!...
...THE ROOM LOOKS A MESS! MOVE!
YES'R!
ZERK! ZERK!
HE MADE YOUR BED!
NOW HE'S PICKING UP STUFF!
YOU'RE REAL "NEATO", LITTLE GUY!
LET'S TAKE HIM OVER TO MY HOUSE!
MAN! LOOK AT HIM WORK!
ZERK! ZERK!
WAIT'LL YOUR MOM MEETS HIM!
I-I-I DON'T BELIEVE IT... I'M DREAMING!
4

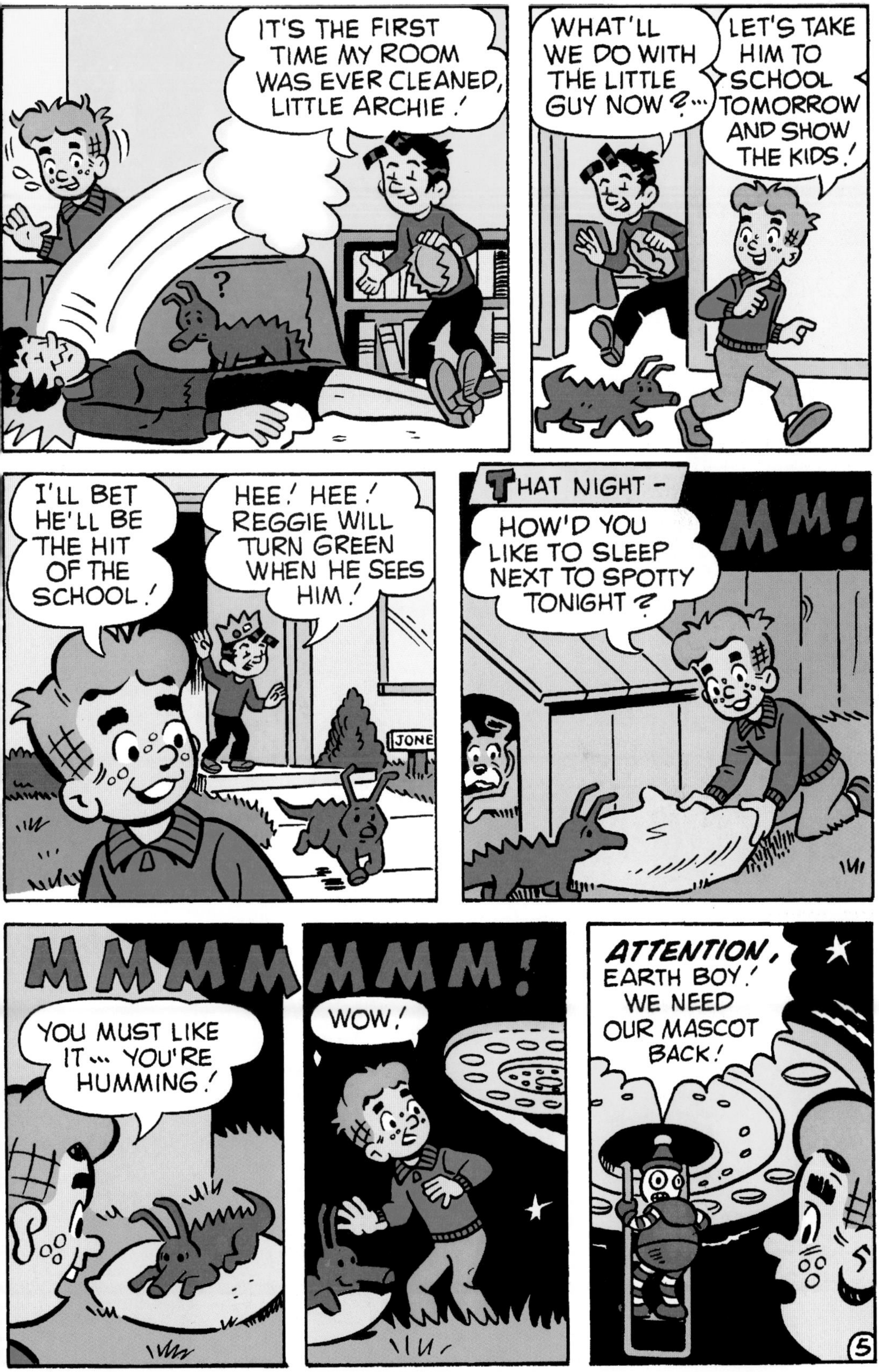
IT'S THE FIRST TIME MY ROOM WAS EVER CLEANED, LITTLE ARCHIE!
WHAT'LL WE DO WITH THE LITTLE GUY NOW?...
LET'S TAKE HIM TO SCHOOL TOMORROW AND SHOW THE KIDS!
I'LL BET HE'LL BE THE HIT OF THE SCHOOL!
HEE! HEE! REGGIE WILL TURN GREEN WHEN HE SEES HIM!
JONE
THAT NIGHT -
HOW'D YOU LIKE TO SLEEP NEXT TO SPOTTY TONIGHT?
MM!
MMMMMMMM!
YOU MUST LIKE IT... YOU'RE HUMMING!
WOW!
ATTENTION, EARTH BOY! WE NEED OUR MASCOT BACK!
5

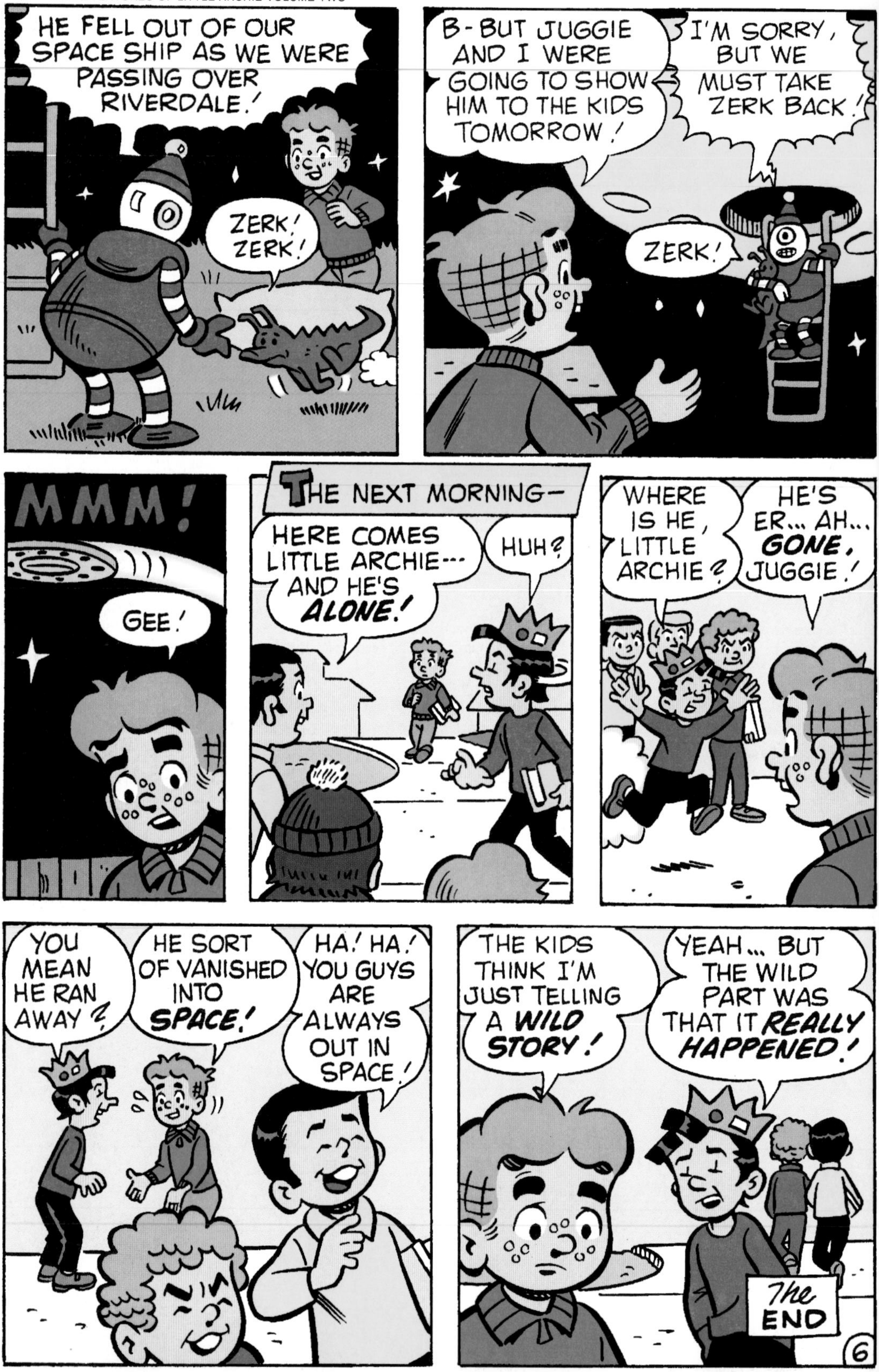
HE FELL OUT OF OUR SPACE SHIP AS WE WERE PASSING OVER RIVERDALE!
ZERK! ZERK!
B-BUT JUGGIE AND I WERE GOING TO SHOW HIM TO THE KIDS TOMORROW!
I'M SORRY, BUT WE MUST TAKE ZERK BACK!
ZERK!
MMM!
GEE!
THE NEXT MORNING—
HERE COMES LITTLE ARCHIE--- AND HE'S ALONE!
HUH?
WHERE IS HE, LITTLE ARCHIE?
HE'S ER... AH... GONE, JUGGIE!
YOU MEAN HE RAN AWAY?
HE SORT OF VANISHED INTO SPACE!
HA! HA! YOU GUYS ARE ALWAYS OUT IN SPACE!
THE KIDS THINK I'M JUST TELLING A WILD STORY!
YEAH... BUT THE WILD PART WAS THAT IT REALLY HAPPENED!
The END
6

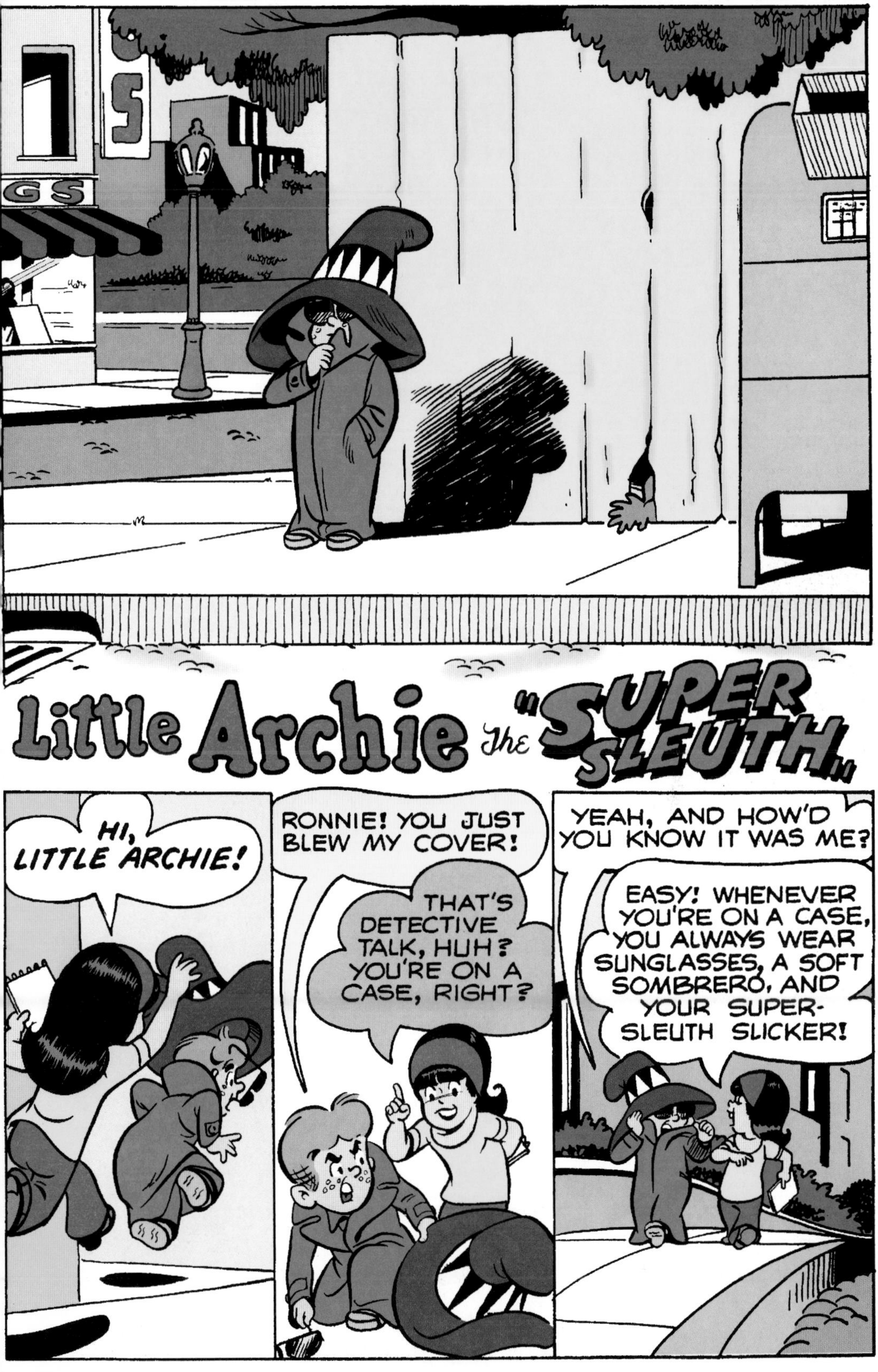
Little Archie
The "SUPER SLEUTH"
HI, LITTLE ARCHIE!
RONNIE! YOU JUST BLEW MY COVER!
THAT'S DETECTIVE TALK, HUH? YOU'RE ON A CASE, RIGHT?
YEAH, AND HOW'D YOU KNOW IT WAS ME?
EASY! WHENEVER YOU'RE ON A CASE, YOU ALWAYS WEAR SUNGLASSES, A SOFT SOMBRERO, AND YOUR SUPER-SLEUTH SLICKER!

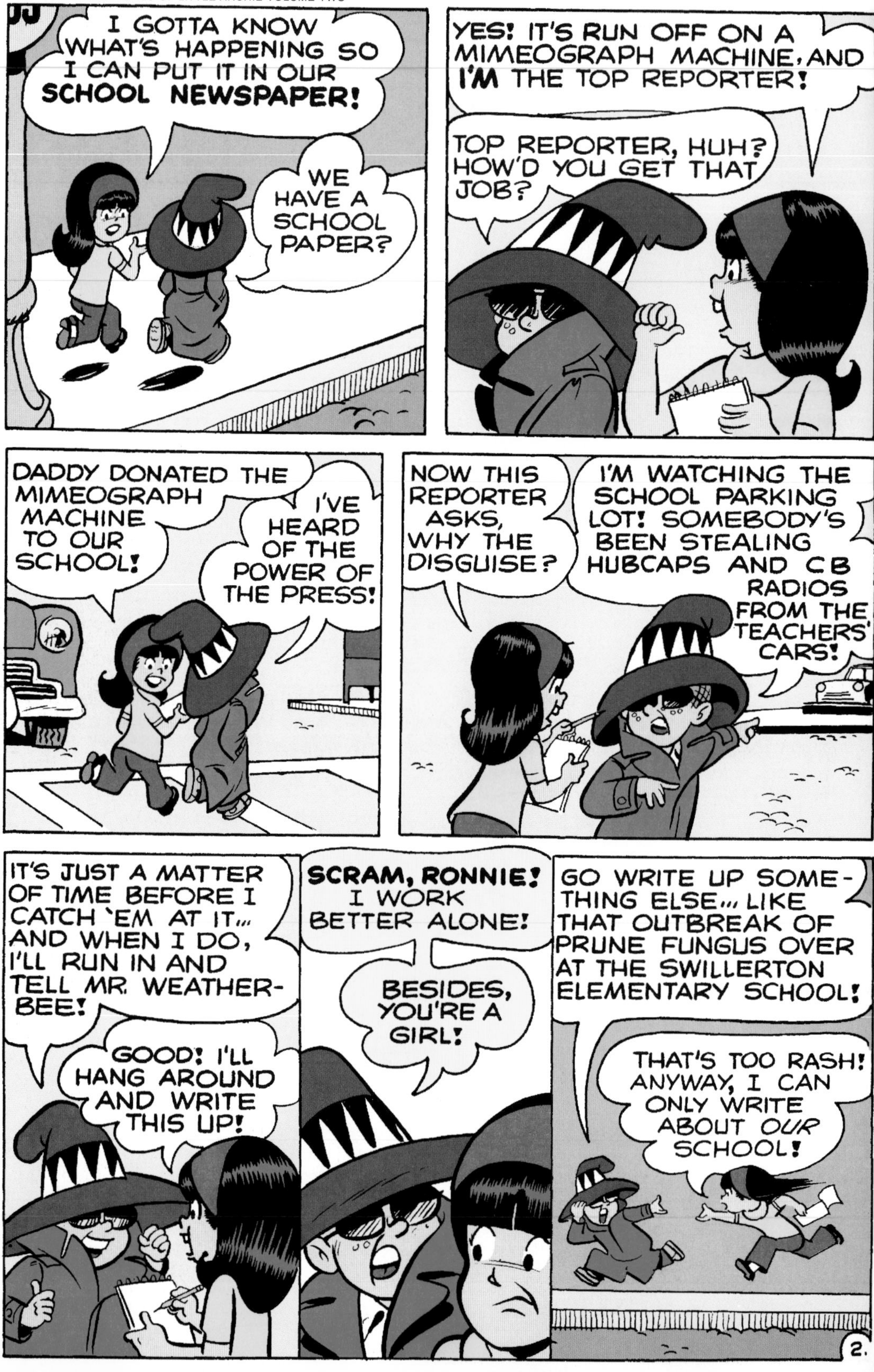
I GOTTA KNOW WHAT'S HAPPENING SO I CAN PUT IT IN OUR SCHOOL NEWSPAPER!
WE HAVE A SCHOOL PAPER?
YES! IT'S RUN OFF ON A MIMEOGRAPH MACHINE, AND I'M THE TOP REPORTER!
TOP REPORTER, HUH? HOW'D YOU GET THAT JOB?
DADDY DONATED THE MIMEOGRAPH MACHINE TO OUR SCHOOL!
I'VE HEARD OF THE POWER OF THE PRESS!
NOW THIS REPORTER ASKS, WHY THE DISGUISE?
I'M WATCHING THE SCHOOL PARKING LOT! SOMEBODY'S BEEN STEALING HUBCAPS AND CB RADIOS FROM THE TEACHERS' CARS!
IT'S JUST A MATTER OF TIME BEFORE I CATCH 'EM AT IT... AND WHEN I DO, I'LL RUN IN AND TELL MR. WEATHERBEE!
GOOD! I'LL HANG AROUND AND WRITE THIS UP!
SCRAM, RONNIE! I WORK BETTER ALONE!
BESIDES, YOU'RE A GIRL!
GO WRITE UP SOMETHING ELSE... LIKE THAT OUTBREAK OF PRUNE FUNGUS OVER AT THE SWILLERTON ELEMENTARY SCHOOL!
THAT'S TOO RASH! ANYWAY, I CAN ONLY WRITE ABOUT OUR SCHOOL!
2.

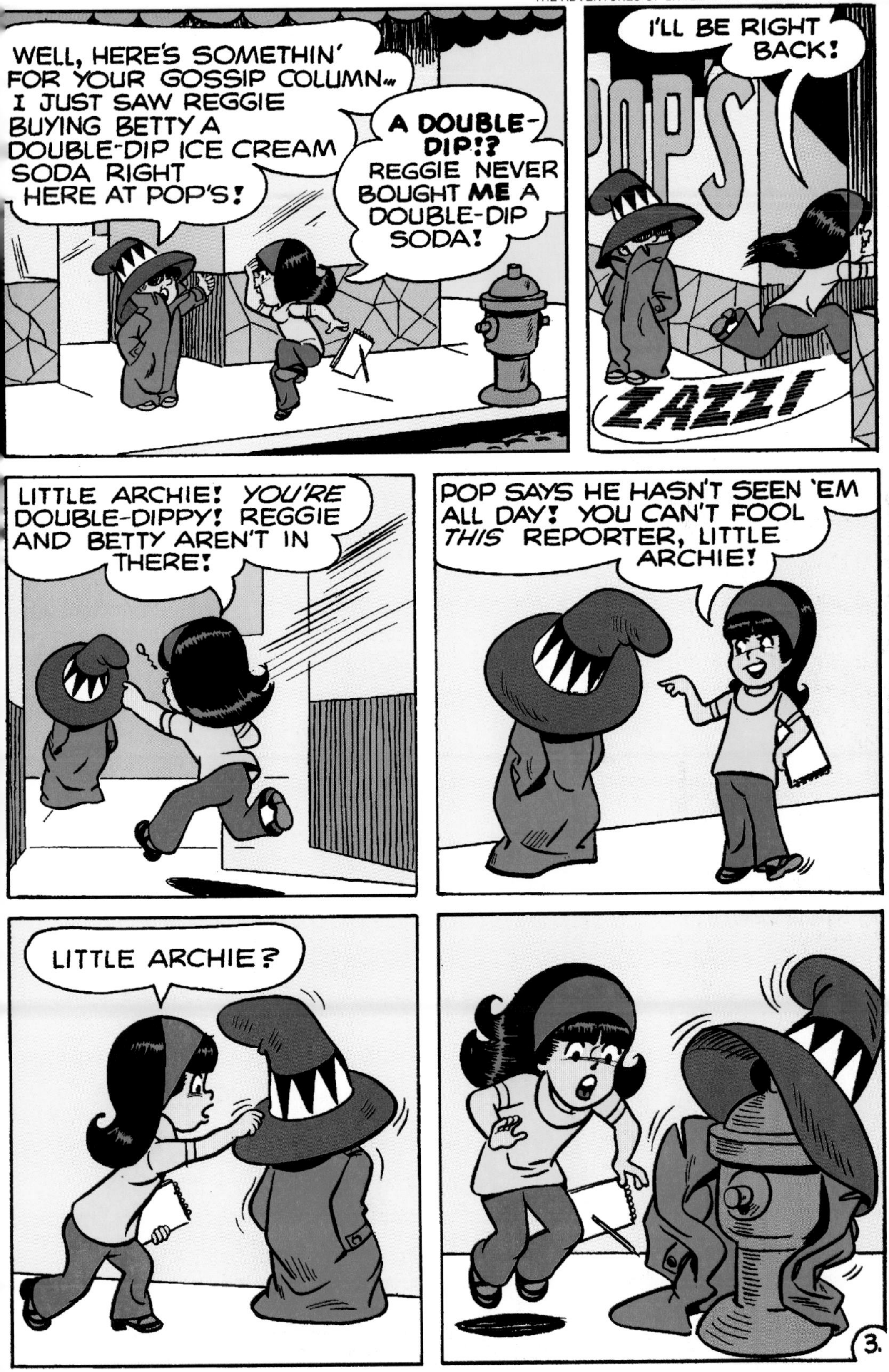
WELL, HERE'S SOMETHIN' FOR YOUR GOSSIP COLUMN... I JUST SAW REGGIE BUYING BETTY A DOUBLE-DIP ICE CREAM SODA RIGHT HERE AT POP'S!
A DOUBLE-DIP!? REGGIE NEVER BOUGHT ME A DOUBLE-DIP SODA!
I'LL BE RIGHT BACK!
POP'S
ZAZZ!
LITTLE ARCHIE! YOU'RE DOUBLE-DIPPY! REGGIE AND BETTY AREN'T IN THERE!
POP SAYS HE HASN'T SEEN 'EM ALL DAY! YOU CAN'T FOOL THIS REPORTER, LITTLE ARCHIE!
LITTLE ARCHIE?
3.

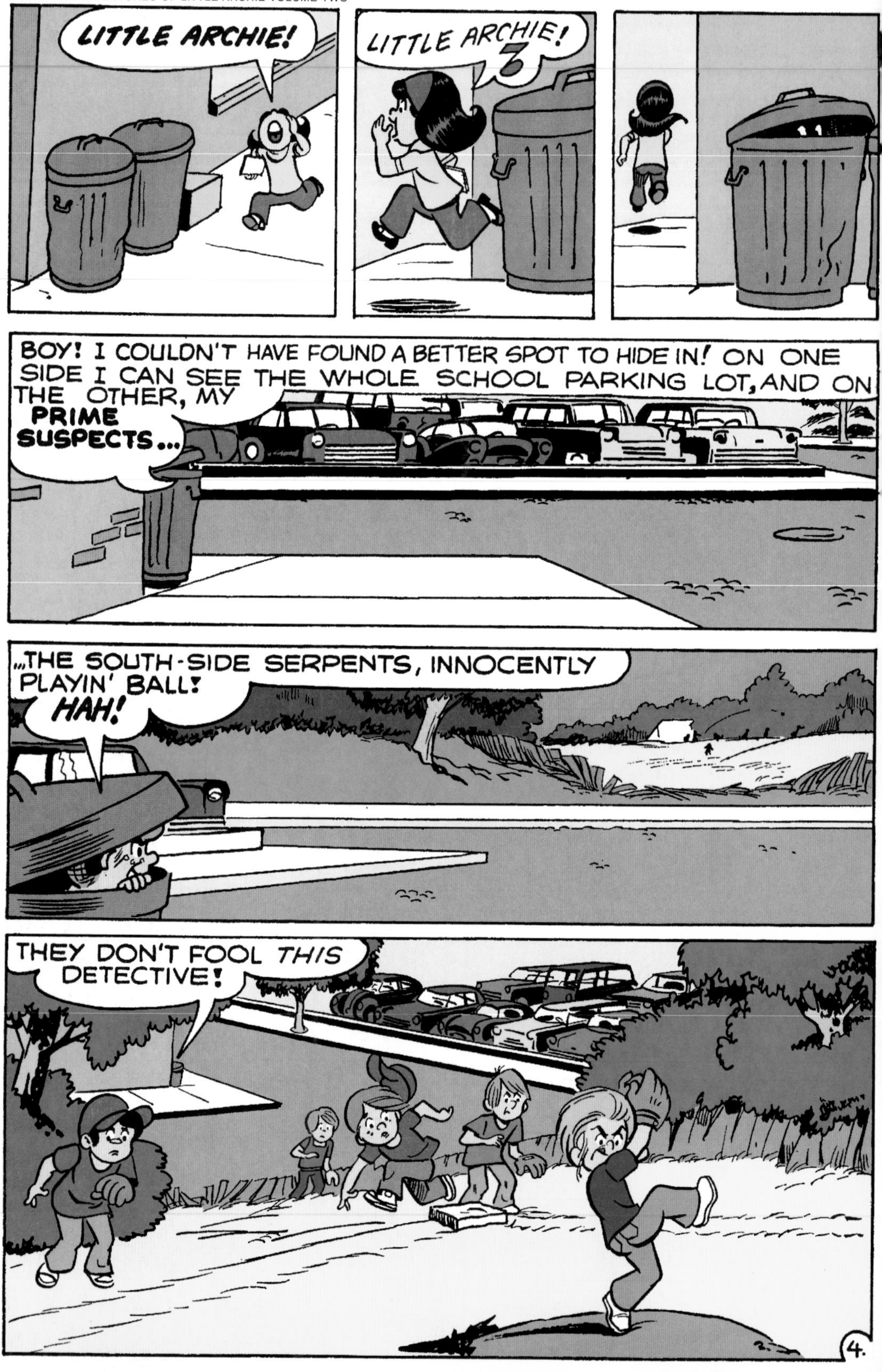
LITTLE ARCHIE!
LITTLE ARCHIE!
BOY! I COULDN'T HAVE FOUND A BETTER SPOT TO HIDE IN! ON ONE SIDE I CAN SEE THE WHOLE SCHOOL PARKING LOT, AND ON THE OTHER, MY PRIME SUSPECTS...
...THE SOUTH-SIDE SERPENTS, INNOCENTLY PLAYIN' BALL! HAH!
THEY DON'T FOOL THIS DETECTIVE!
4.

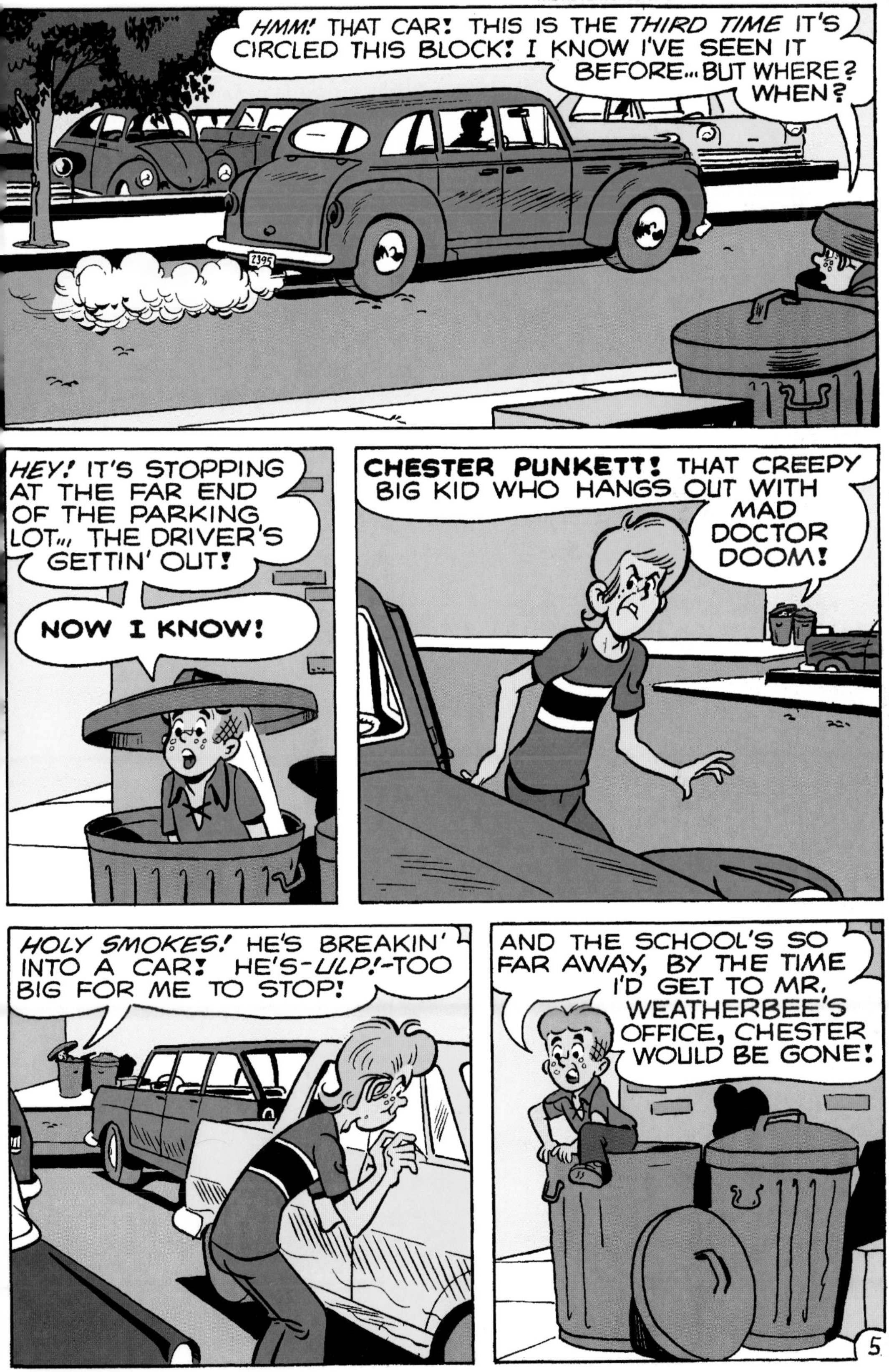
HMM! THAT CAR! THIS IS THE THIRD TIME IT'S CIRCLED THIS BLOCK! I KNOW I'VE SEEN IT BEFORE... BUT WHERE? WHEN?
2395
HEY! IT'S STOPPING AT THE FAR END OF THE PARKING LOT... THE DRIVER'S GETTIN' OUT!
NOW I KNOW!
CHESTER PUNKETT! THAT CREEPY BIG KID WHO HANGS OUT WITH MAD DOCTOR DOOM!
HOLY SMOKES! HE'S BREAKIN' INTO A CAR! HE'S-ULP!-TOO BIG FOR ME TO STOP!
AND THE SCHOOL'S SO FAR AWAY, BY THE TIME I'D GET TO MR. WEATHERBEE'S OFFICE, CHESTER WOULD BE GONE!
5

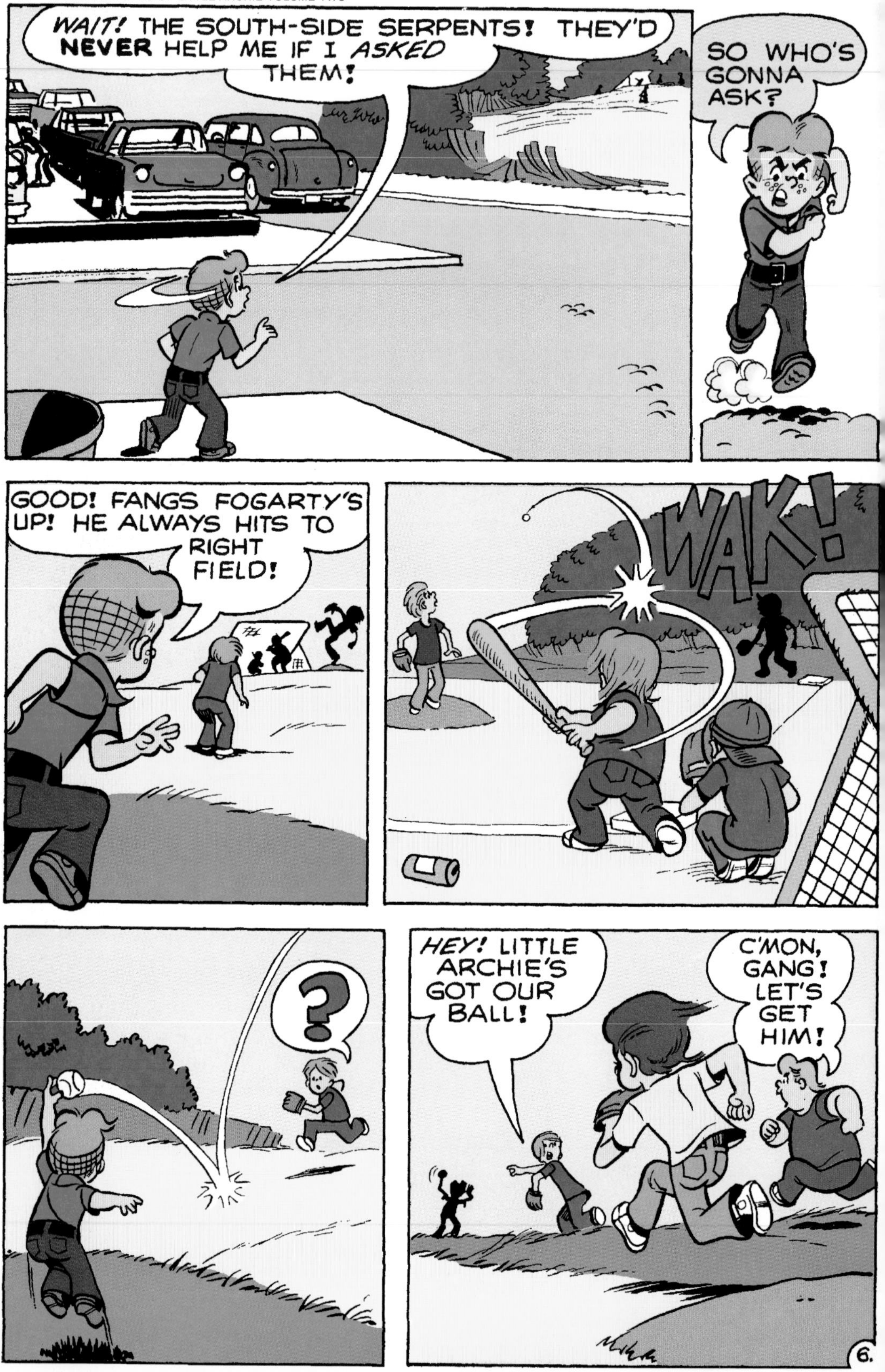
WAIT! THE SOUTH-SIDE SERPENTS! THEY'D NEVER HELP ME IF I ASKED THEM!
SO WHO'S GONNA ASK?
GOOD! FANGS FOGARTY'S UP! HE ALWAYS HITS TO RIGHT FIELD!
WAK!
?
HEY! LITTLE ARCHIE'S GOT OUR BALL!
C'MON, GANG! LET'S GET HIM!
6.

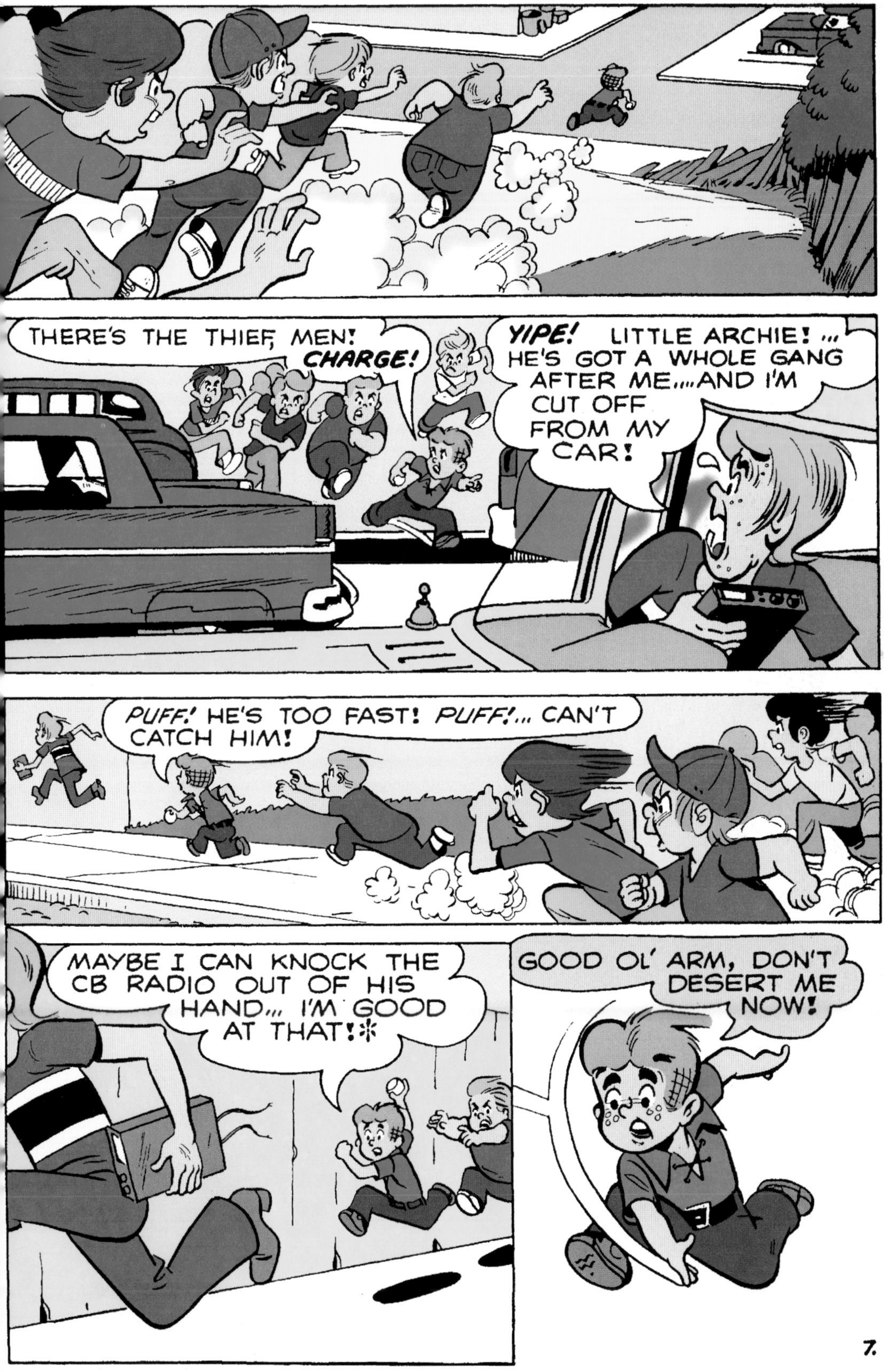
THERE'S THE THIEF, MEN! CHARGE!
YIPE! LITTLE ARCHIE! ... HE'S GOT A WHOLE GANG AFTER ME....AND I'M CUT OFF FROM MY CAR!
PUFF! HE'S TOO FAST! PUFF!... CAN'T CATCH HIM!
MAYBE I CAN KNOCK THE CB RADIO OUT OF HIS HAND... I'M GOOD AT THAT!*
GOOD OL' ARM, DON'T DESERT ME NOW!

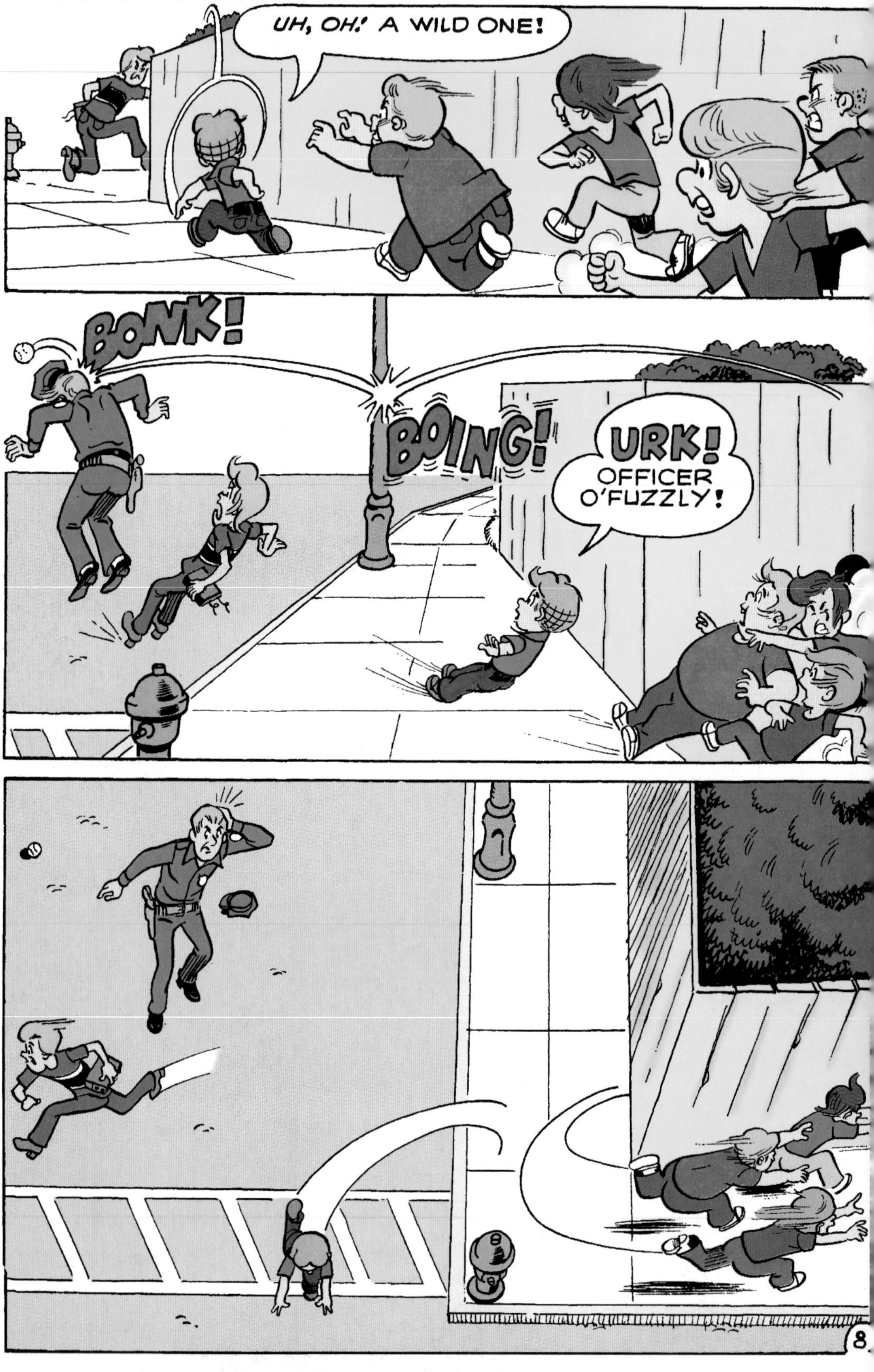
UH, OH! A WILD ONE!
BONK!
BOING!
URK! OFFICER O'FUZZLY!
8

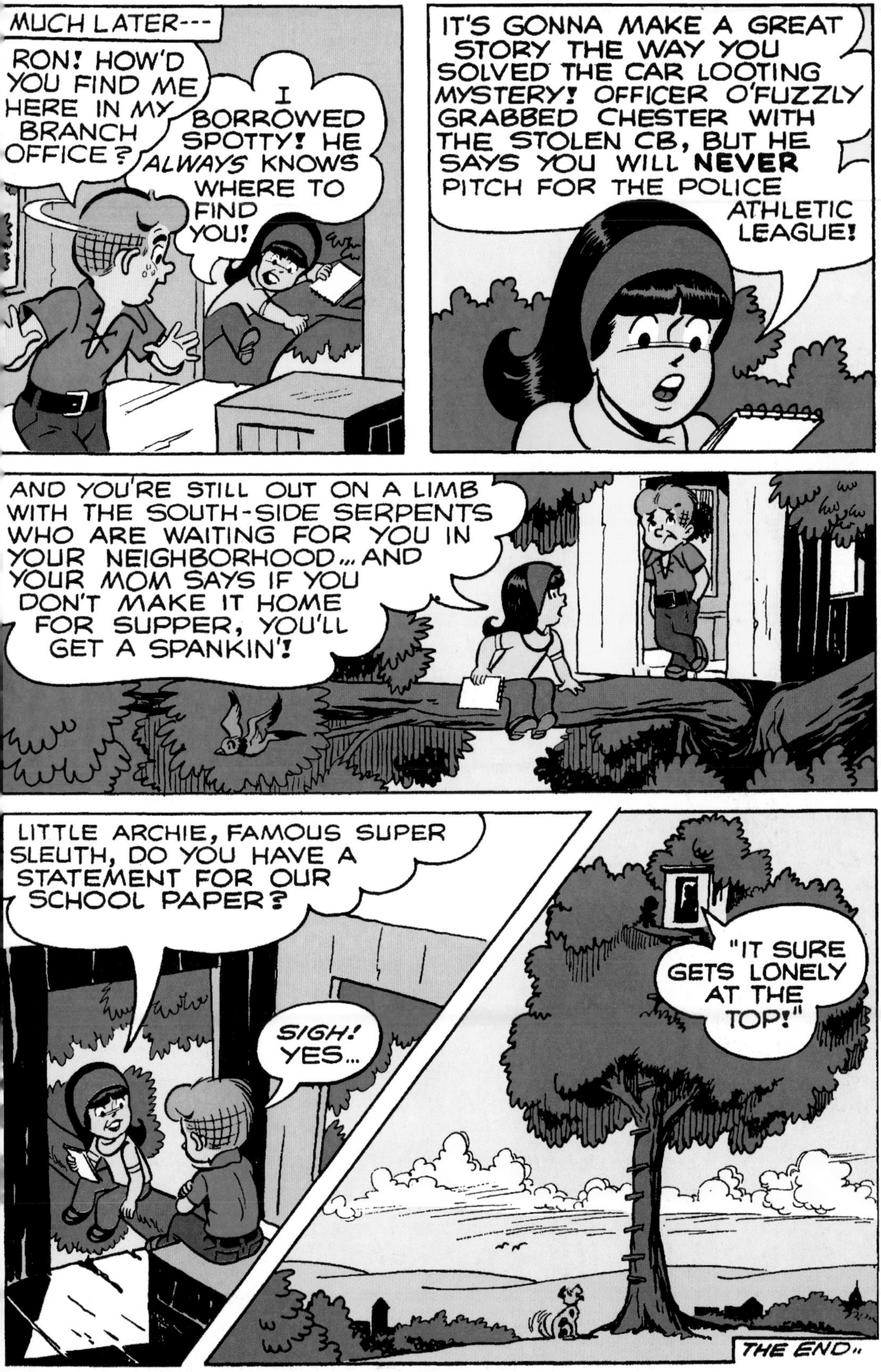
MUCH LATER---
RON! HOW'D YOU FIND ME HERE IN MY BRANCH OFFICE?
I BORROWED SPOTTY! HE ALWAYS KNOWS WHERE TO FIND YOU!
IT'S GONNA MAKE A GREAT STORY THE WAY YOU SOLVED THE CAR LOOTING MYSTERY! OFFICER O'FUZZLY GRABBED CHESTER WITH THE STOLEN CB, BUT HE SAYS YOU WILL NEVER PITCH FOR THE POLICE ATHLETIC LEAGUE!
AND YOU'RE STILL OUT ON A LIMB WITH THE SOUTH-SIDE SERPENTS WHO ARE WAITING FOR YOU IN YOUR NEIGHBORHOOD... AND YOUR MOM SAYS IF YOU DON'T MAKE IT HOME FOR SUPPER, YOU'LL GET A SPANKIN'!
LITTLE ARCHIE, FAMOUS SUPER SLEUTH, DO YOU HAVE A STATEMENT FOR OUR SCHOOL PAPER?
SIGH! YES...
"IT SURE GETS LONELY AT THE TOP!"
THE END..

CHECK OUT THESE GREAT ARCHIE COMIC GRAPHIC NOVELS...

ARCHIE AMERICANA SERIES

BEST OF THE FORTIES
BEST OF THE FORTIES: BOOK 2
BEST OF THE FIFTIES
BEST OF THE FIFTIES: BOOK 2
BEST OF THE SIXTIES
BEST OF THE SIXTIES: BOOK 2
BEST OF THE SEVENTIES
BEST OF THE EIGHTIES
BEST OF THE NINETIES

MORE GREAT GRAPHIC NOVELS

BETTY & VERONICA: SUMMER FUN
BETTY & VERONICA: BAD BOY TROUBLE
THE ADVENTURES OF LITTLE ARCHIE VOL. 1
THE BEST OF JOSIE & THE PUSSYCATS
KATY KEENE:
MODEL BEHAVIOR
SABRINA THE TEENAGE WITCH:
THE MAGIC REVISITED
ARCHIE'S CLASSIC CHRISTMAS STORIES
ARCHIE'S CAMP TALES
THE ARCHIES GREATEST HITS
ARCHIE: DAY BY DAY
ARCHIE: LOVE SHOWDOWN

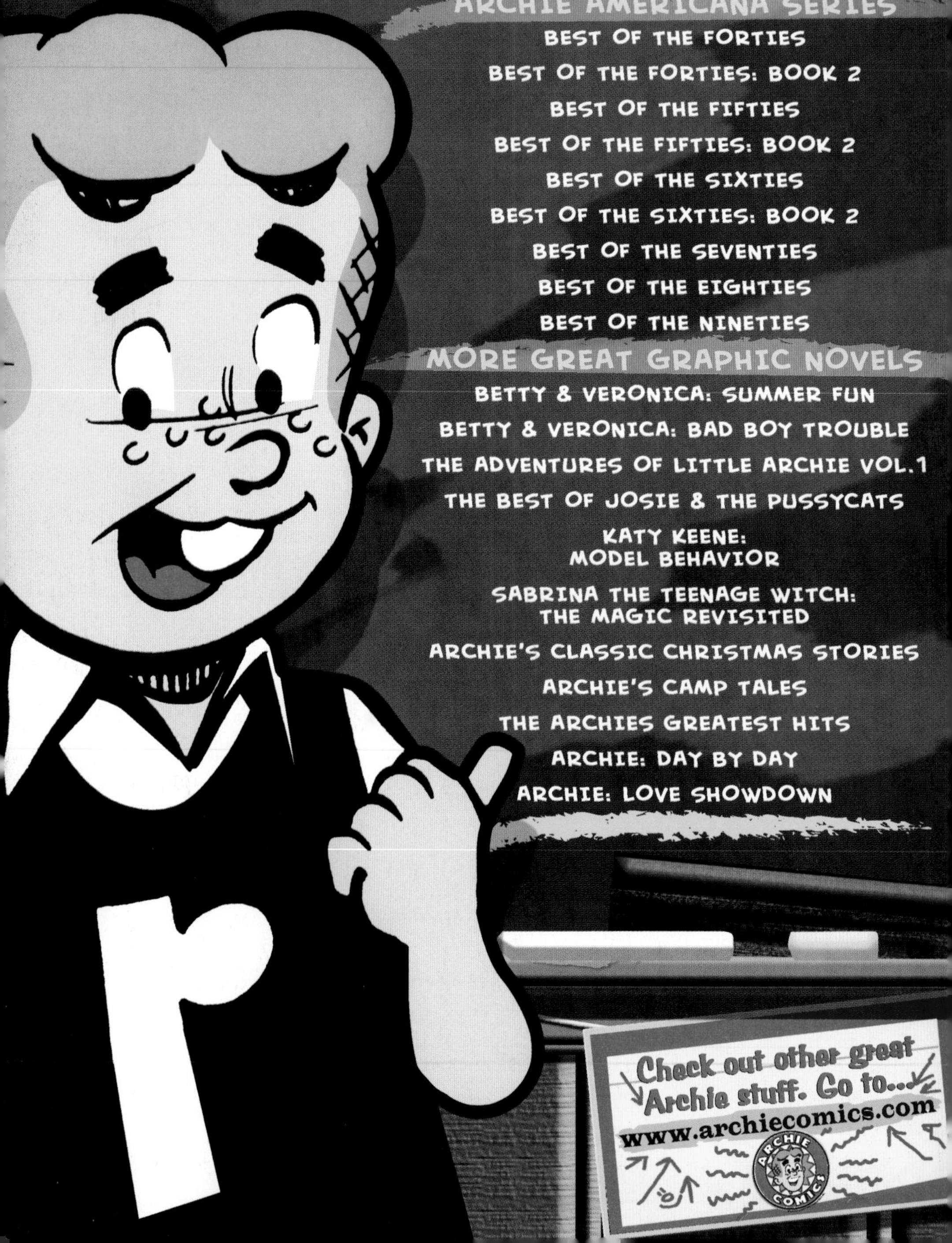
Check out other great
Archie stuff. Go to...
www.archiecomics.com
ARCHIE COMICS